IN TRAINING

No. 1

ZEUS AND THE THUNDERBOLT OF DOOM

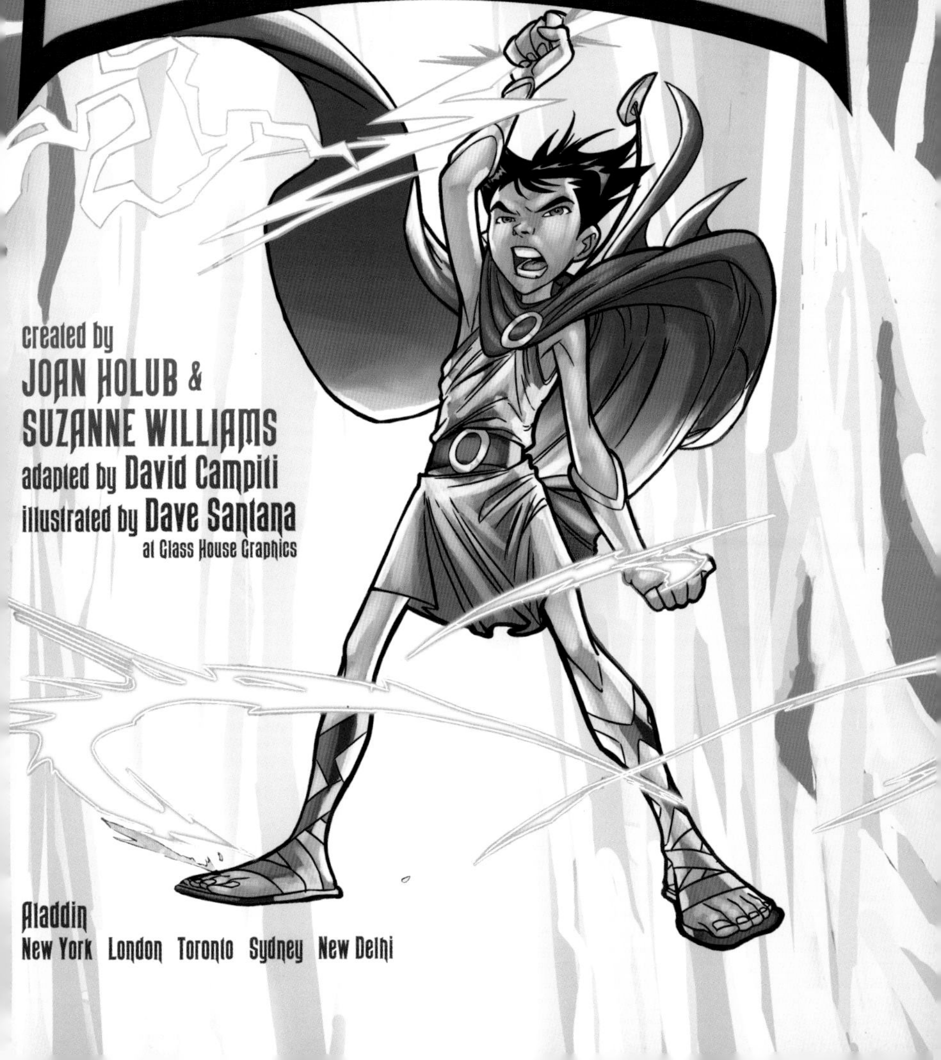

created by
JOAN HOLUB &
SUZANNE WILLIAMS
adapted by David Campiti
illustrated by Dave Santana
at Glass House Graphics

Aladdin
New York London Toronto Sydney New Delhi

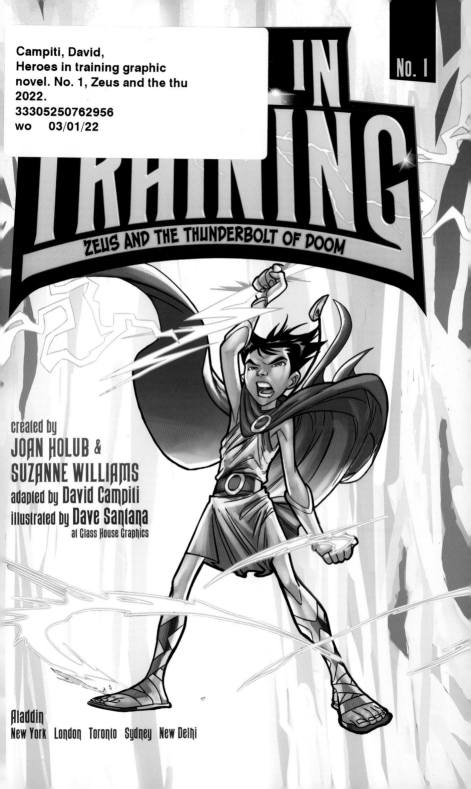

ALADDIN

An imprint of Simon & Schuster Children's Publishing Division
1230 Avenue of the Americas, New York, New York 10020
First Aladdin edition February 2022
Text copyright © 2022 by Joan Holub and Suzanne Williams
Illustrations copyright © 2022 by Glass House Graphics
Art by Dave Santana. Inks by Flávio Soares with João Zod and Juan Araujo. Colors by Felipe Felix and João Zod. Lettering by Marcos Inoue. Art services by Glass House Graphics.
All rights reserved, including the right of
reproduction in whole or in part in any form.
ALADDIN and related logo are registered
trademarks of Simon & Schuster, Inc.
For information about special discounts for bulk purchases, please contact Simon & Schuster Special Sales
at 1-866-506-1949 or business@simonandschuster.com.
The Simon & Schuster Speakers Bureau can bring authors to your live event. For more information or to book an event contact the Simon & Schuster Speakers Bureau at 1-866-248-3049 or visit our website at www.simonspeakers.com.
Designed by Nicholas Sciacca
The text of this book was set in CCMonologus.
Manufactured in China 1121 SCP
10 9 8 7 6 5 4 3 2 1
Library of Congress Cataloging-in-Publication Data
Names: Holub, Joan, author. · Williams, Suzanne, 1953- author. · Campiti, David, author. · Glass House Graphics, illustrator. · Title: Zeus and the thunderbolt of doom / created by Joan Holub and Suzanne Williams ; adapted by David Campiti ; illustrated by Glass House Graphics. · Description: First Aladdin hardcover edition. · New York : Aladdin, 2022. · Series: Heroes in training graphic novel ; book 1 · Audience: Ages 8 to 12 · Summary: Ten-year-old Zeus is kidnapped by the terrible Titans, merciless giants who enjoy snacking on humans, and when in self-defense he pulls a magical thunderbolt from a stone, he begins an adventure to rescue his fellow Olympians from the evil Cronus. · Identifiers: LCCN 2021015454 (print) · LCCN 2021015455 (ebook) · ISBN 9781534481152 (hardcover) · ISBN 9781534481145 (paperback) · ISBN 9781534481169 (ebook) · Subjects: LCSH: Graphic novels. · CYAC: Graphic novels. · Zeus (Greek deity)—Fiction. · Gods, Greek—Fiction. · Mythology, Greek—Fiction. · Adventure and adventurers—Fiction. · Classification: LCC PZ7.7.H656 Ze 2022 (print) · LCC PZ7.7.H656 (ebook)
DDC 741.5/973—dc23
LC record available at https://lccn.loc.gov/2021015454
LC ebook record available at https://lccn.loc.gov/2021015455

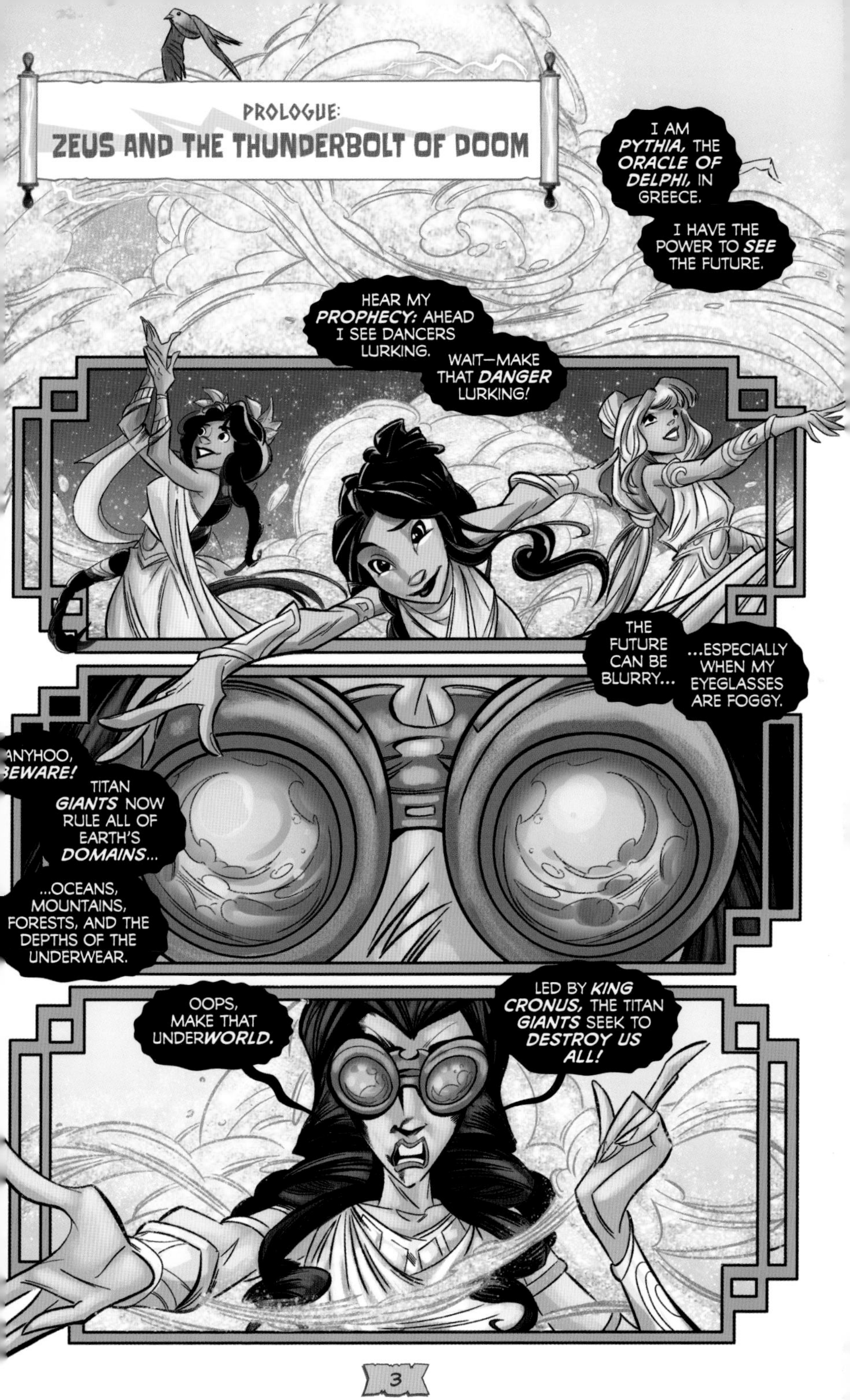
PROLOGUE:
ZEUS AND THE THUNDERBOLT OF DOOM
I AM PYTHIA, THE ORACLE OF DELPHI, IN GREECE.
I HAVE THE POWER TO SEE THE FUTURE.
HEAR MY PROPHECY: AHEAD I SEE DANCERS LURKING.
WAIT—MAKE THAT DANGER LURKING!
THE FUTURE CAN BE BLURRY...
...ESPECIALLY WHEN MY EYEGLASSES ARE FOGGY.
ANYHOO, BEWARE!
TITAN GIANTS NOW RULE ALL OF EARTH'S DOMAINS...
...OCEANS, MOUNTAINS, FORESTS, AND THE DEPTHS OF THE UNDERWEAR.
OOPS, MAKE THAT UNDERWORLD.
LED BY KING CRONUS, THE TITAN GIANTS SEEK TO DESTROY US ALL!

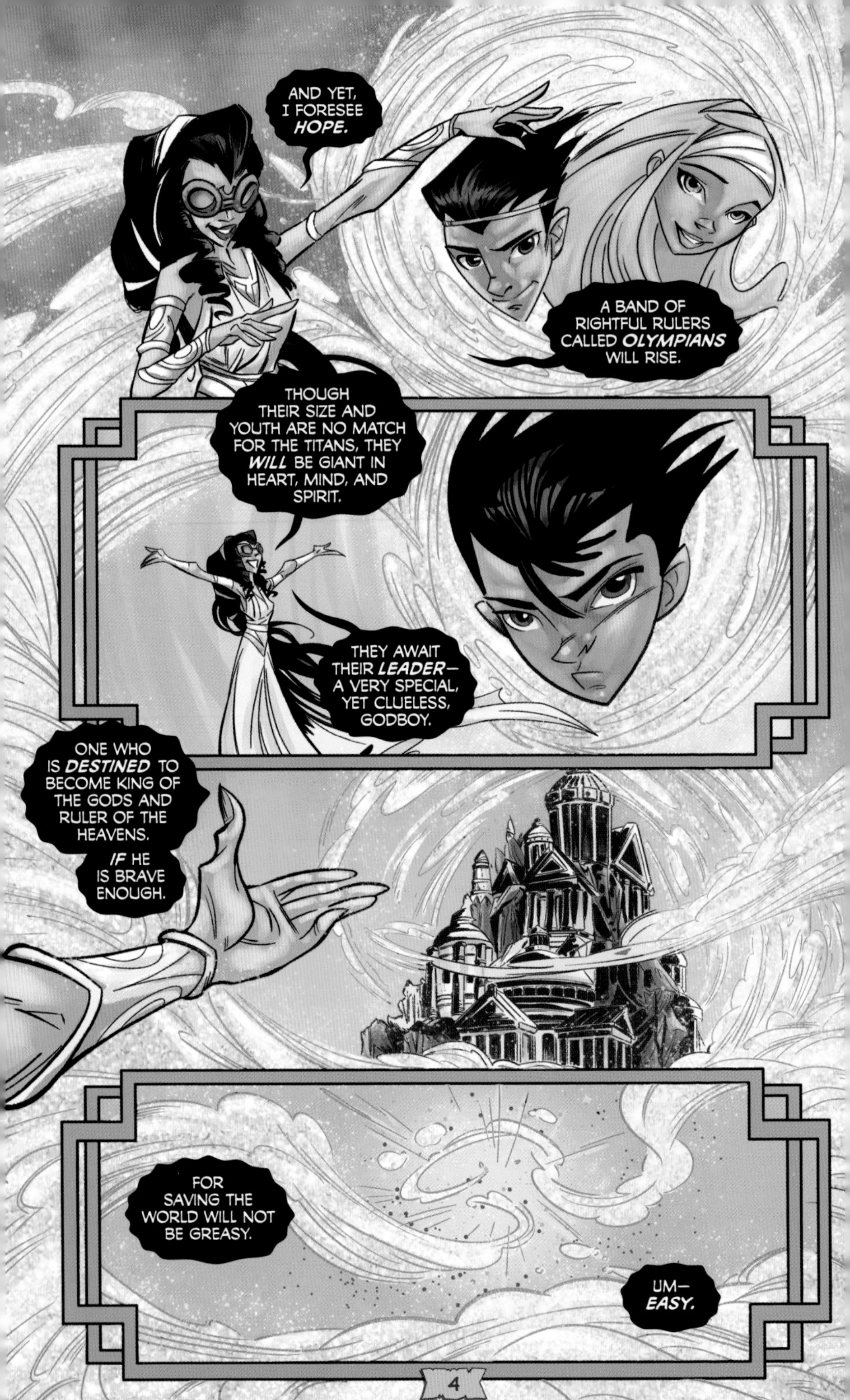

AND YET, I FORESEE HOPE.
A BAND OF RIGHTFUL RULERS CALLED OLYMPIANS WILL RISE.
THOUGH THEIR SIZE AND YOUTH ARE NO MATCH FOR THE TITANS, THEY WILL BE GIANT IN HEART, MIND, AND SPIRIT.
THEY AWAIT THEIR LEADER— A VERY SPECIAL, YET CLUELESS, GODBOY.
ONE WHO IS DESTINED TO BECOME KING OF THE GODS AND RULER OF THE HEAVENS.
IF HE IS BRAVE ENOUGH.
FOR SAVING THE WORLD WILL NOT BE GREASY.
UM— EASY.

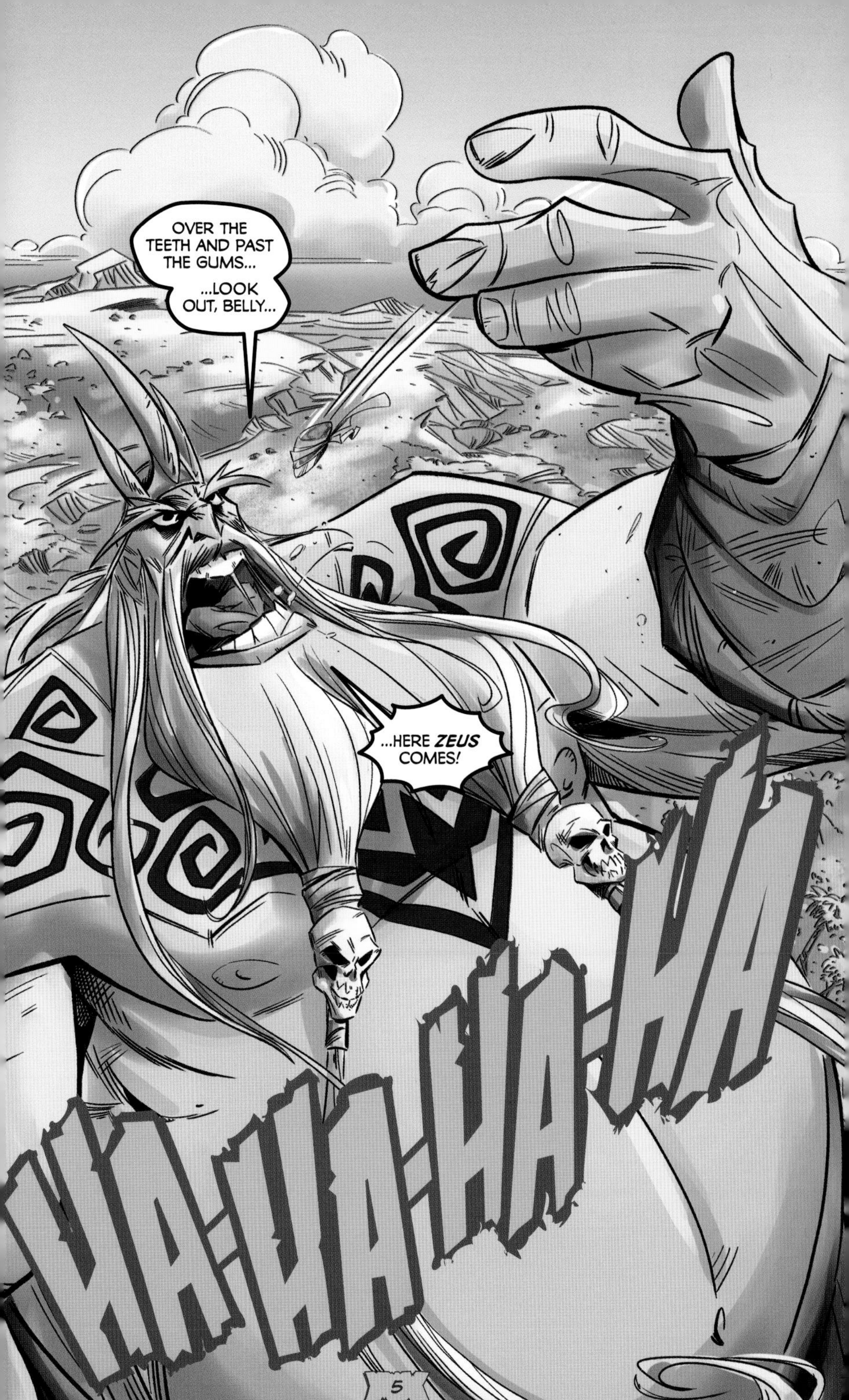
OVER THE TEETH AND PAST THE GUMS...
...LOOK OUT, BELLY...
...HERE *ZEUS* COMES!
HA-HA-HA-HA-HA

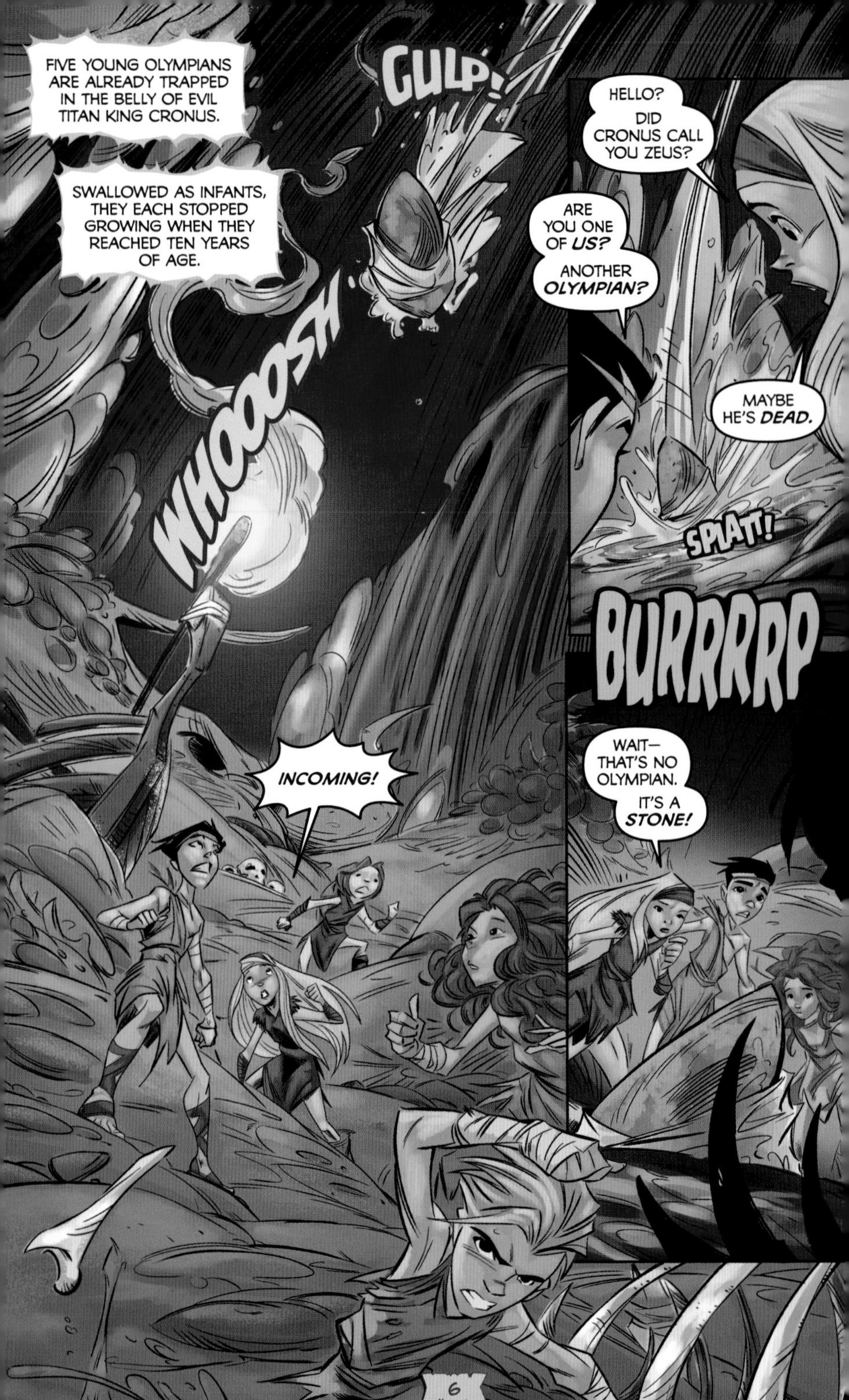
FIVE YOUNG OLYMPIANS ARE ALREADY TRAPPED IN THE BELLY OF EVIL TITAN KING CRONUS.
SWALLOWED AS INFANTS, THEY EACH STOPPED GROWING WHEN THEY REACHED TEN YEARS OF AGE.
GULP!
WHOOOSH
INCOMING!
HELLO?
DID CRONUS CALL YOU ZEUS?
ARE YOU ONE OF US?
ANOTHER OLYMPIAN?
MAYBE HE'S DEAD.
SPLATT!
BURRRRP
WAIT—THAT'S NO OLYMPIAN.
IT'S A STONE!

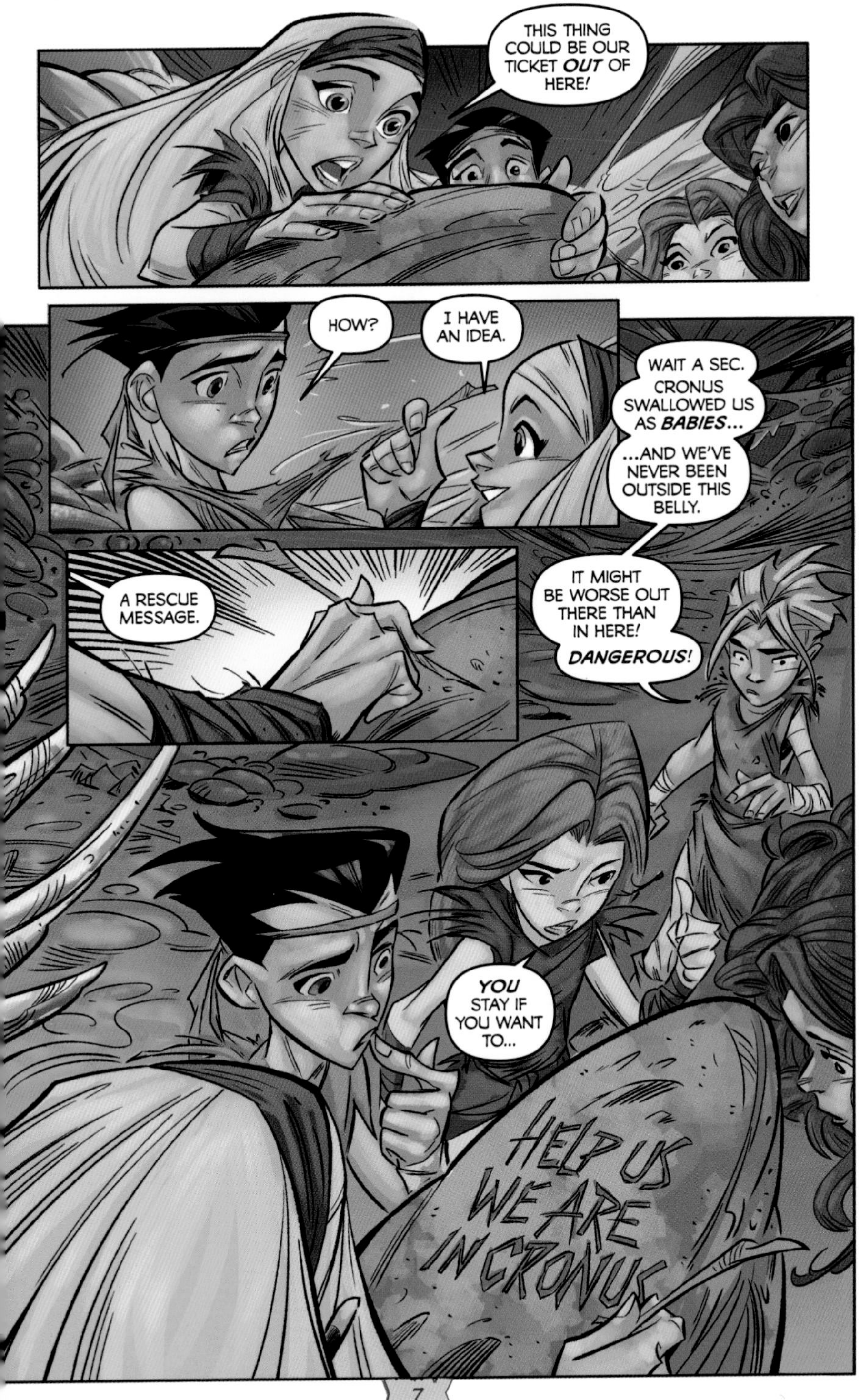
THIS THING COULD BE OUR TICKET *OUT* OF HERE!
HOW?
I HAVE AN IDEA.
A RESCUE MESSAGE.
WAIT A SEC. CRONUS SWALLOWED US AS *BABIES*...
...AND WE'VE NEVER BEEN OUTSIDE THIS BELLY.
IT MIGHT BE WORSE OUT THERE THAN IN HERE! *DANGEROUS*!
YOU STAY IF YOU WANT TO...
HELP US WE ARE IN CRONUS

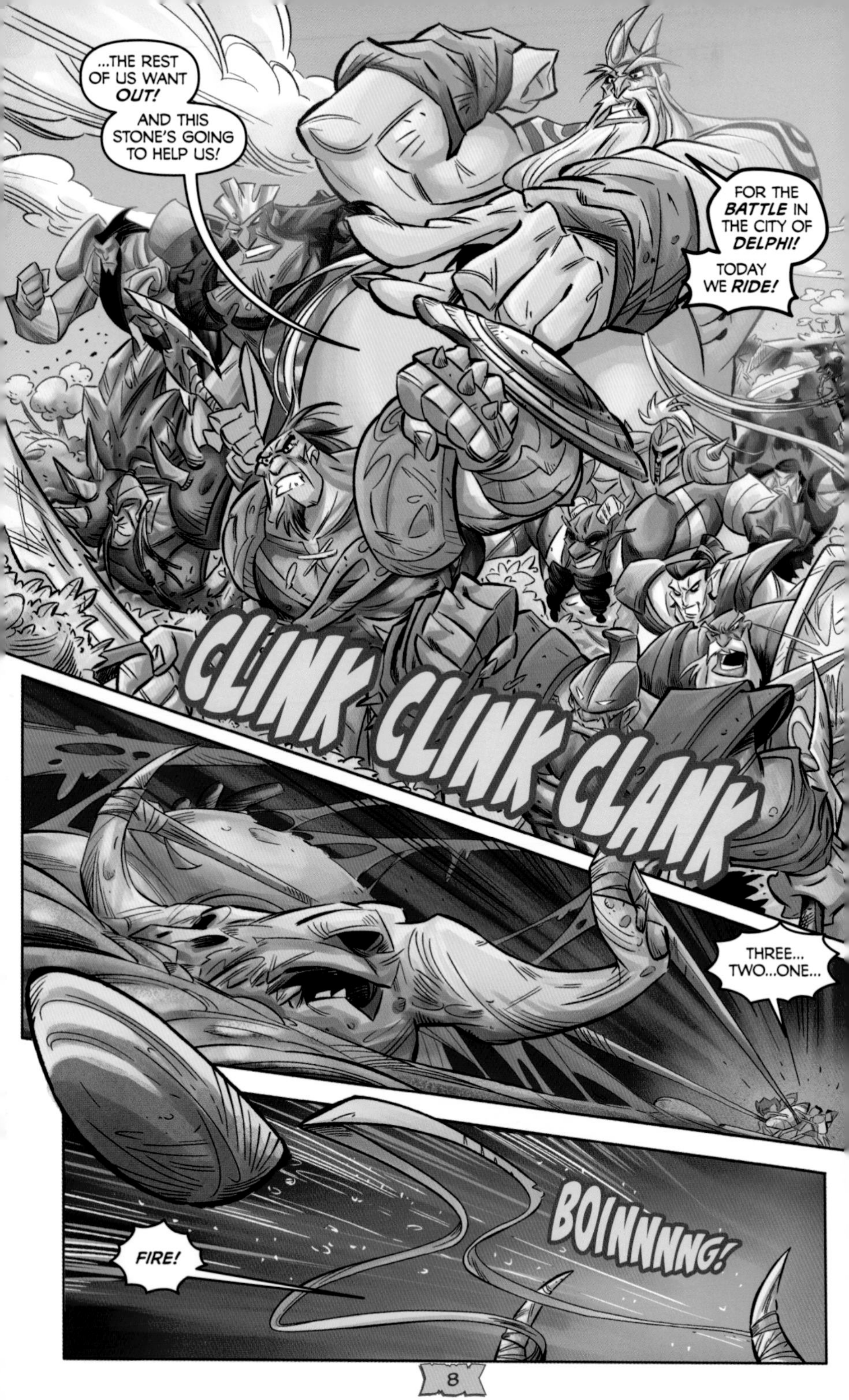
...THE REST OF US WANT *OUT!*
AND THIS STONE'S GOING TO HELP US!
FOR THE *BATTLE* IN THE CITY OF *DELPHI!*
TODAY WE *RIDE!*
CLINK CLINK CLANK
THREE... TWO...ONE...
FIRE!
BOINNNNG!

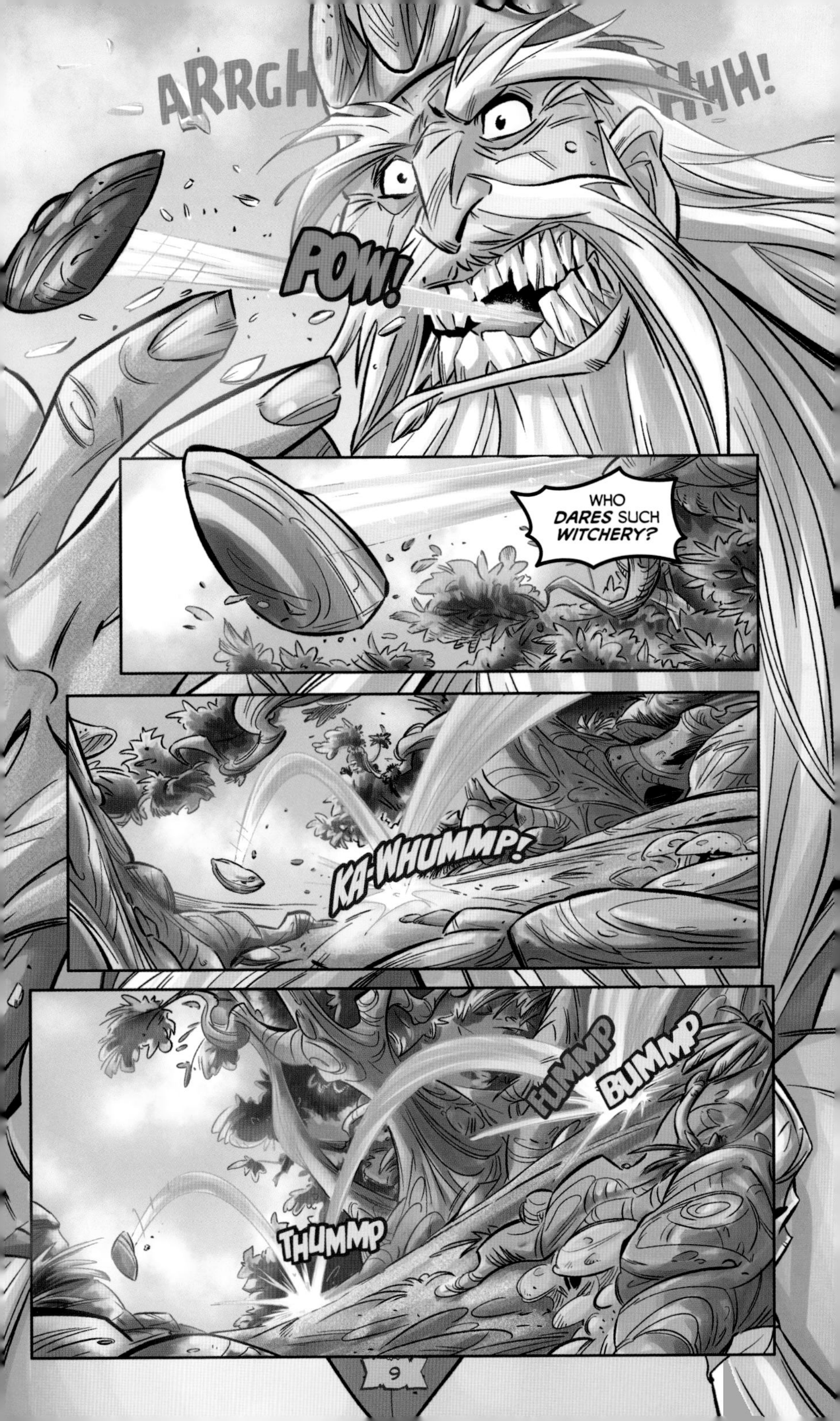
ARRGH
HHH!
POW!
WHO DARES SUCH WITCHERY?
KA-WHUMMP!
THUMMP
HUMMP
BUMMP

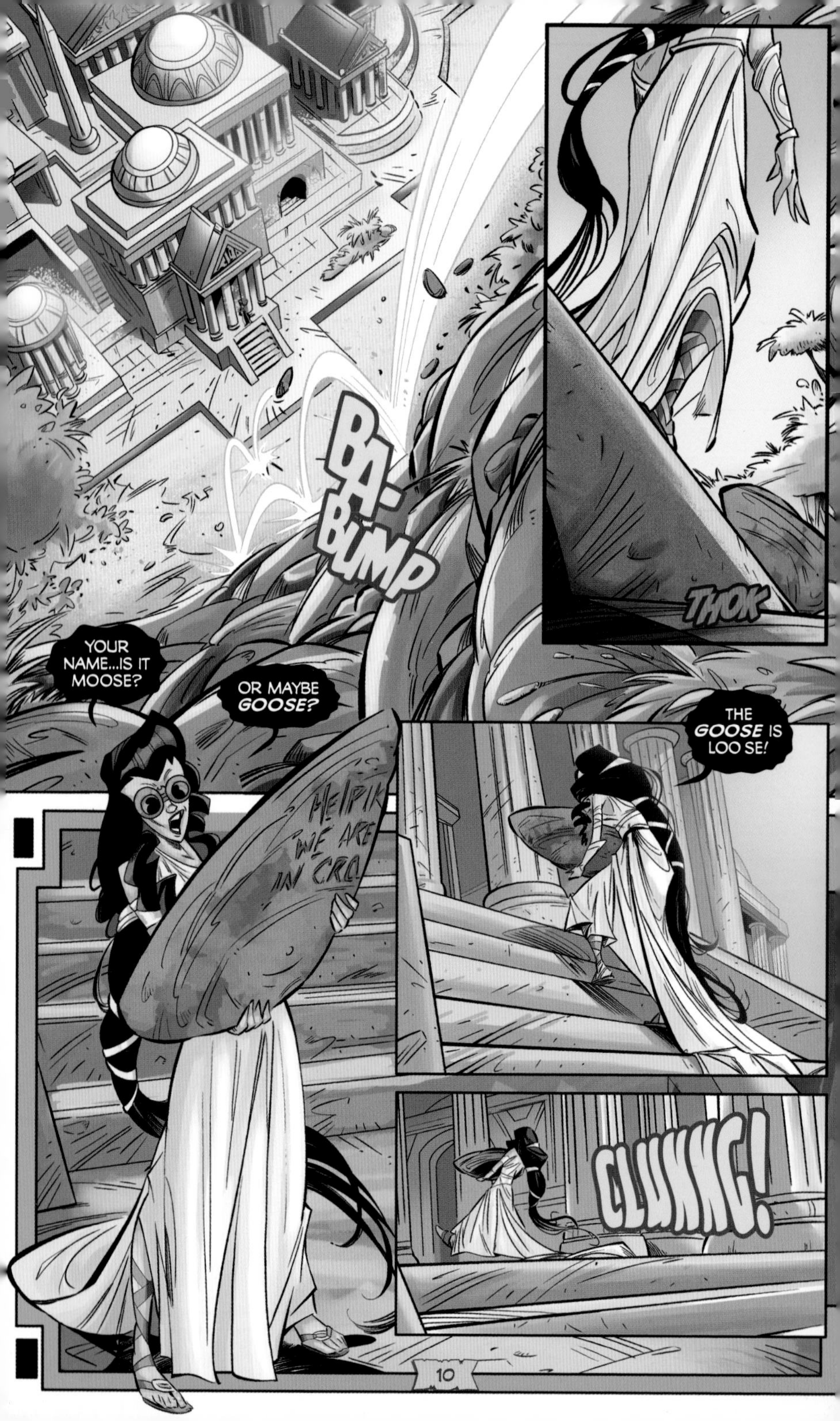
BA-BUMP
THOK
YOUR NAME...IS IT MOOSE?
OR MAYBE *GOOSE?*
THE *GOOSE* IS LOO SE!
CLUNNG!

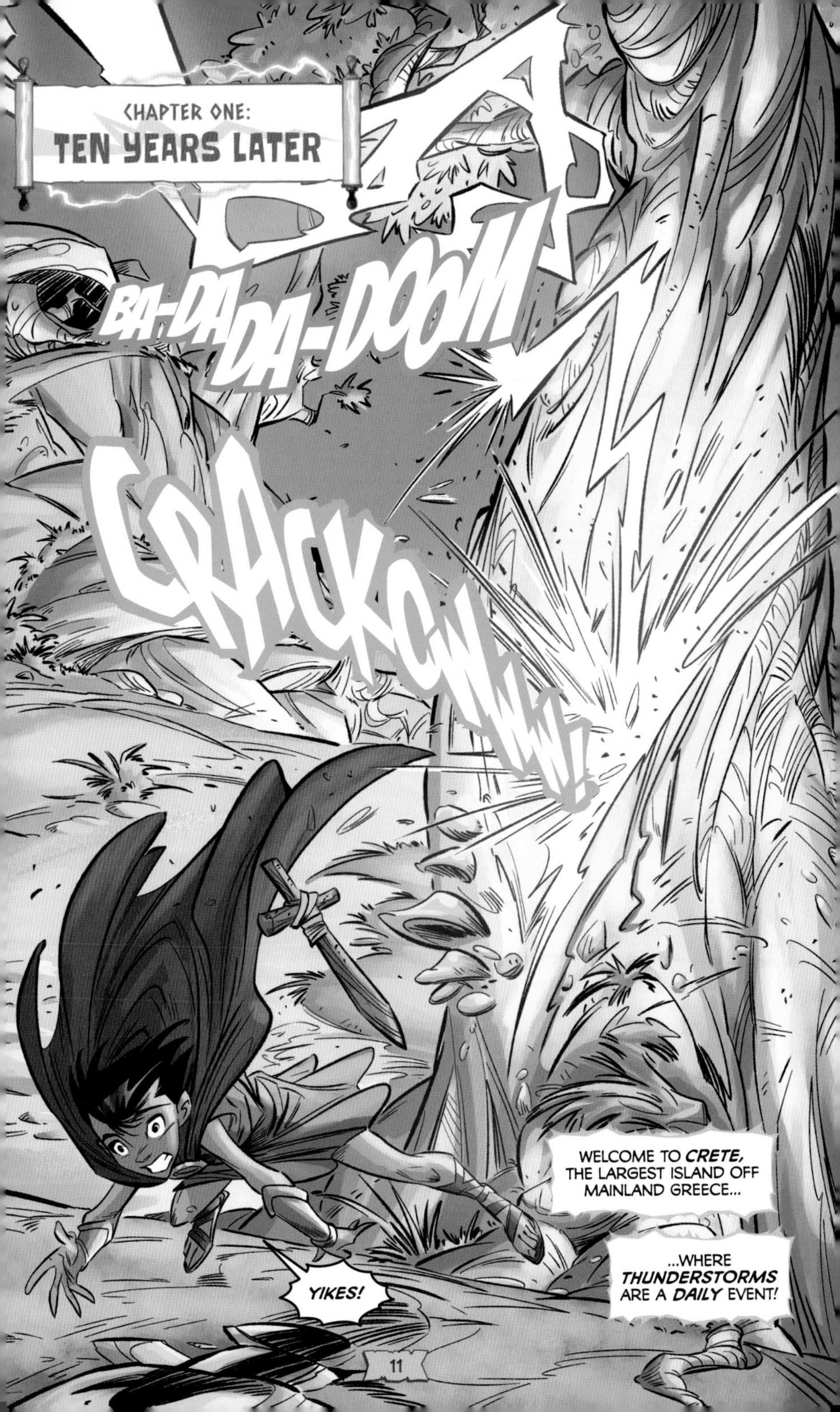
CHAPTER ONE:
TEN YEARS LATER
BA-DA DA-DOOM
CRACKOOM!
WELCOME TO *CRETE,* THE LARGEST ISLAND OFF MAINLAND GREECE...
...WHERE *THUNDERSTORMS* ARE A *DAILY* EVENT!
YIKES!

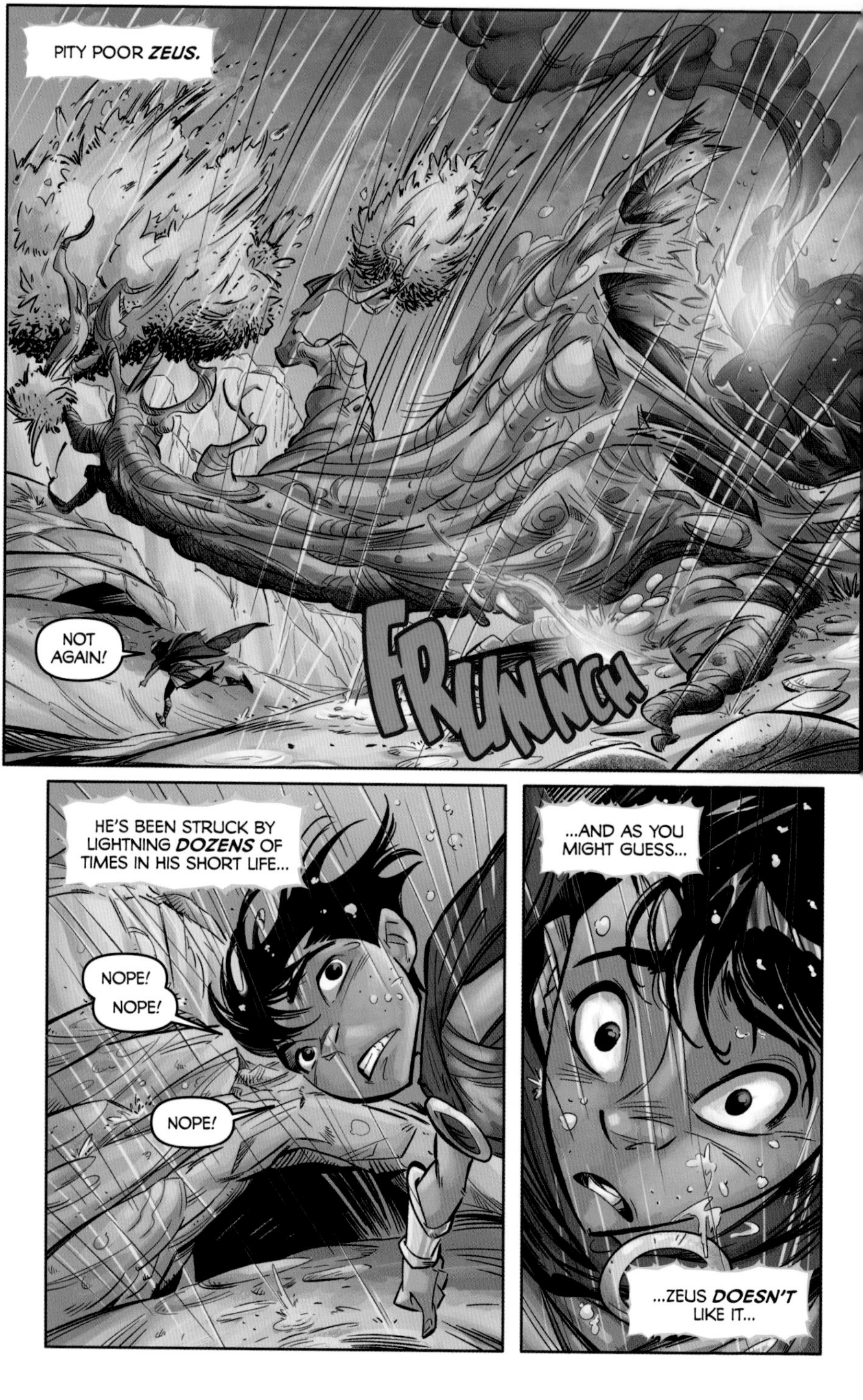
PITY POOR ZEUS.
NOT AGAIN!
FRUNNCH
HE'S BEEN STRUCK BY LIGHTNING DOZENS OF TIMES IN HIS SHORT LIFE...
NOPE! NOPE!
NOPE!
...AND AS YOU MIGHT GUESS...
...ZEUS DOESN'T LIKE IT...

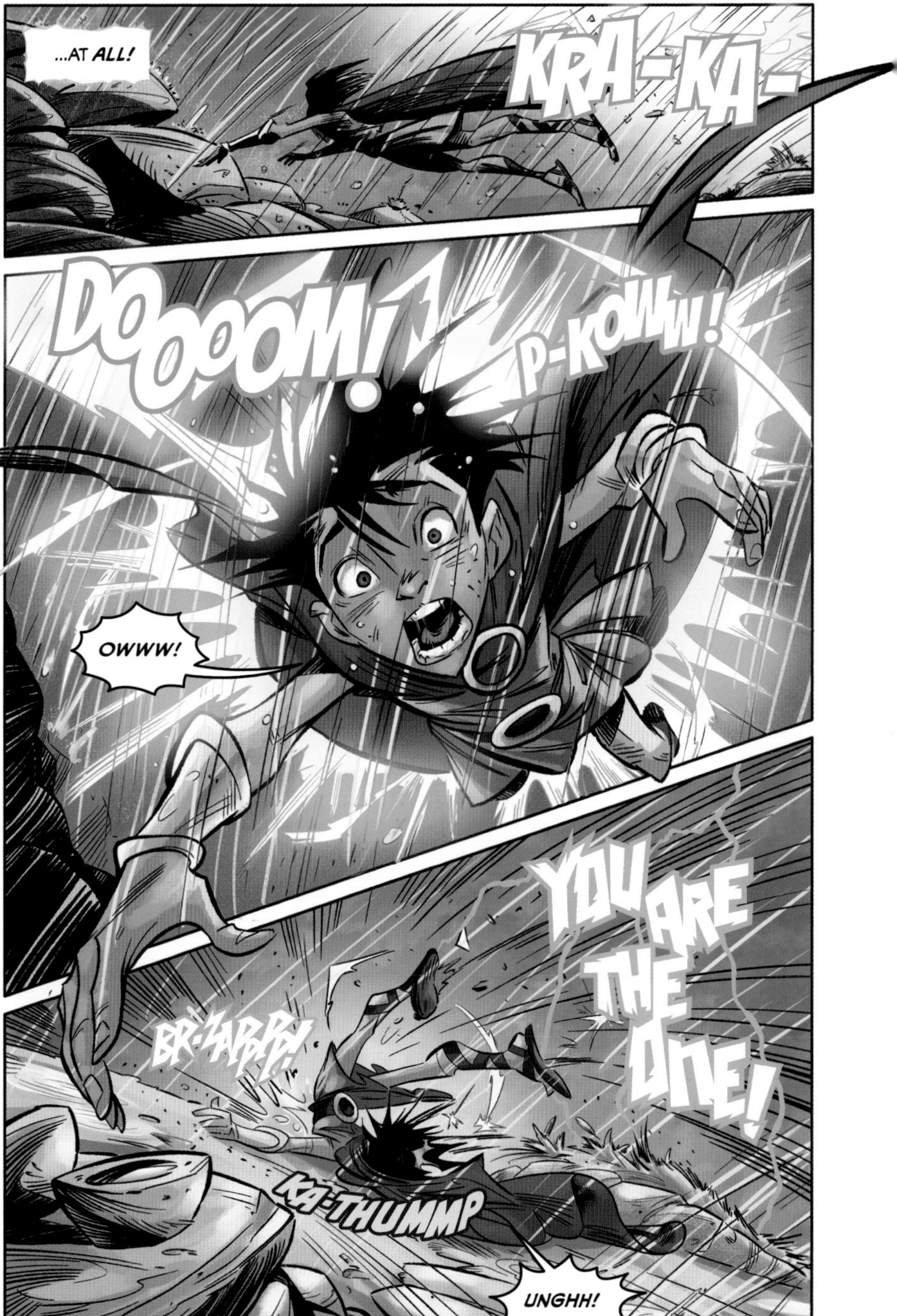
...AT ALL!
KRA-KA-
DOOOOOM!
P-KOWW!
OWWW!
YOU ARE THE ONE!
BR-ZARRP!
KA-THUMMP
UNGHH!

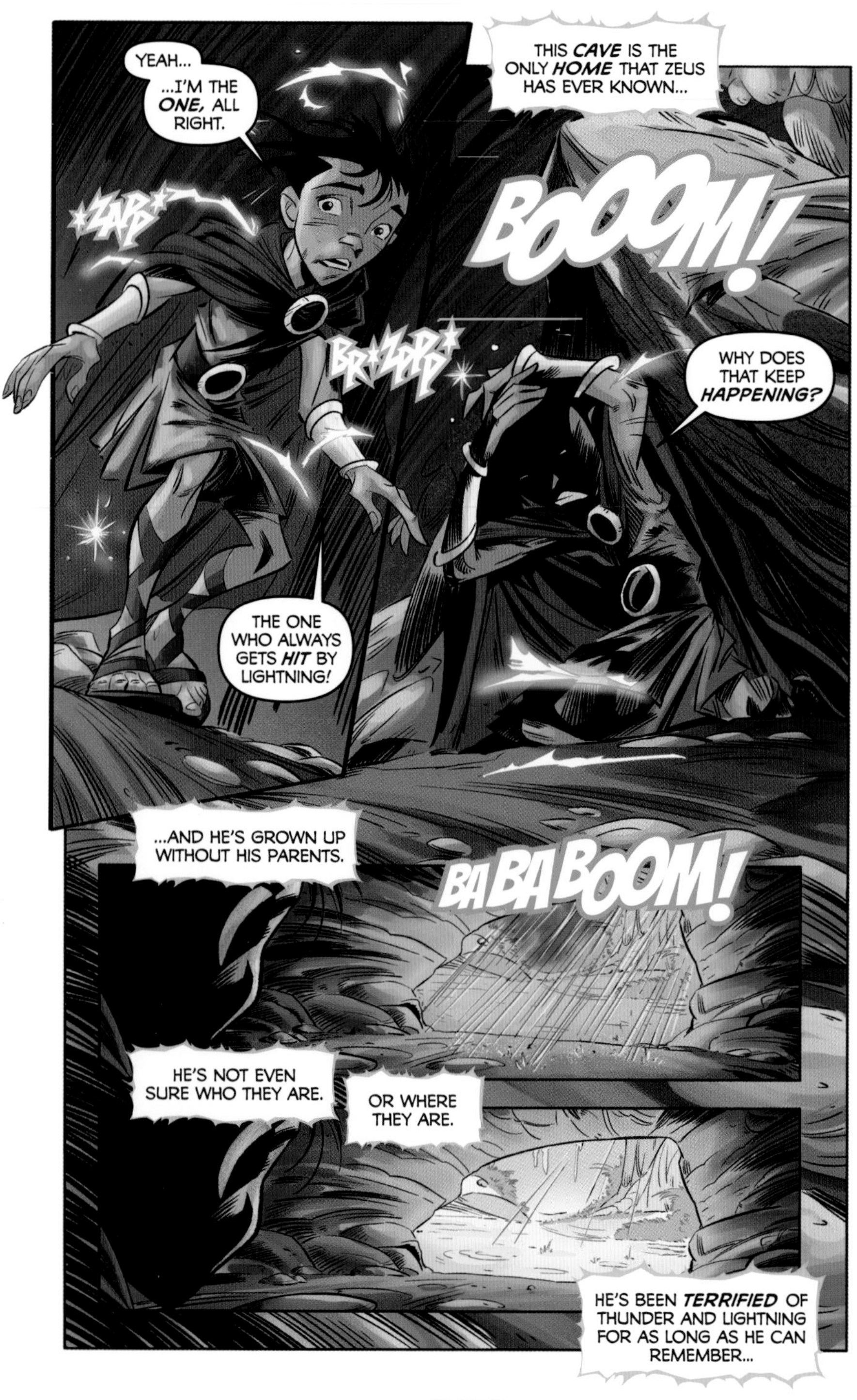
YEAH... ...I'M THE ONE, ALL RIGHT.
THIS CAVE IS THE ONLY HOME THAT ZEUS HAS EVER KNOWN...
ZAP
BOOOM!
BR*ZPP*
WHY DOES THAT KEEP HAPPENING?
THE ONE WHO ALWAYS GETS HIT BY LIGHTNING!
...AND HE'S GROWN UP WITHOUT HIS PARENTS.
BABABOOM!
HE'S NOT EVEN SURE WHO THEY ARE.
OR WHERE THEY ARE.
HE'S BEEN TERRIFIED OF THUNDER AND LIGHTNING FOR AS LONG AS HE CAN REMEMBER...

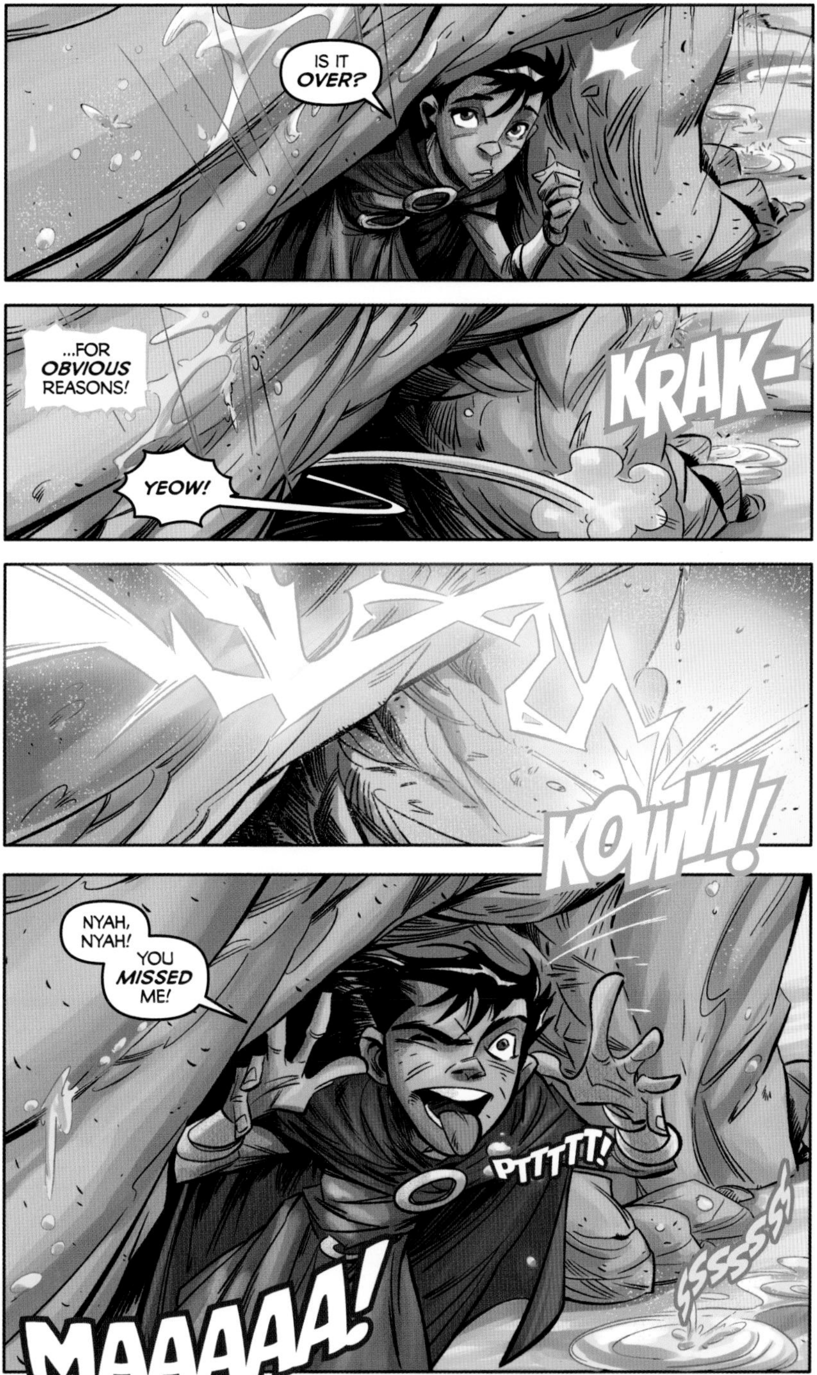
IS IT OVER?
...FOR OBVIOUS REASONS!
KRAK-
YEOW!
KOWW!
NYAH, NYAH!
YOU MISSED ME!
PTTTTT!
SSSSSS
MAAAAA!

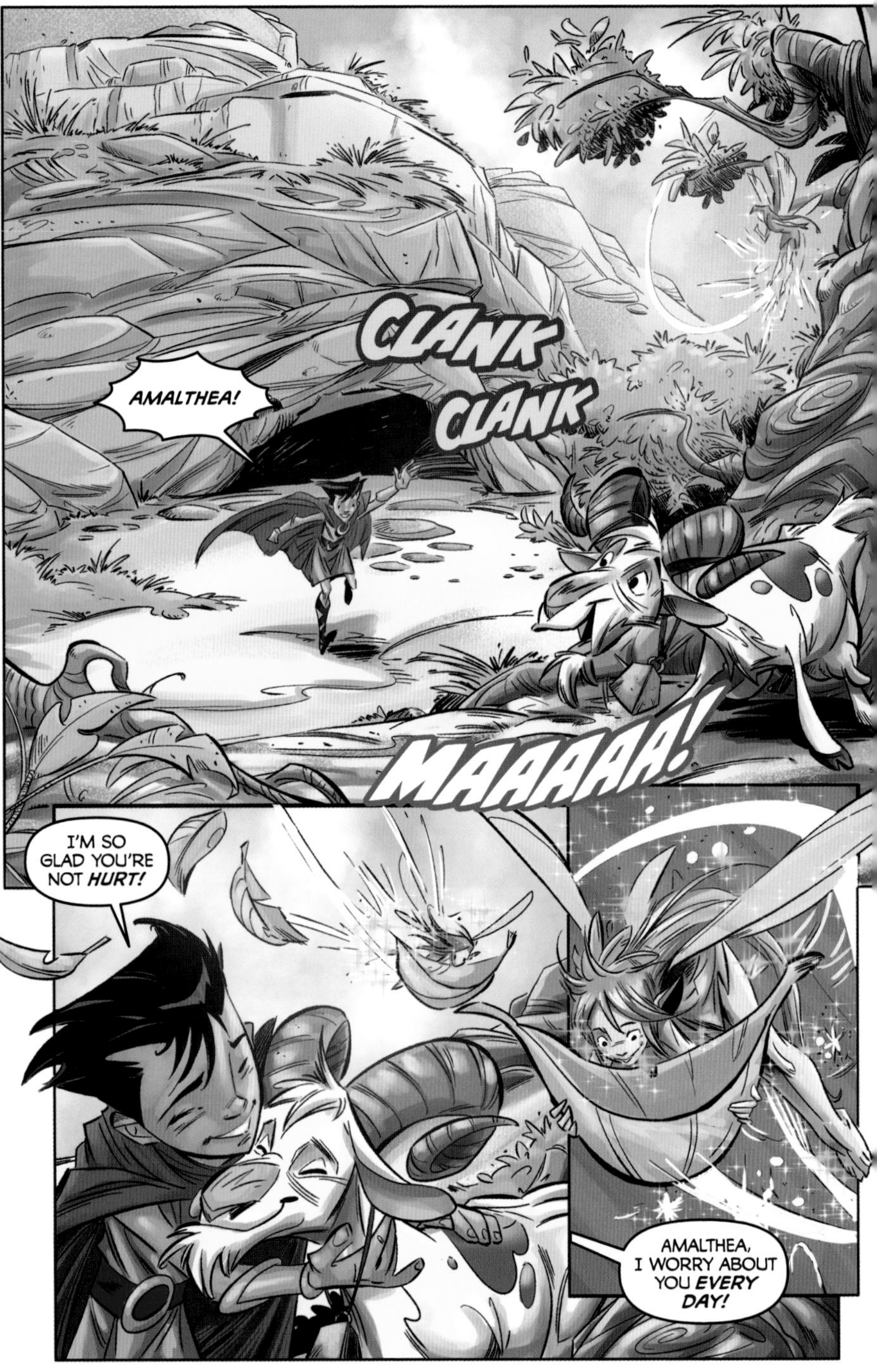
CLANK
CLANK
AMALTHEA!
MAAAAAA!
I'M SO GLAD YOU'RE NOT *HURT!*
AMALTHEA, I WORRY ABOUT YOU *EVERY DAY!*

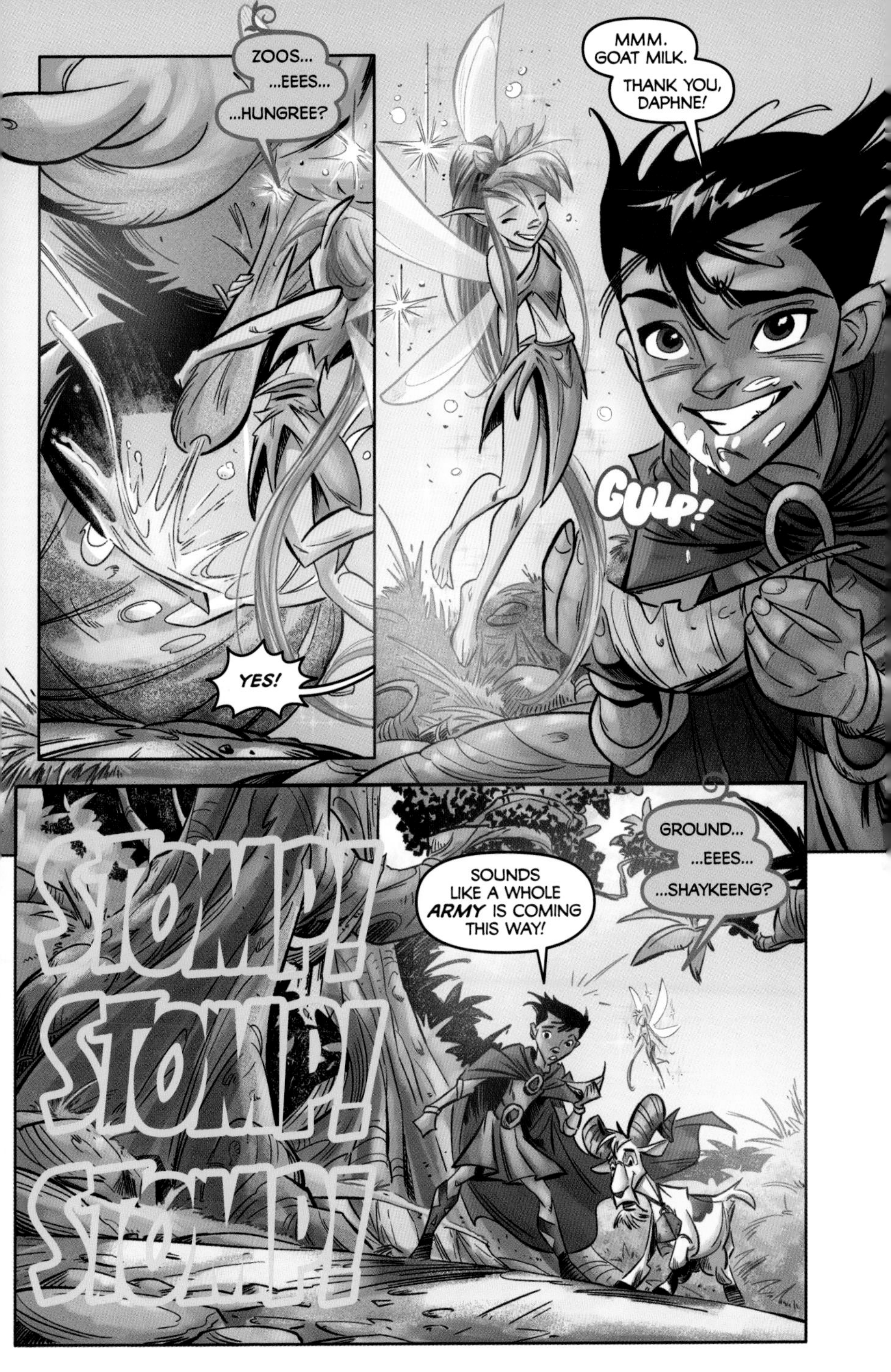

ZOOS... ...EEES... ...HUNGREE?
YES!
MMM. GOAT MILK.
THANK YOU, DAPHNE!
GULP!
STOMP! STOMP! STOMP!
SOUNDS LIKE A WHOLE *ARMY* IS COMING THIS WAY!
GROUND... ...EEES... ...SHAYKEENG?

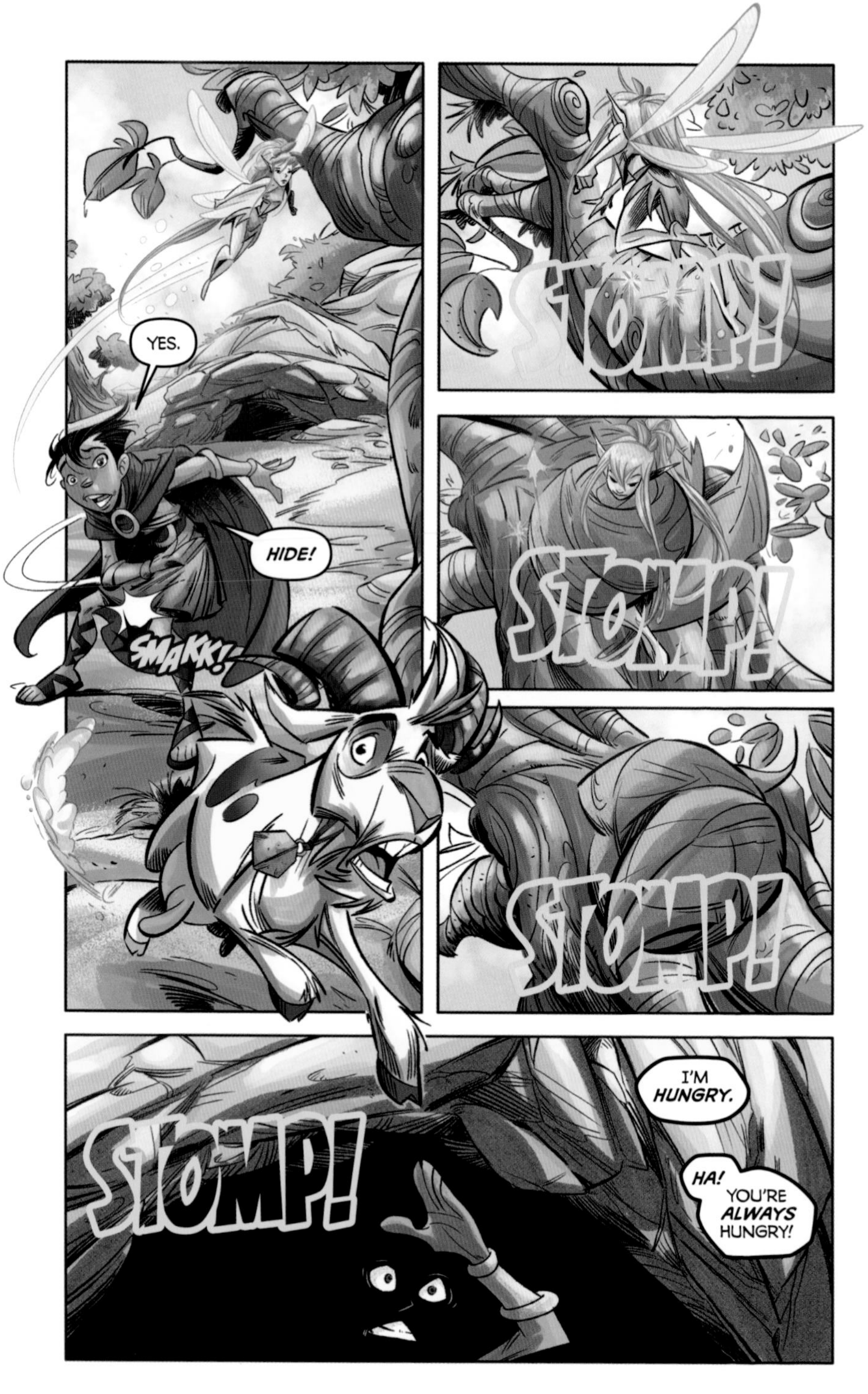
YES.
HIDE!
SMAKK!
STOMP!
STOMP!
STOMP!
STOMP!
I'M *HUNGRY.*
HA! YOU'RE *ALWAYS* HUNGRY!

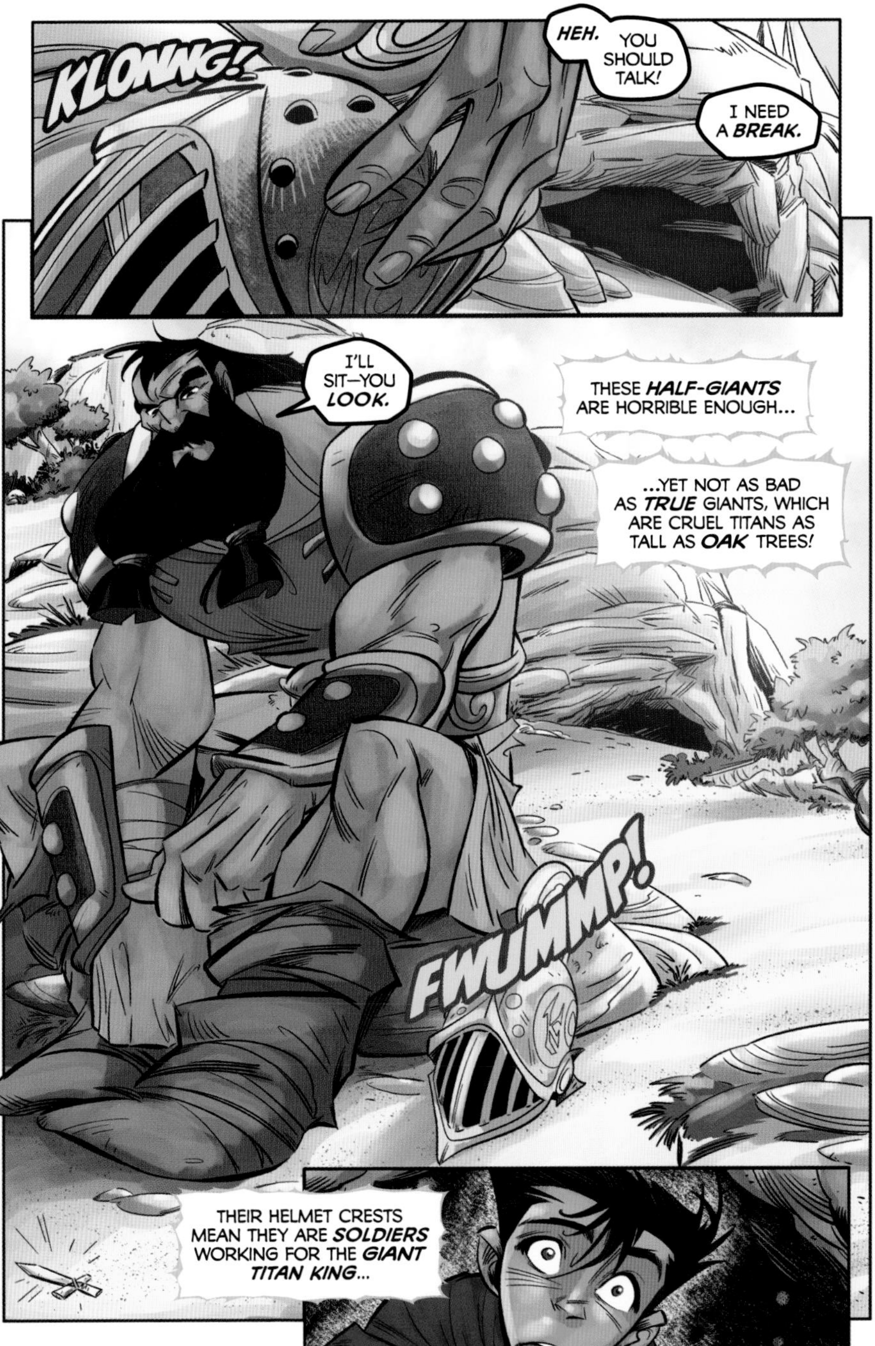
KLONNG!
HEH. YOU SHOULD TALK!
I NEED A BREAK.
I'LL SIT—YOU LOOK.
THESE HALF-GIANTS ARE HORRIBLE ENOUGH...
...YET NOT AS BAD AS TRUE GIANTS, WHICH ARE CRUEL TITANS AS TALL AS OAK TREES!
FWUMMP!
THEIR HELMET CRESTS MEAN THEY ARE SOLDIERS WORKING FOR THE GIANT TITAN KING...

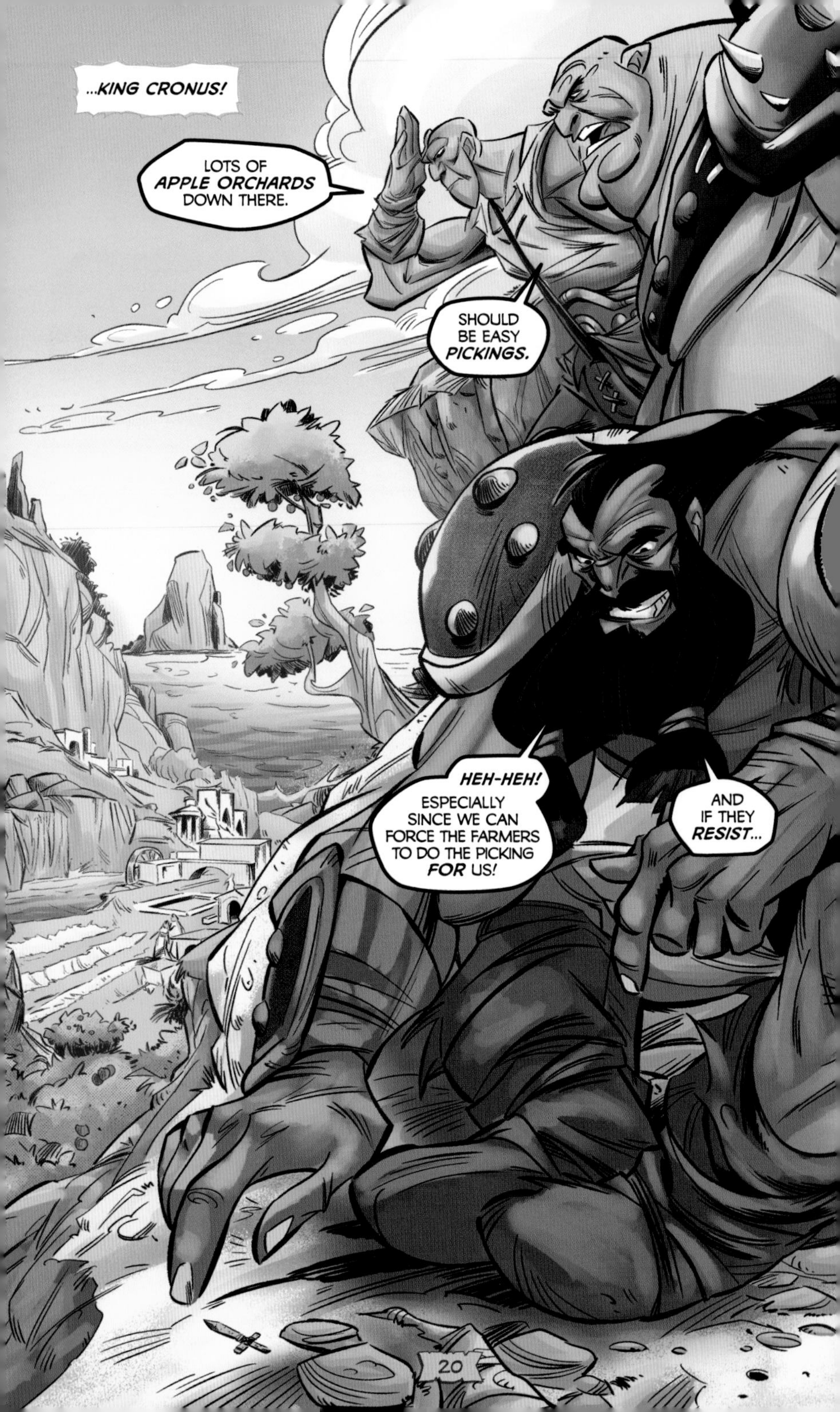
...KING CRONUS!
LOTS OF APPLE ORCHARDS DOWN THERE.
SHOULD BE EASY PICKINGS.
HEH-HEH! ESPECIALLY SINCE WE CAN FORCE THE FARMERS TO DO THE PICKING FOR US!
AND IF THEY RESIST...

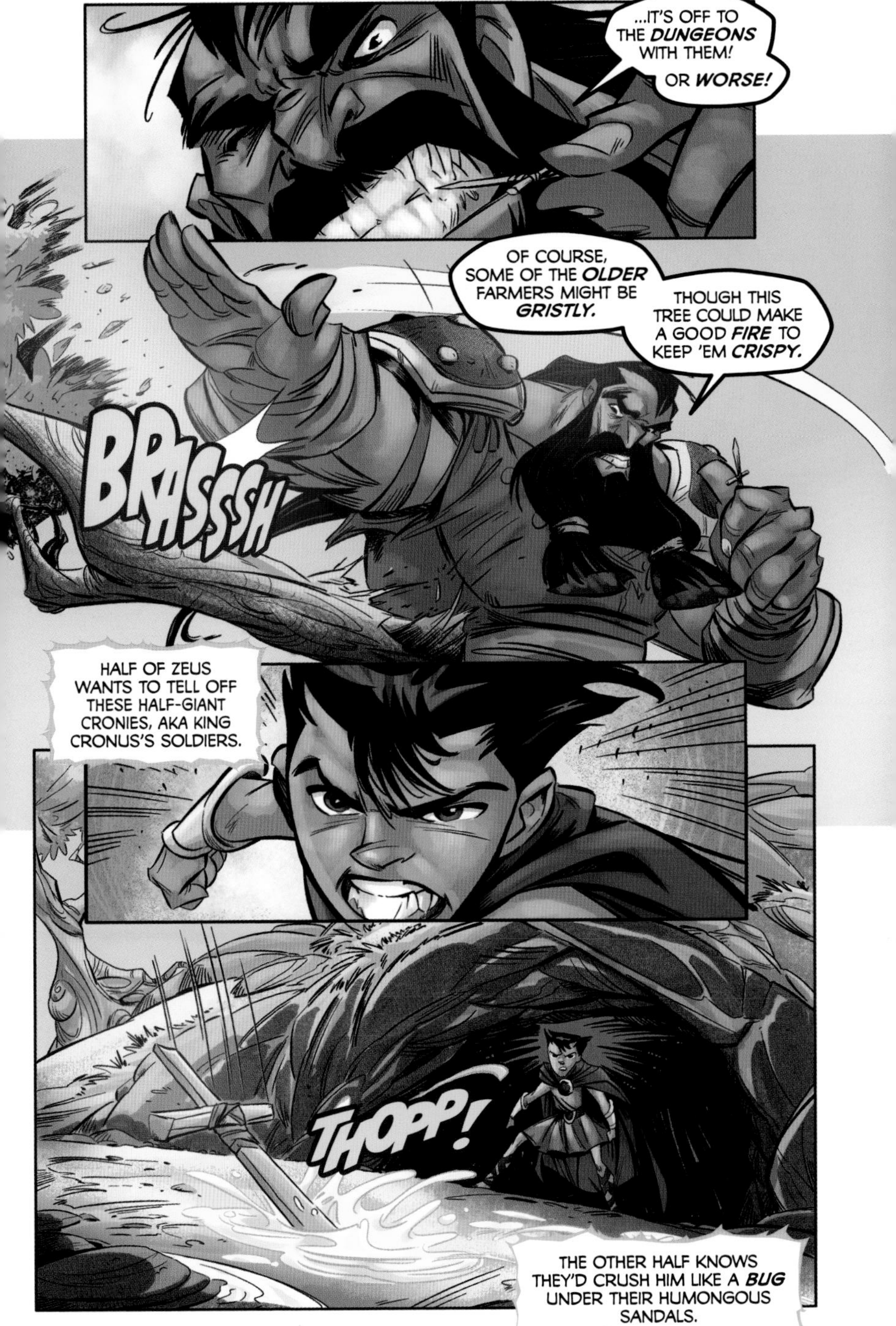
...IT'S OFF TO THE DUNGEONS WITH THEM!
OR WORSE!
OF COURSE, SOME OF THE OLDER FARMERS MIGHT BE GRISTLY.
THOUGH THIS TREE COULD MAKE A GOOD FIRE TO KEEP 'EM CRISPY.
BRASSSH
HALF OF ZEUS WANTS TO TELL OFF THESE HALF-GIANT CRONIES, AKA KING CRONUS'S SOLDIERS.
THOPP!
THE OTHER HALF KNOWS THEY'D CRUSH HIM LIKE A BUG UNDER THEIR HUMONGOUS SANDALS.

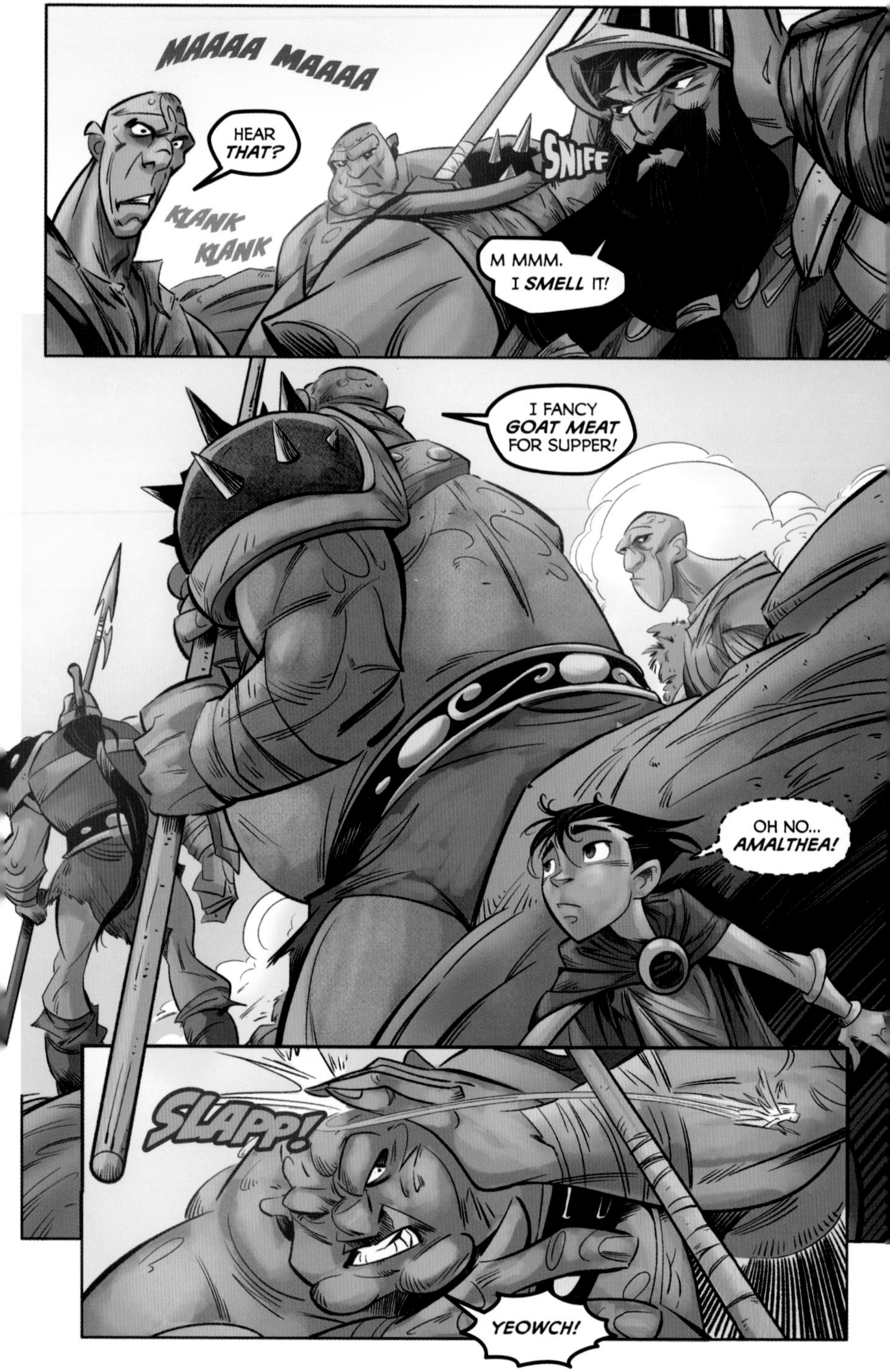
MAAAA MAAAA
HEAR *THAT?*
KLANK KLANK
SNIFF
M MMM. I *SMELL* IT!
I FANCY *GOAT MEAT* FOR SUPPER!
OH NO... *AMALTHEA!*
SLAPP!
YEOWCH!

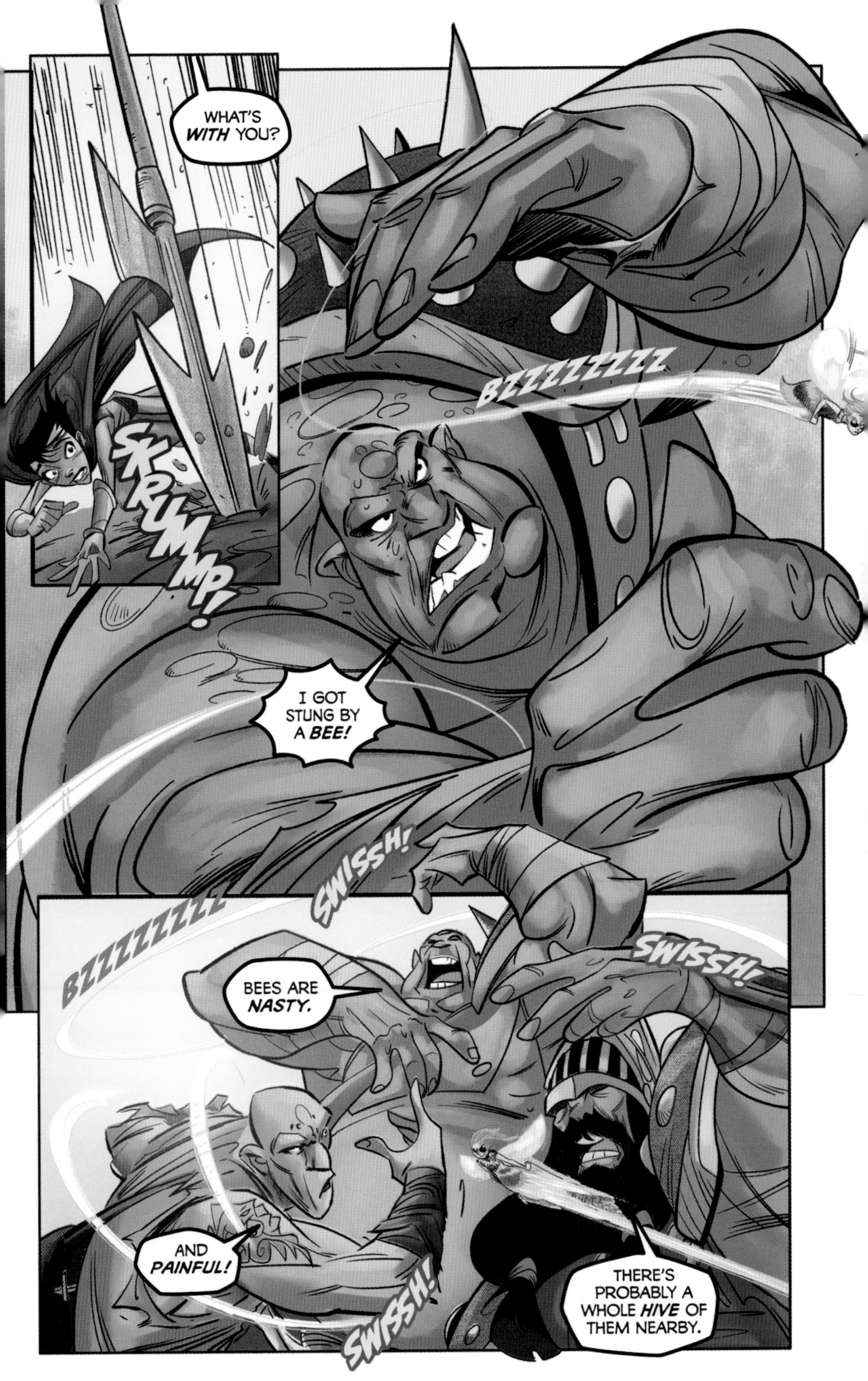

WHAT'S WITH YOU?
SKRUMMP!
BZZZZZZZZZ
I GOT STUNG BY A BEE!
SWISSH!
BZZZZZZZZ
SWISSH!
BEES ARE NASTY.
AND PAINFUL!
SWISSH!
THERE'S PROBABLY A WHOLE HIVE OF THEM NEARBY.

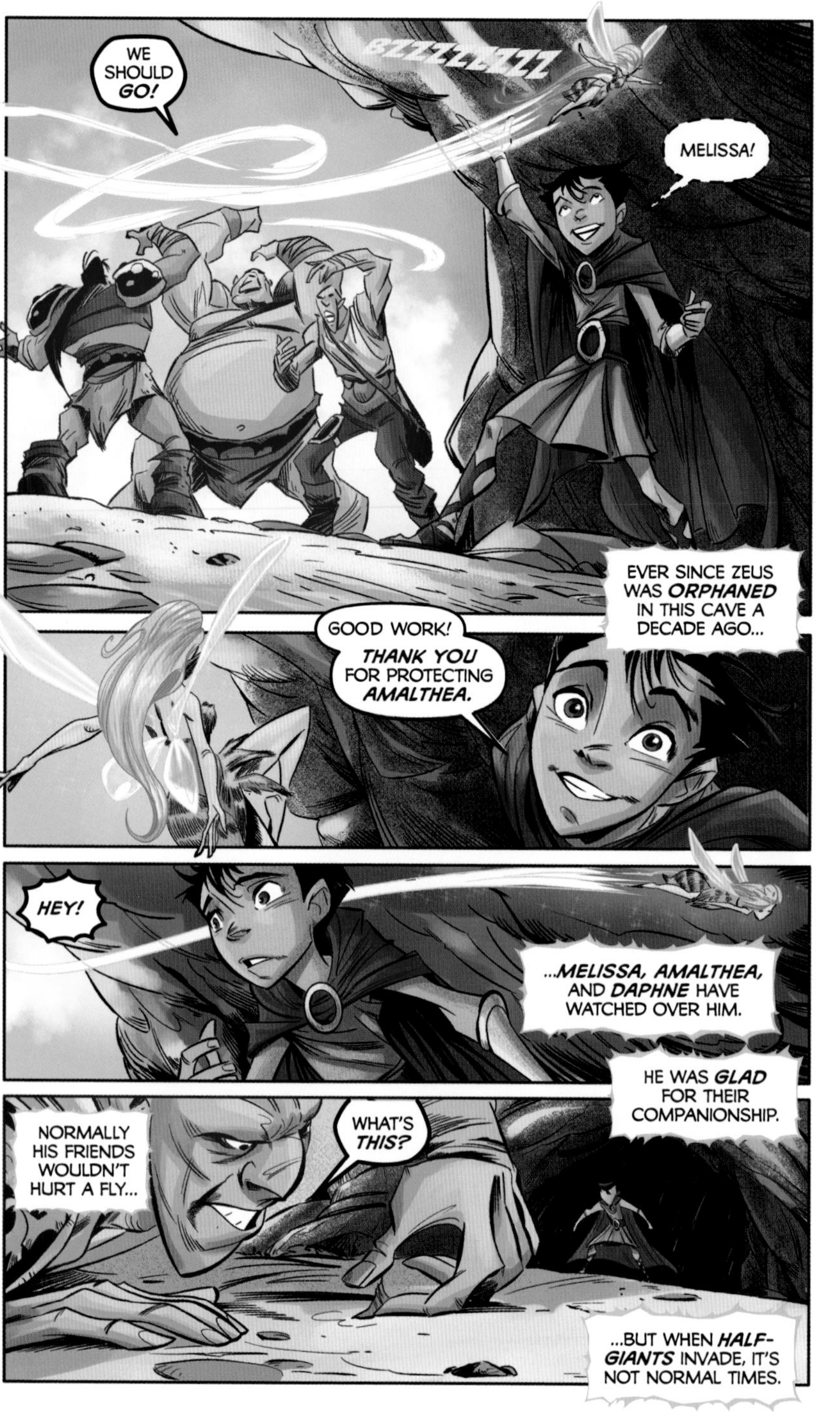
WE SHOULD *GO!*
BZZZZZZZZZ
MELISSA!
EVER SINCE ZEUS WAS *ORPHANED* IN THIS CAVE A DECADE AGO...
GOOD WORK! *THANK YOU* FOR PROTECTING *AMALTHEA.*
HEY!
...*MELISSA, AMALTHEA,* AND *DAPHNE* HAVE WATCHED OVER HIM.
HE WAS *GLAD* FOR THEIR COMPANIONSHIP.
NORMALLY HIS FRIENDS WOULDN'T HURT A FLY...
WHAT'S *THIS?*
...BUT WHEN *HALF-GIANTS* INVADE, IT'S NOT NORMAL TIMES.

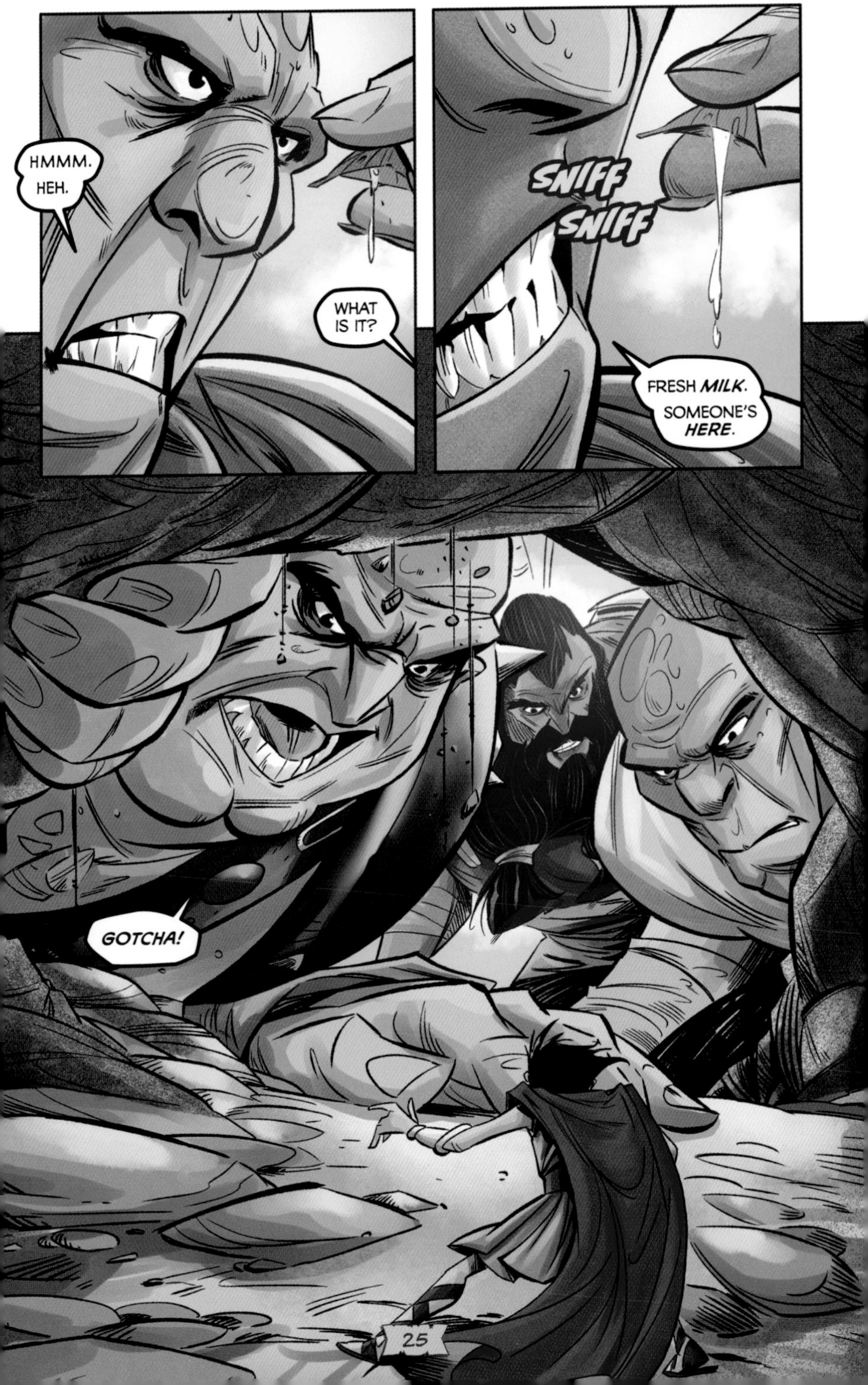
HMMM. HEH.
WHAT IS IT?
SNIFF SNIFF
FRESH MILK. SOMEONE'S HERE.
GOTCHA!

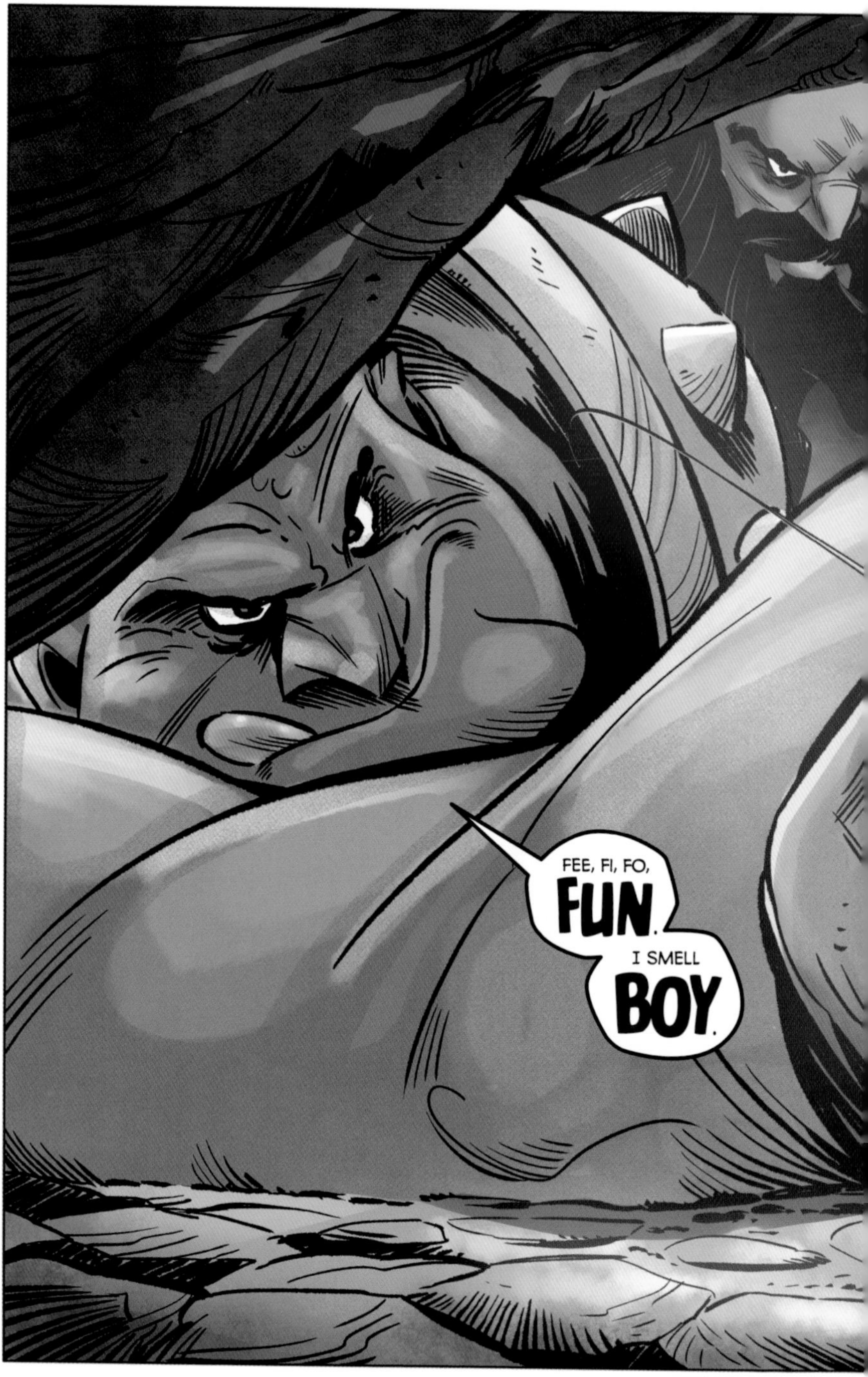
FEE, FI, FO,
FUN.
I SMELL
BOY.

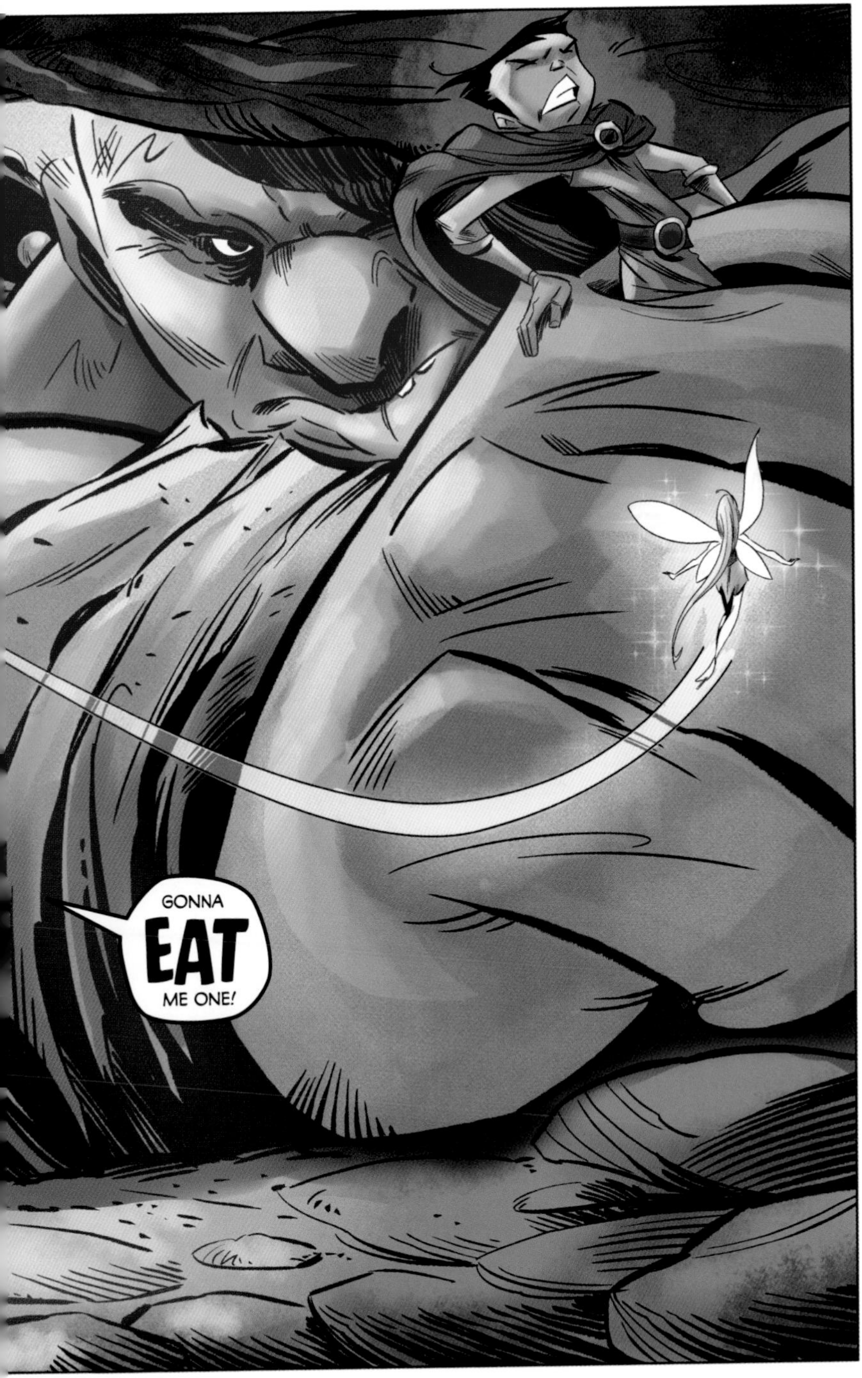
GONNA EAT ME ONE!

CHAPTER TWO:
GOODBYE, CRETE!

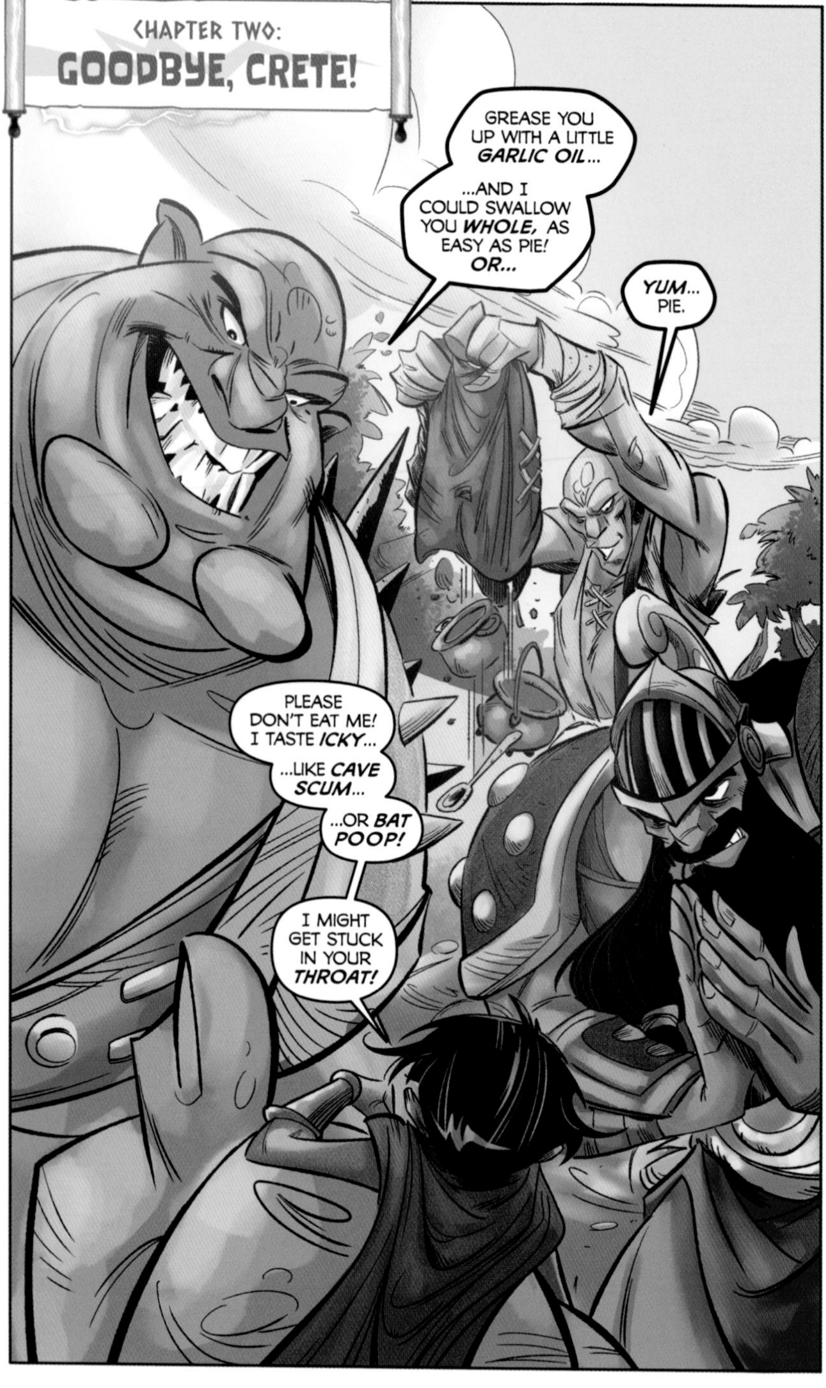
GREASE YOU UP WITH A LITTLE GARLIC OIL...
...AND I COULD SWALLOW YOU WHOLE, AS EASY AS PIE! OR...
YUM... PIE.
PLEASE DON'T EAT ME! I TASTE ICKY...
...LIKE CAVE SCUM...
...OR BAT POOP!
I MIGHT GET STUCK IN YOUR THROAT!

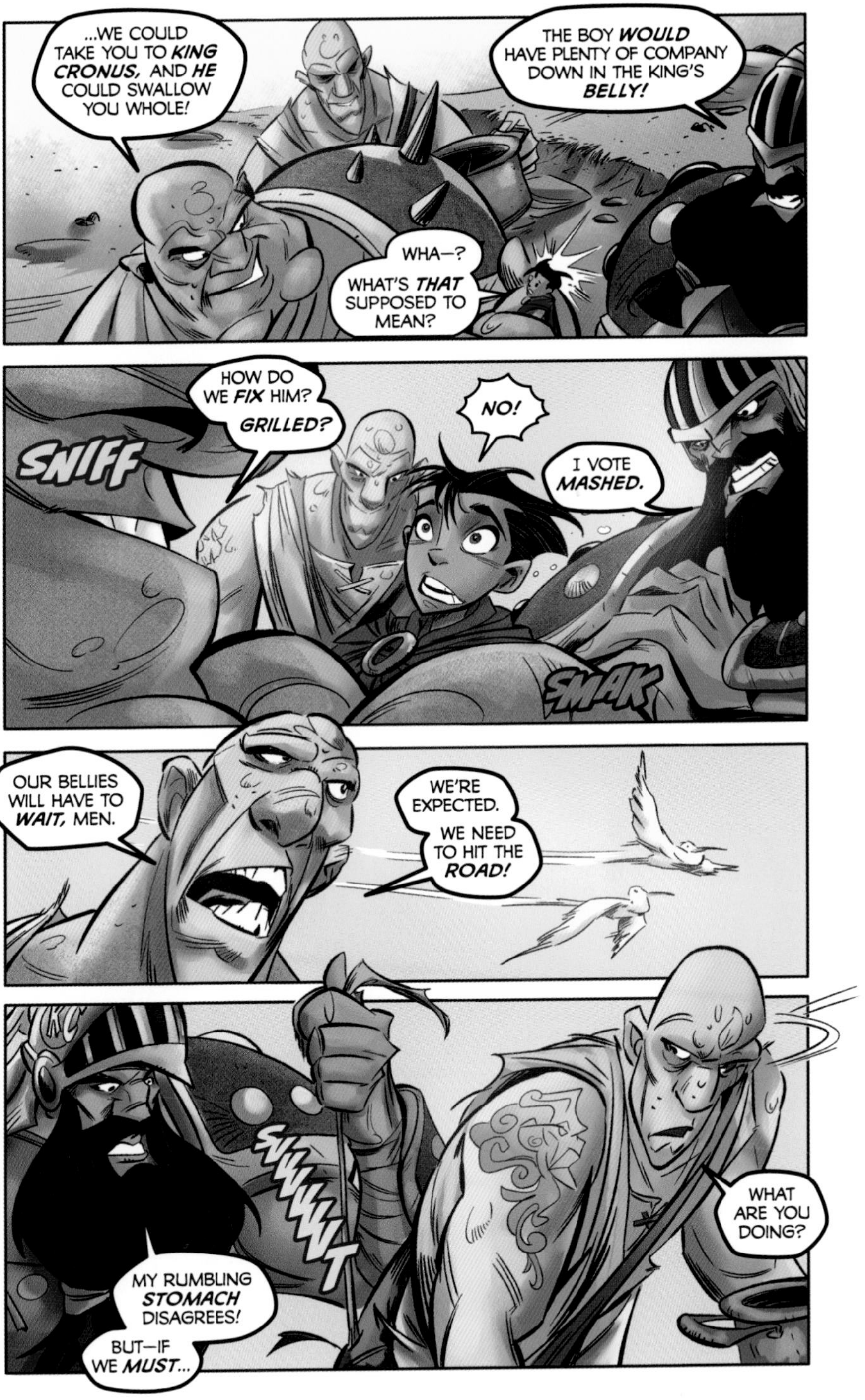
...WE COULD TAKE YOU TO KING CRONUS, AND HE COULD SWALLOW YOU WHOLE!
THE BOY WOULD HAVE PLENTY OF COMPANY DOWN IN THE KING'S BELLY!
WHA—? WHAT'S THAT SUPPOSED TO MEAN?
HOW DO WE FIX HIM? GRILLED?
NO!
I VOTE MASHED.
SNIFF
SMAK
OUR BELLIES WILL HAVE TO WAIT, MEN.
WE'RE EXPECTED. WE NEED TO HIT THE ROAD!
SWWWNT
WHAT ARE YOU DOING?
MY RUMBLING STOMACH DISAGREES!
BUT—IF WE MUST...

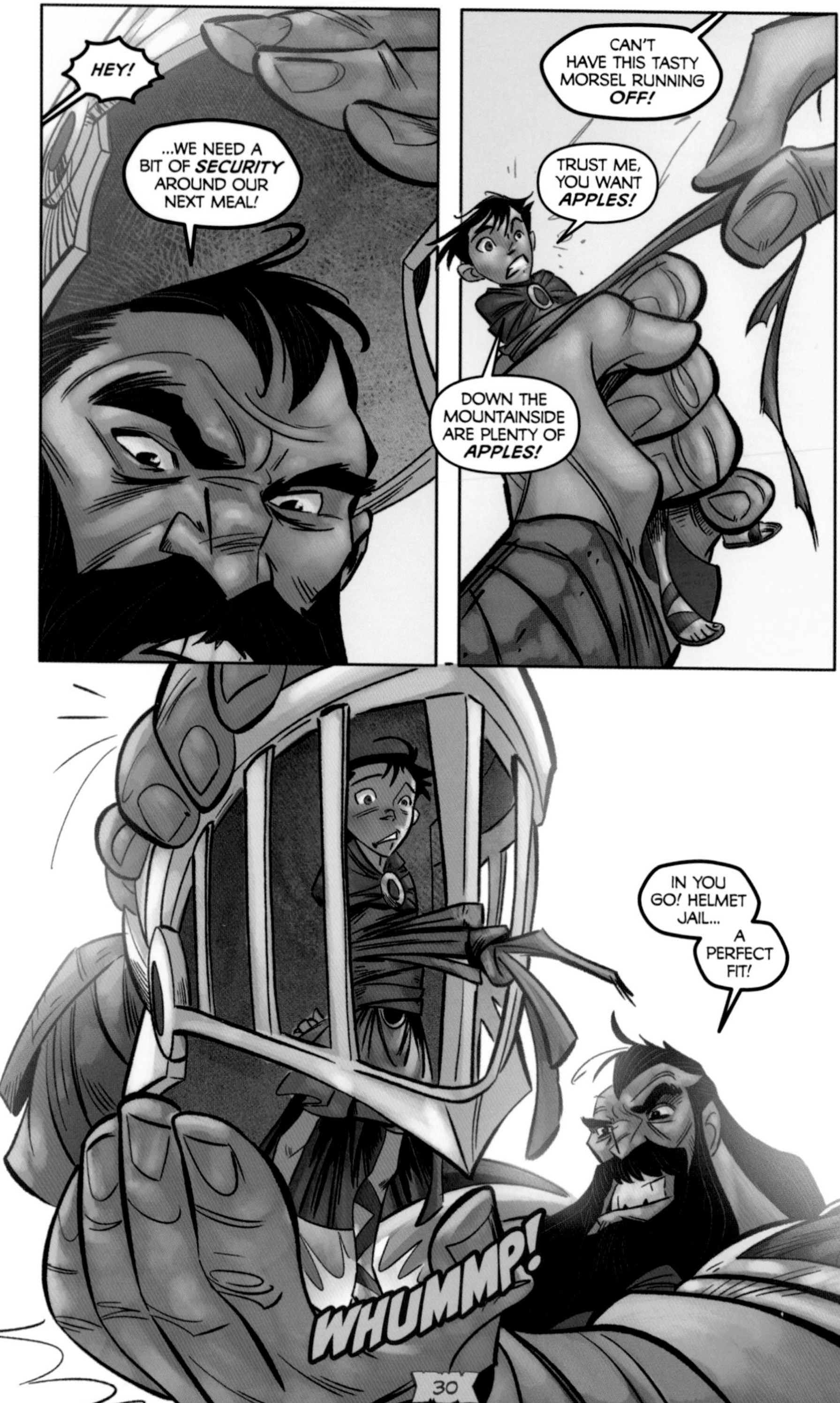
HEY!
...WE NEED A BIT OF SECURITY AROUND OUR NEXT MEAL!
CAN'T HAVE THIS TASTY MORSEL RUNNING OFF!
TRUST ME, YOU WANT APPLES!
DOWN THE MOUNTAINSIDE ARE PLENTY OF APPLES!
IN YOU GO! HELMET JAIL... A PERFECT FIT!
WHUMMP!

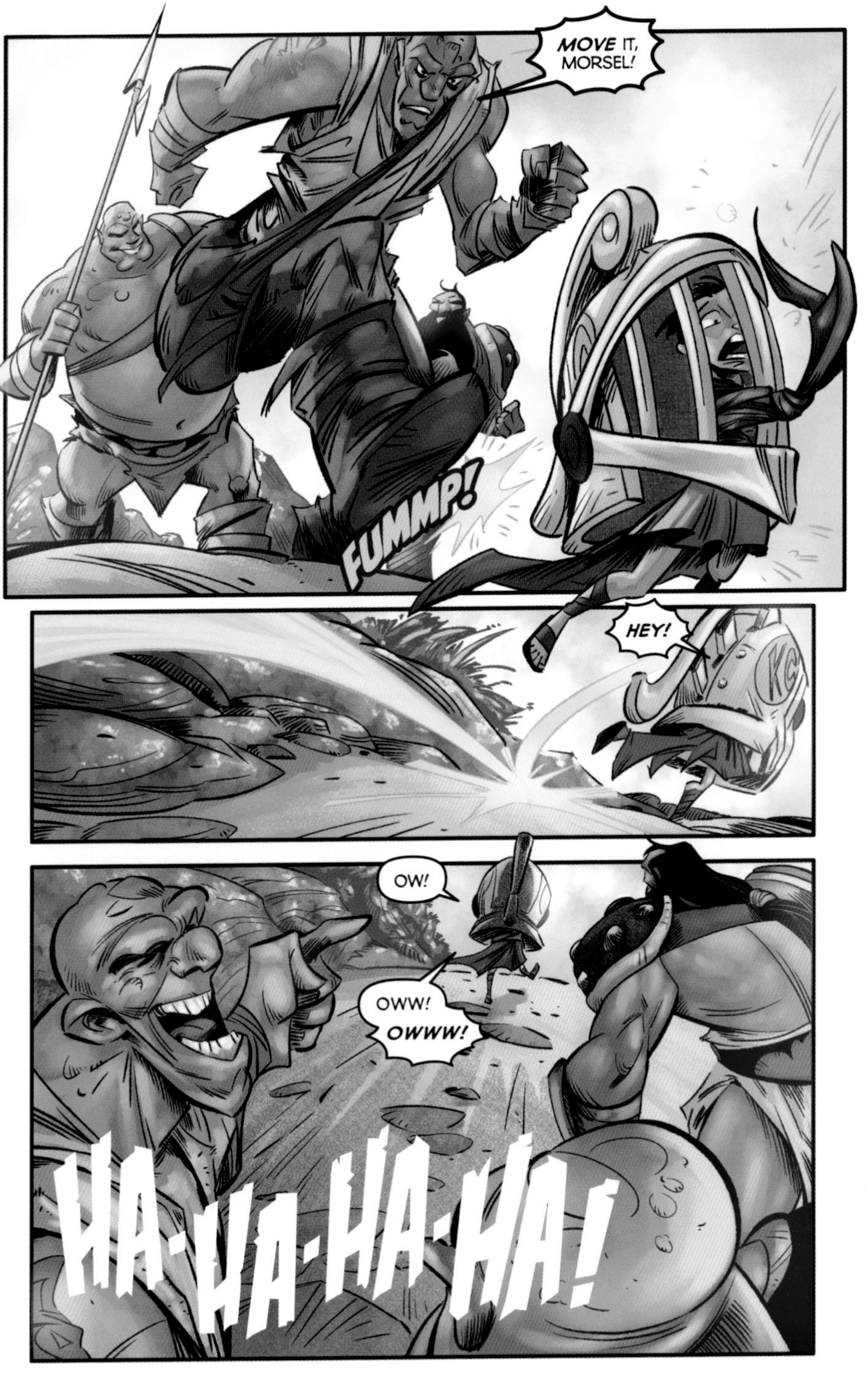
MOVE IT, MORSEL!
FUMMP!
HEY!
KC
OW!
OWW! OWWW!
HA-HA-HA-HA-HA!

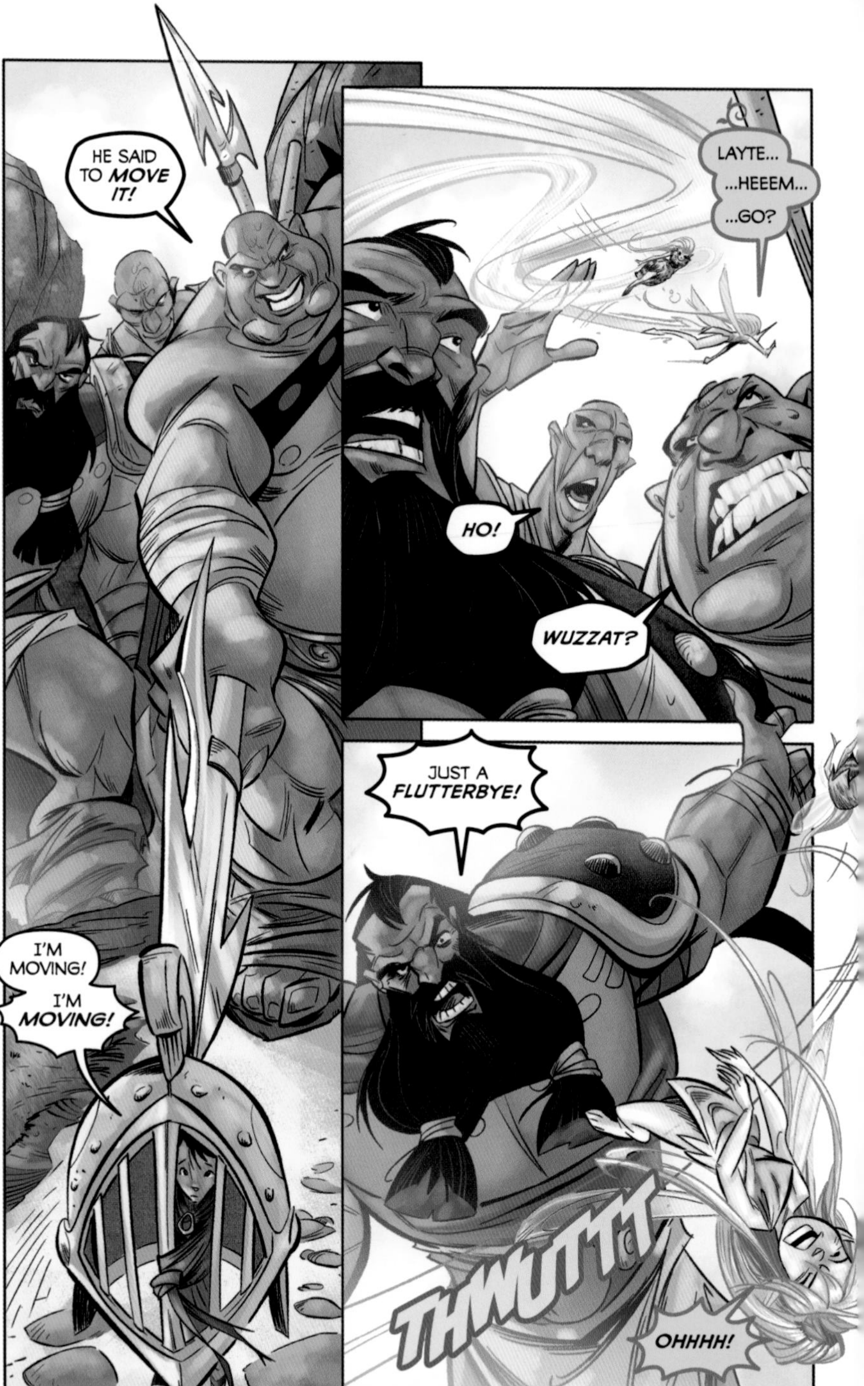
HE SAID TO MOVE IT!
I'M MOVING!
I'M MOVING!
LAYTE... ...HEEEM... ...GO?
HO!
WUZZAT?
JUST A FLUTTERBYE!
THWUTTTT
OHHHH!

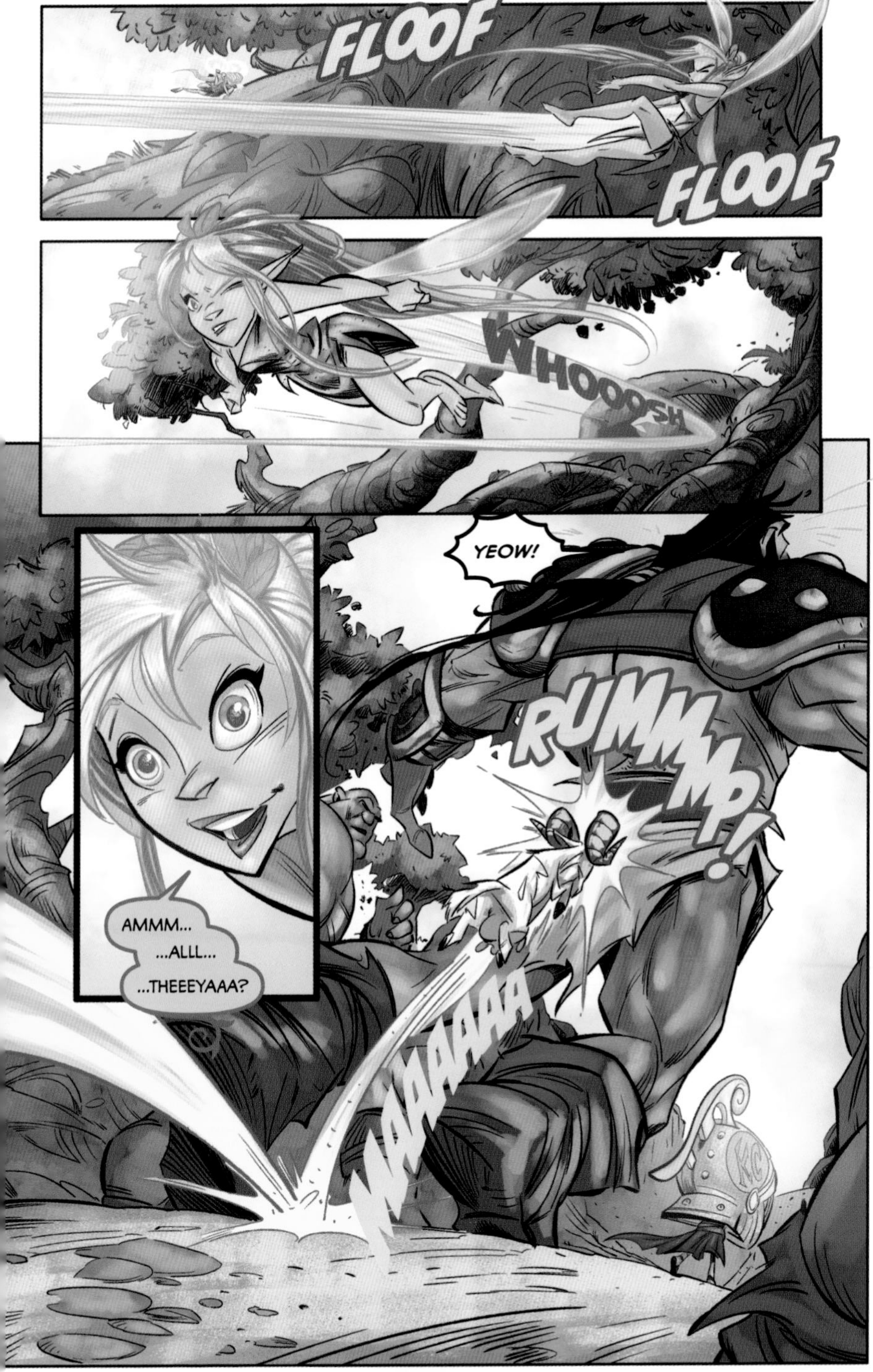
FLOOF
FLOOF
WHOOOOSH
YEOW!
RUMMMP!
AMMM...
...ALLL...
...THEEEYAAA?
MAAAAAA

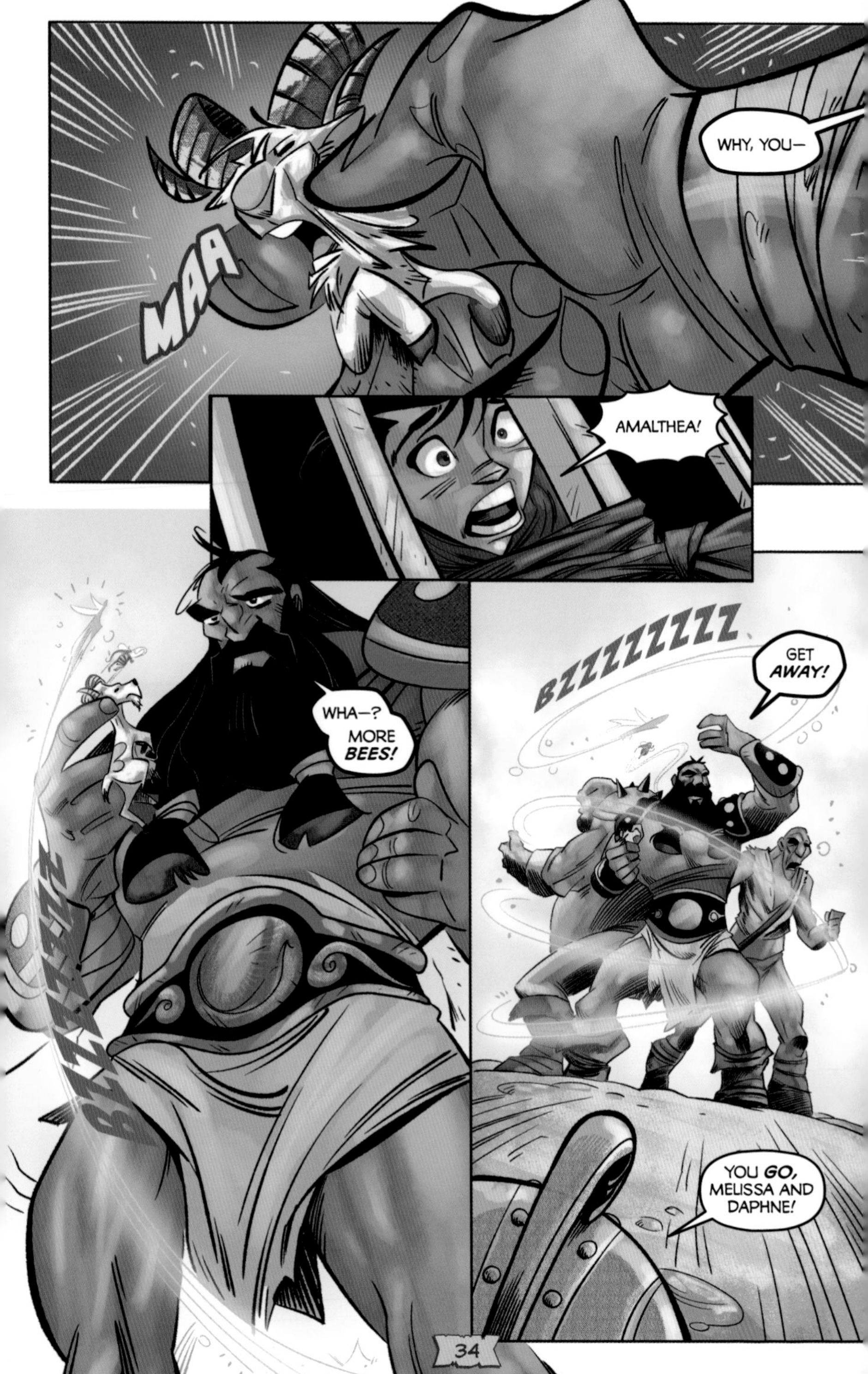
WHY, YOU—
MAA
AMALTHEA!
WHA—? MORE *BEES!*
BZZZZZZZZ
GET *AWAY!*
BZZZZZZZ
YOU *GO,* MELISSA AND DAPHNE!

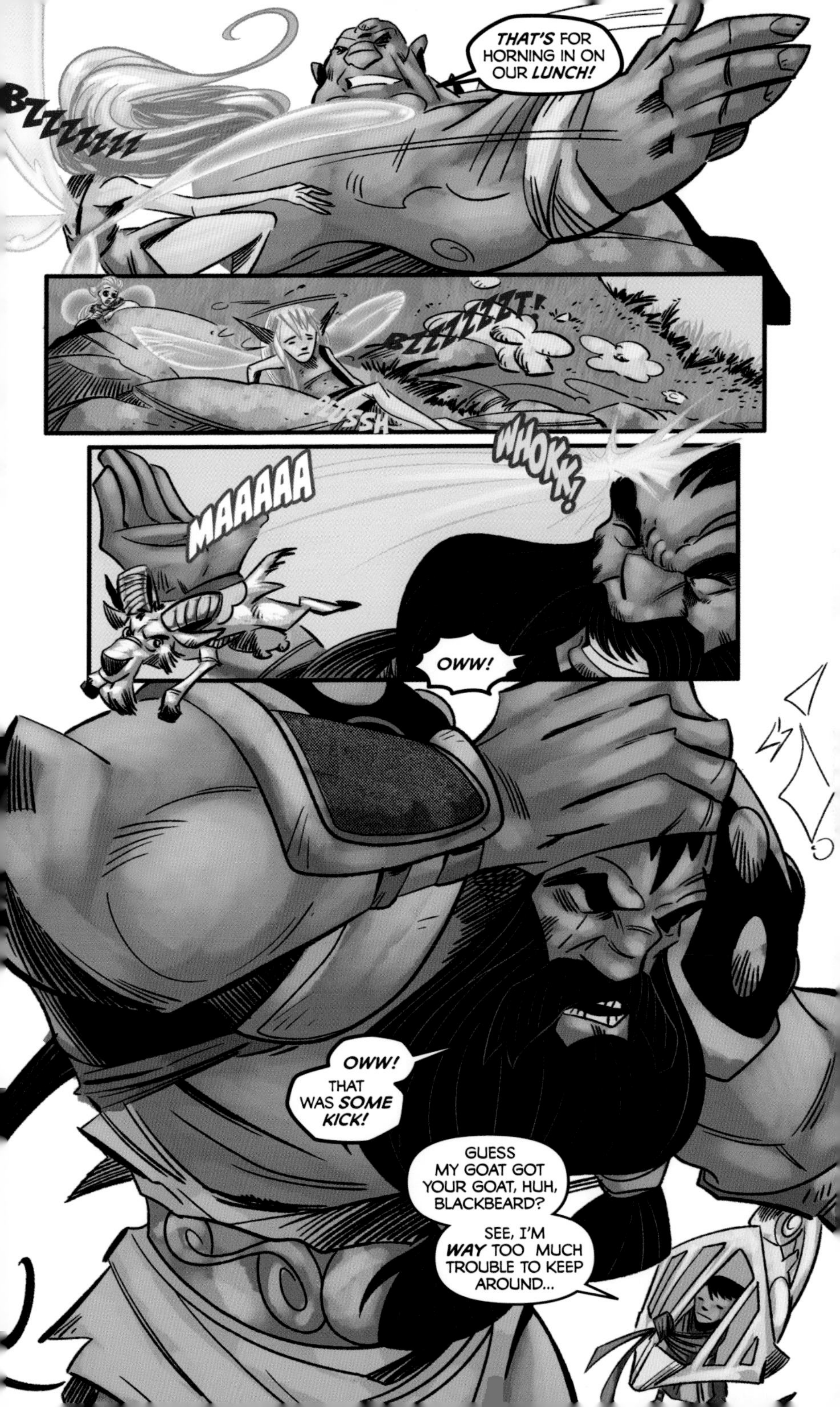
THAT'S FOR HORNING IN ON OUR LUNCH!
BZZZZZZZZ
BZZZZZZZT!
PLUSSH
MAAAAA
WHOKK!
OWW!
OWW! THAT WAS SOME KICK!
GUESS MY GOAT GOT YOUR GOAT, HUH, BLACKBEARD?
SEE, I'M WAY TOO MUCH TROUBLE TO KEEP AROUND...

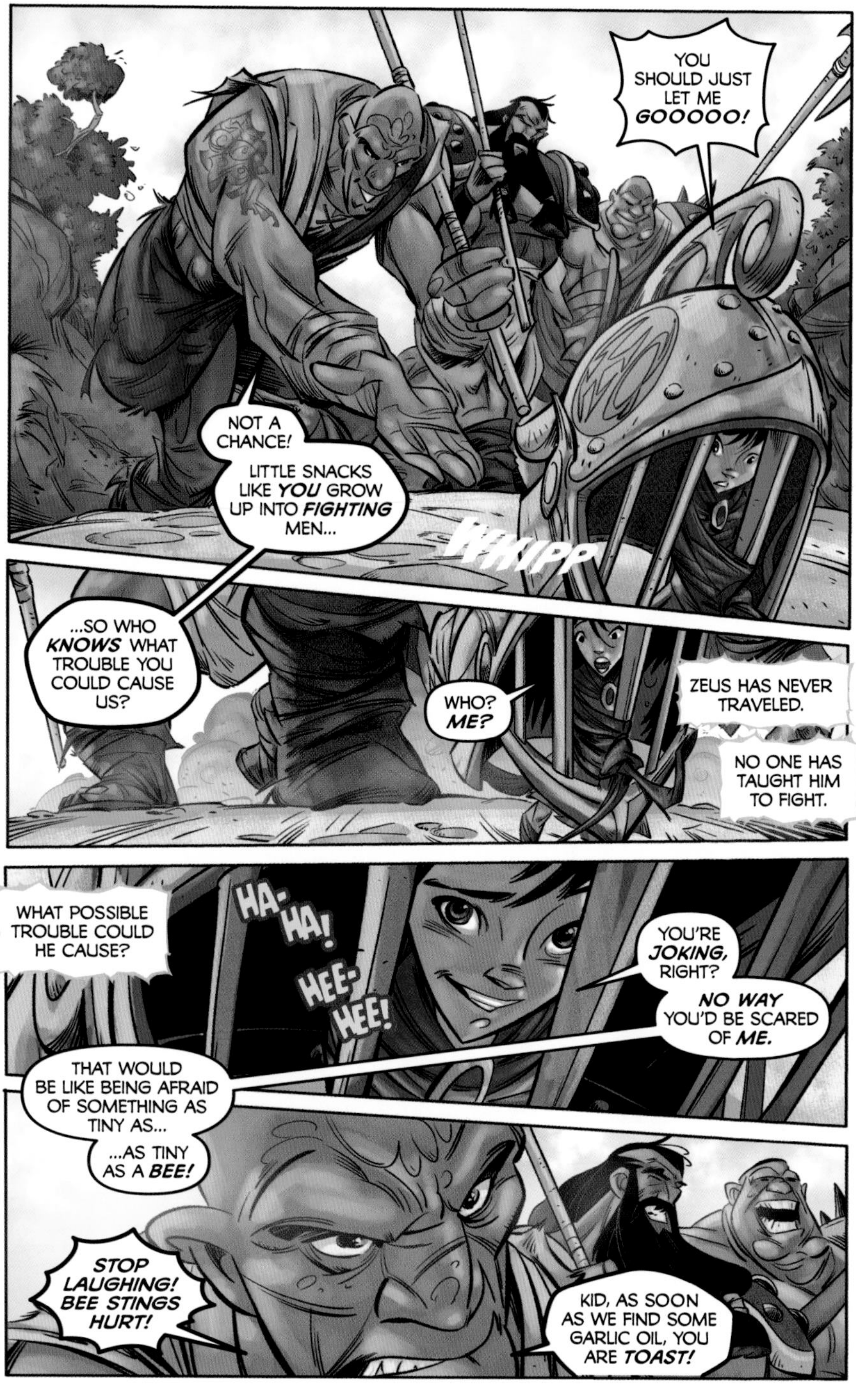
YOU SHOULD JUST LET ME GOOOOO!
NOT A CHANCE!
LITTLE SNACKS LIKE YOU GROW UP INTO FIGHTING MEN...
WHIPP
...SO WHO KNOWS WHAT TROUBLE YOU COULD CAUSE US?
WHO? ME?
ZEUS HAS NEVER TRAVELED.
NO ONE HAS TAUGHT HIM TO FIGHT.
WHAT POSSIBLE TROUBLE COULD HE CAUSE?
HA-HA!
HEE-HEE!
YOU'RE JOKING, RIGHT?
NO WAY YOU'D BE SCARED OF ME.
THAT WOULD BE LIKE BEING AFRAID OF SOMETHING AS TINY AS...
...AS TINY AS A BEE!
STOP LAUGHING! BEE STINGS HURT!
KID, AS SOON AS WE FIND SOME GARLIC OIL, YOU ARE TOAST!

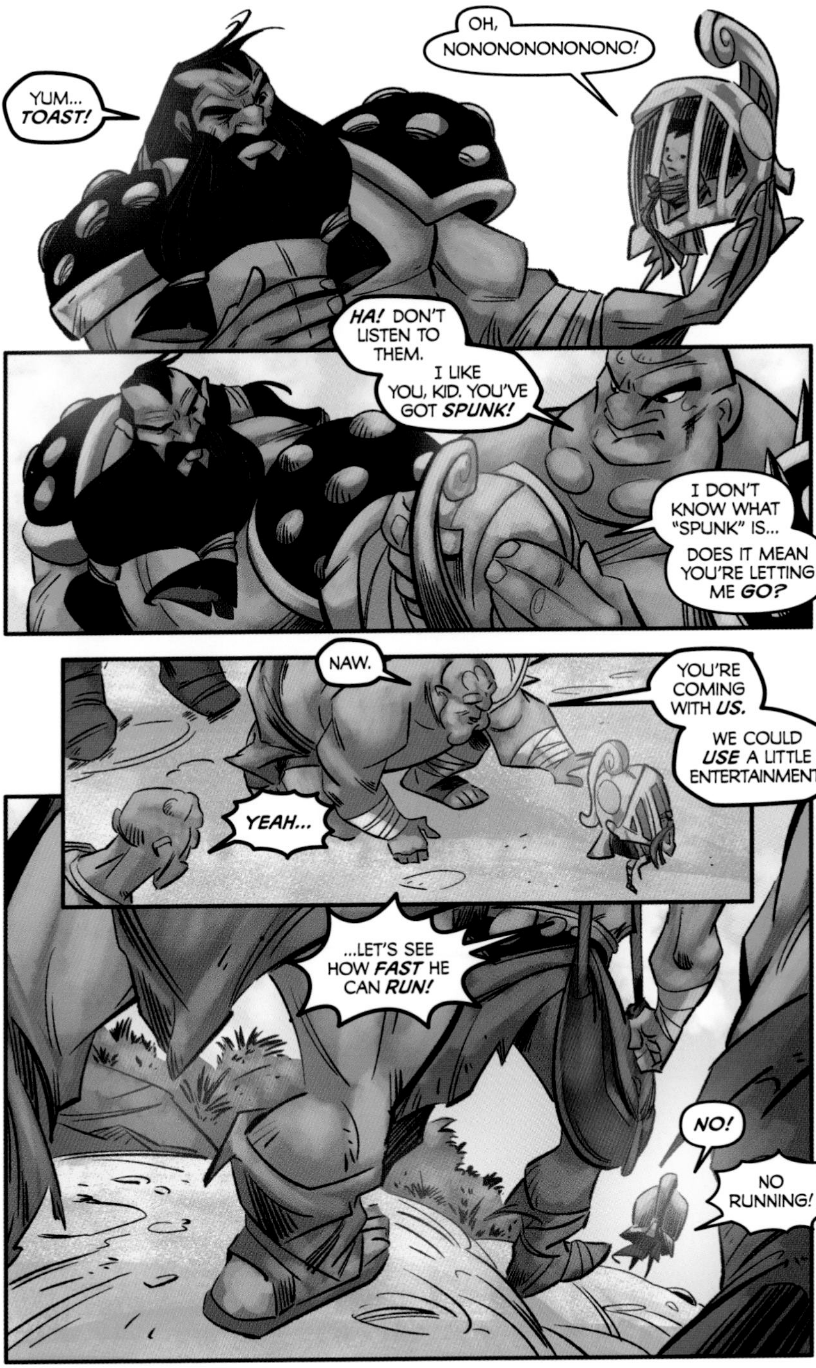
YUM... TOAST!
OH, NONONONONONONO!
HA! DON'T LISTEN TO THEM.
I LIKE YOU, KID. YOU'VE GOT SPUNK!
I DON'T KNOW WHAT "SPUNK" IS...
DOES IT MEAN YOU'RE LETTING ME GO?
NAW.
YOU'RE COMING WITH US.
WE COULD USE A LITTLE ENTERTAINMENT!
YEAH...
...LET'S SEE HOW FAST HE CAN RUN!
NO!
NO RUNNING!

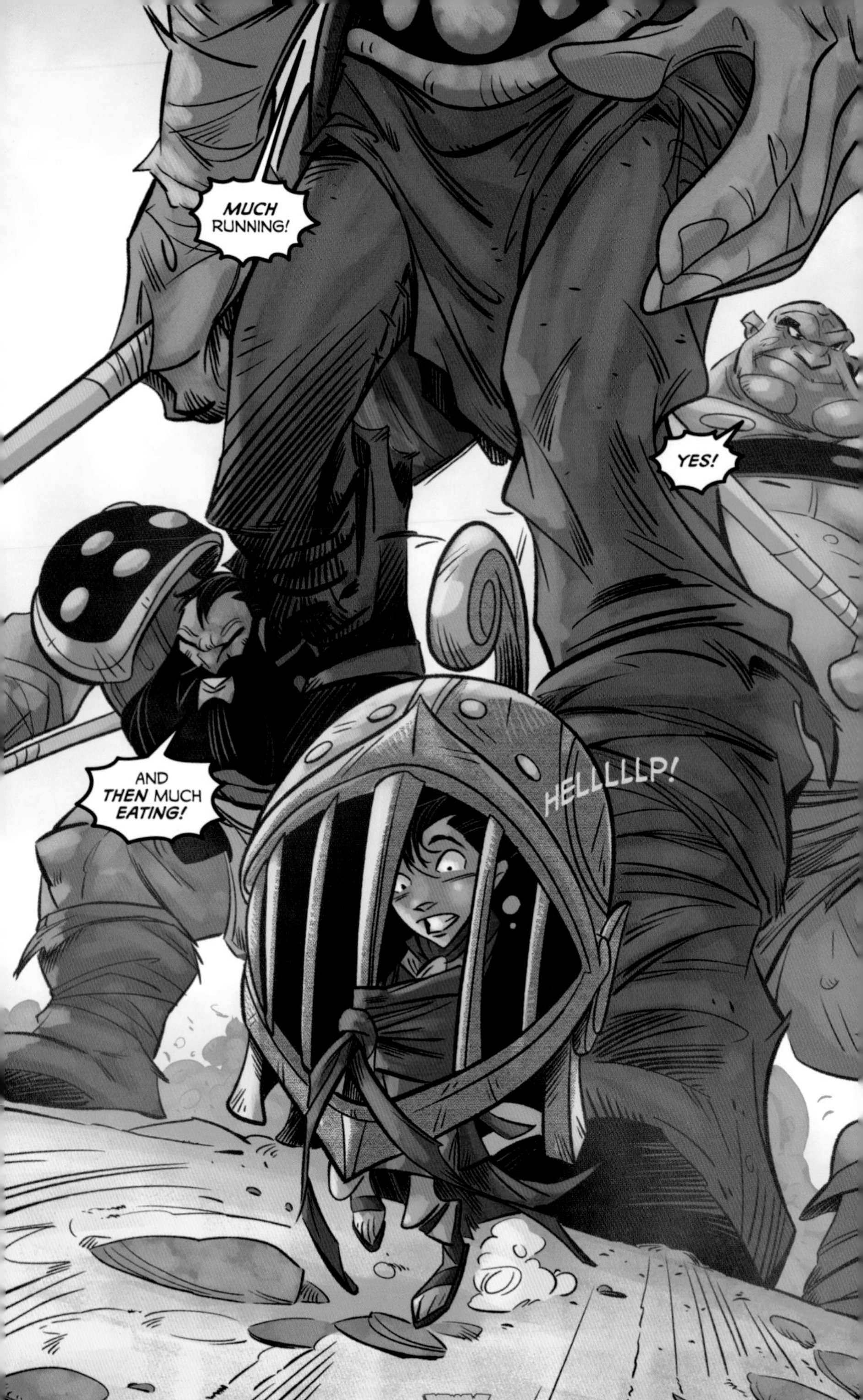
MUCH RUNNING!
YES!
AND THEN MUCH EATING!
HELLLLLP!

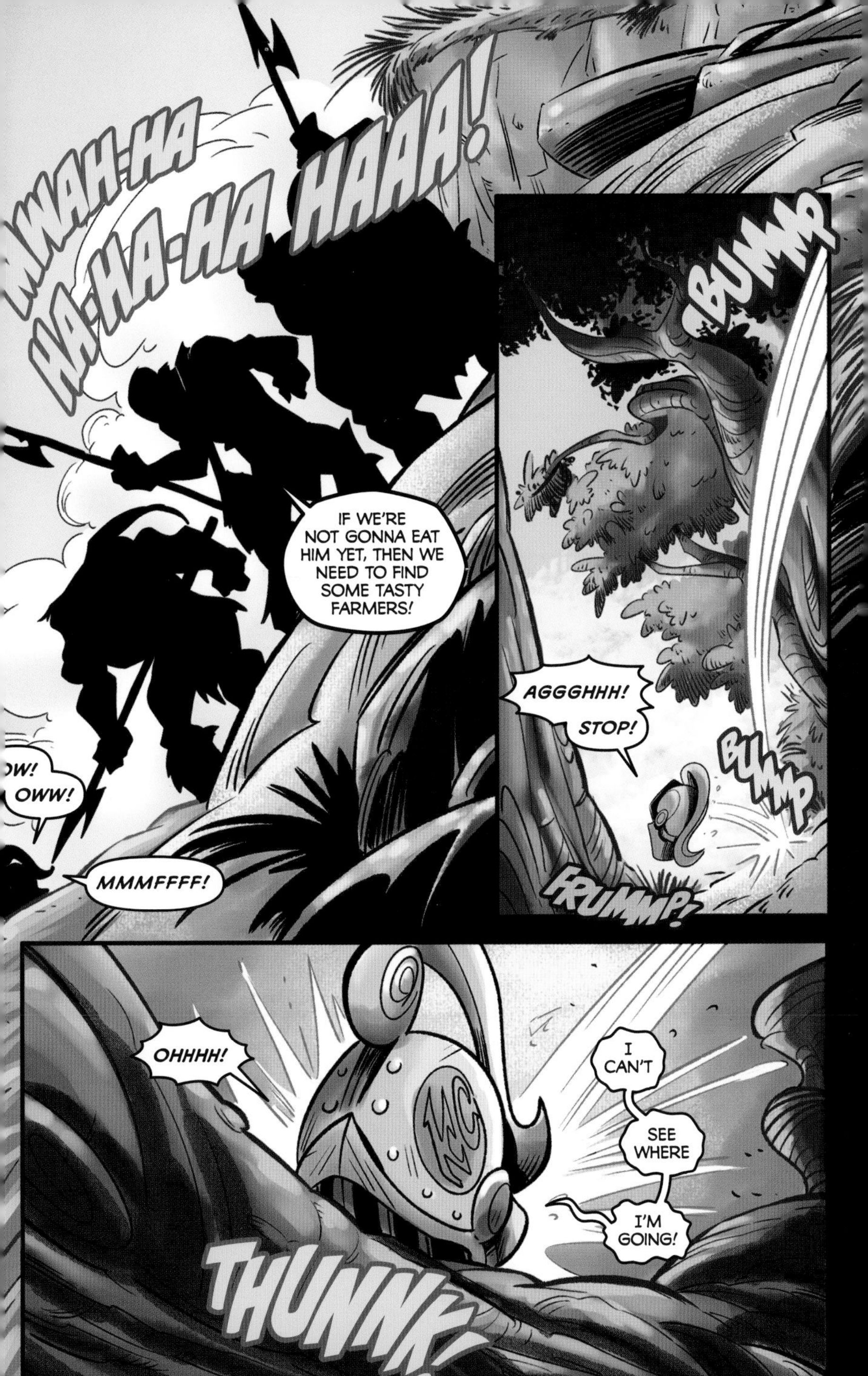
MWAH-HA HA-HA-HA HAAA!
IF WE'RE NOT GONNA EAT HIM YET, THEN WE NEED TO FIND SOME TASTY FARMERS!
OW! OWW!
MMMFFFF!
BUMMP
AGGGHHH! STOP!
BUMMP
FRUMMP!
OHHHH!
I CAN'T
SEE WHERE
I'M GOING!
THUNNK!

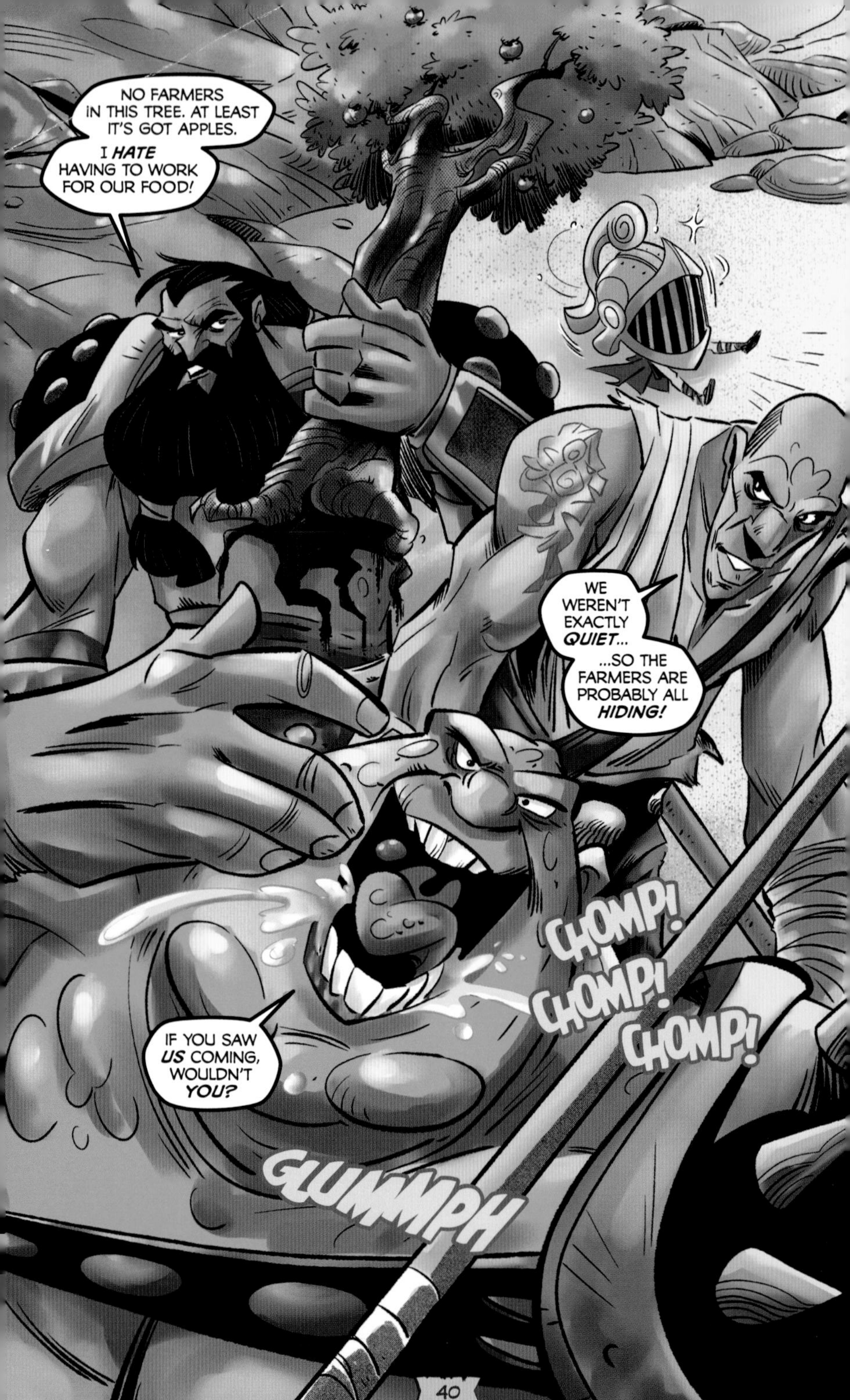

NO FARMERS IN THIS TREE. AT LEAST IT'S GOT APPLES.
I **HATE** HAVING TO WORK FOR OUR FOOD!
WE WEREN'T EXACTLY ***QUIET***...
...SO THE FARMERS ARE PROBABLY ALL ***HIDING!***
CHOMP! CHOMP! CHOMP!
IF YOU SAW ***US*** COMING, WOULDN'T ***YOU?***
GLUMMPH

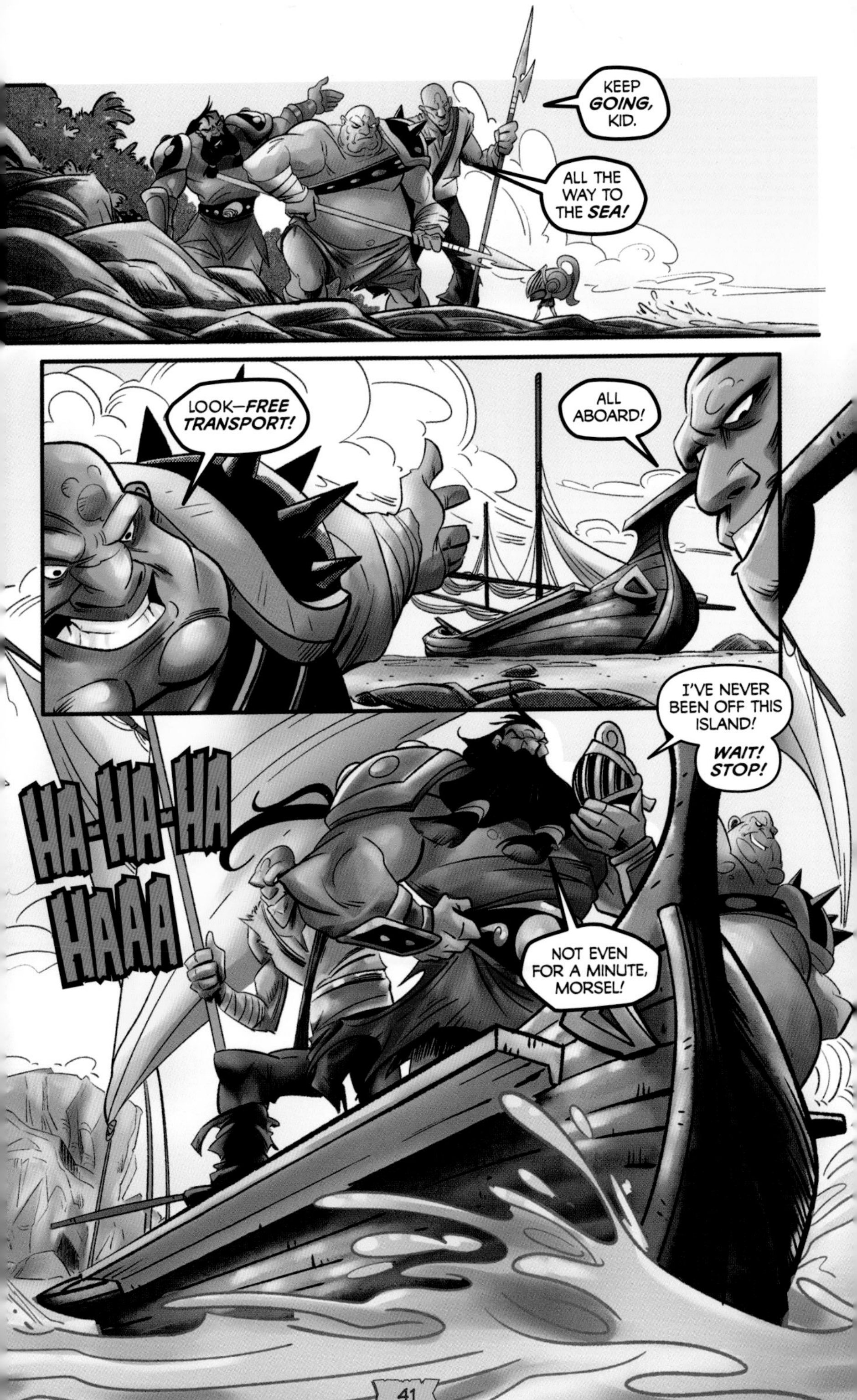
KEEP *GOING,* KID.
ALL THE WAY TO THE *SEA!*
LOOK—*FREE TRANSPORT!*
ALL ABOARD!
I'VE NEVER BEEN OFF THIS ISLAND!
WAIT! STOP!
HA-HA-HA HAAA
NOT EVEN FOR A MINUTE, MORSEL!

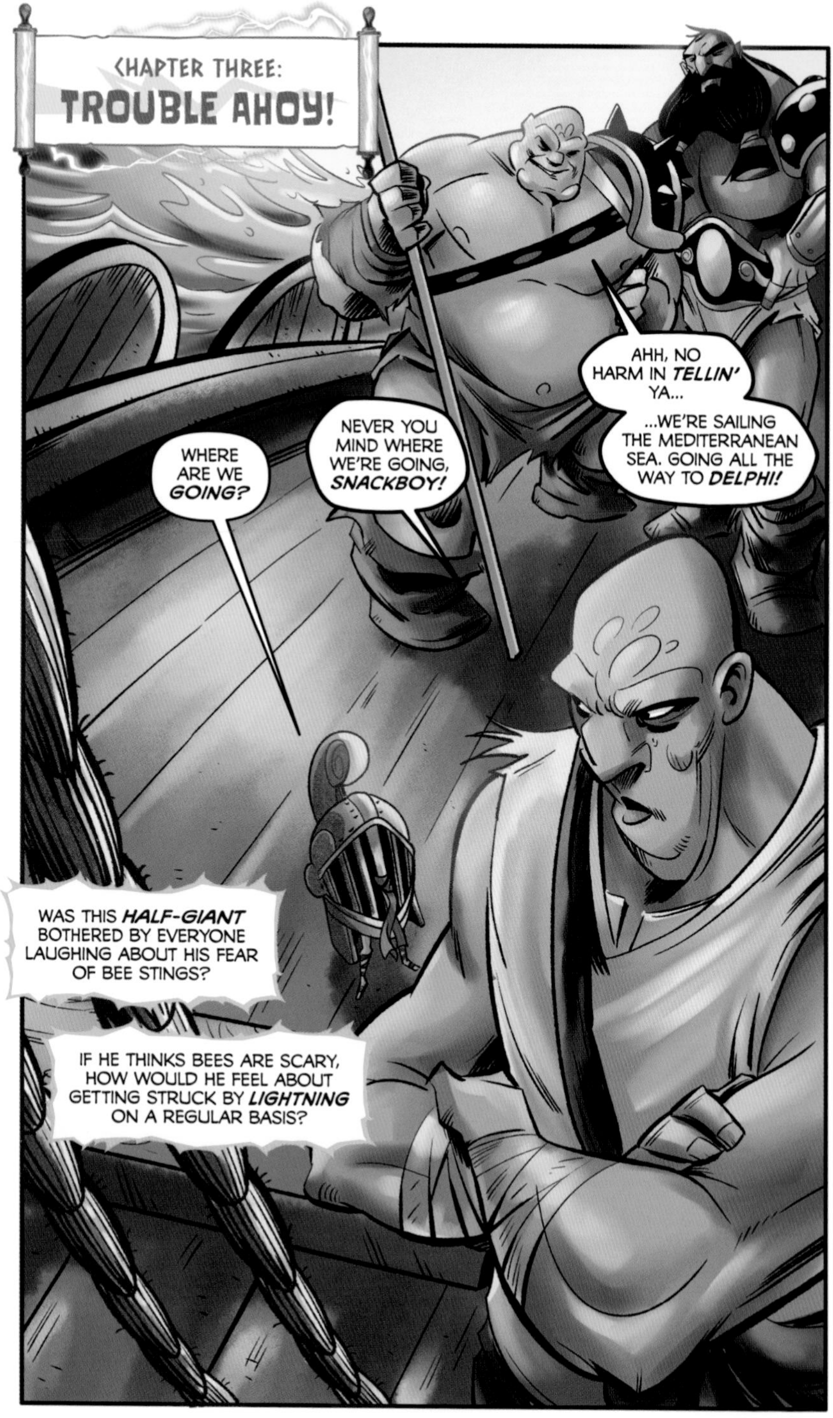
CHAPTER THREE:
TROUBLE AHOY!
WHERE ARE WE *GOING?*
NEVER YOU MIND WHERE WE'RE GOING, *SNACKBOY!*
AHH, NO HARM IN *TELLIN'* YA...
...WE'RE SAILING THE MEDITERRANEAN SEA. GOING ALL THE WAY TO *DELPHI!*
WAS THIS *HALF-GIANT* BOTHERED BY EVERYONE LAUGHING ABOUT HIS FEAR OF BEE STINGS?
IF HE THINKS BEES ARE SCARY, HOW WOULD HE FEEL ABOUT GETTING STRUCK BY *LIGHTNING* ON A REGULAR BASIS?

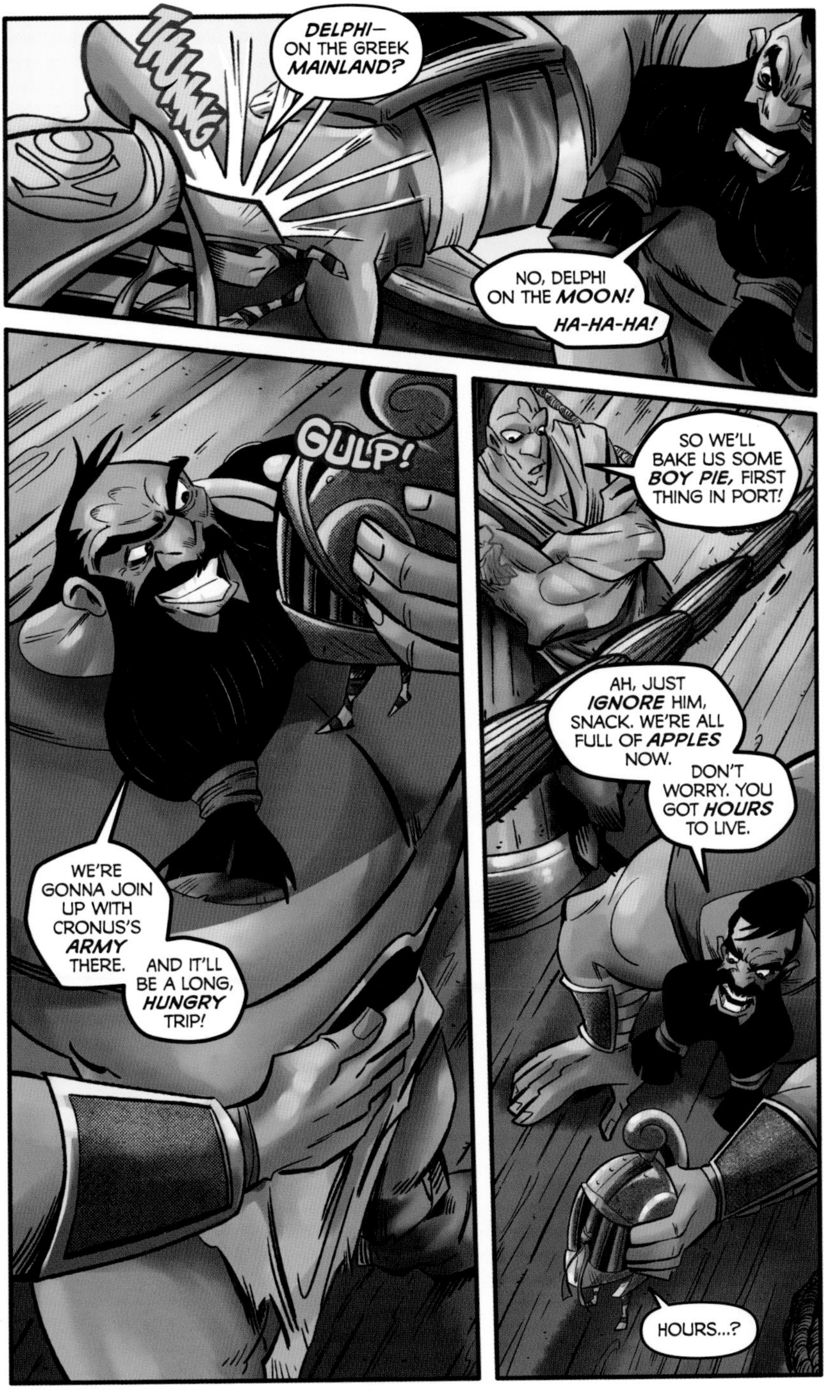
THWANG
DELPHI—
ON THE GREEK
MAINLAND?
NO, DELPHI
ON THE MOON!
HA-HA-HA!
GULP!
WE'RE GONNA JOIN UP WITH CRONUS'S ARMY THERE.
AND IT'LL BE A LONG, HUNGRY TRIP!
SO WE'LL BAKE US SOME BOY PIE, FIRST THING IN PORT!
AH, JUST IGNORE HIM, SNACK. WE'RE ALL FULL OF APPLES NOW.
DON'T WORRY. YOU GOT HOURS TO LIVE.
HOURS...?

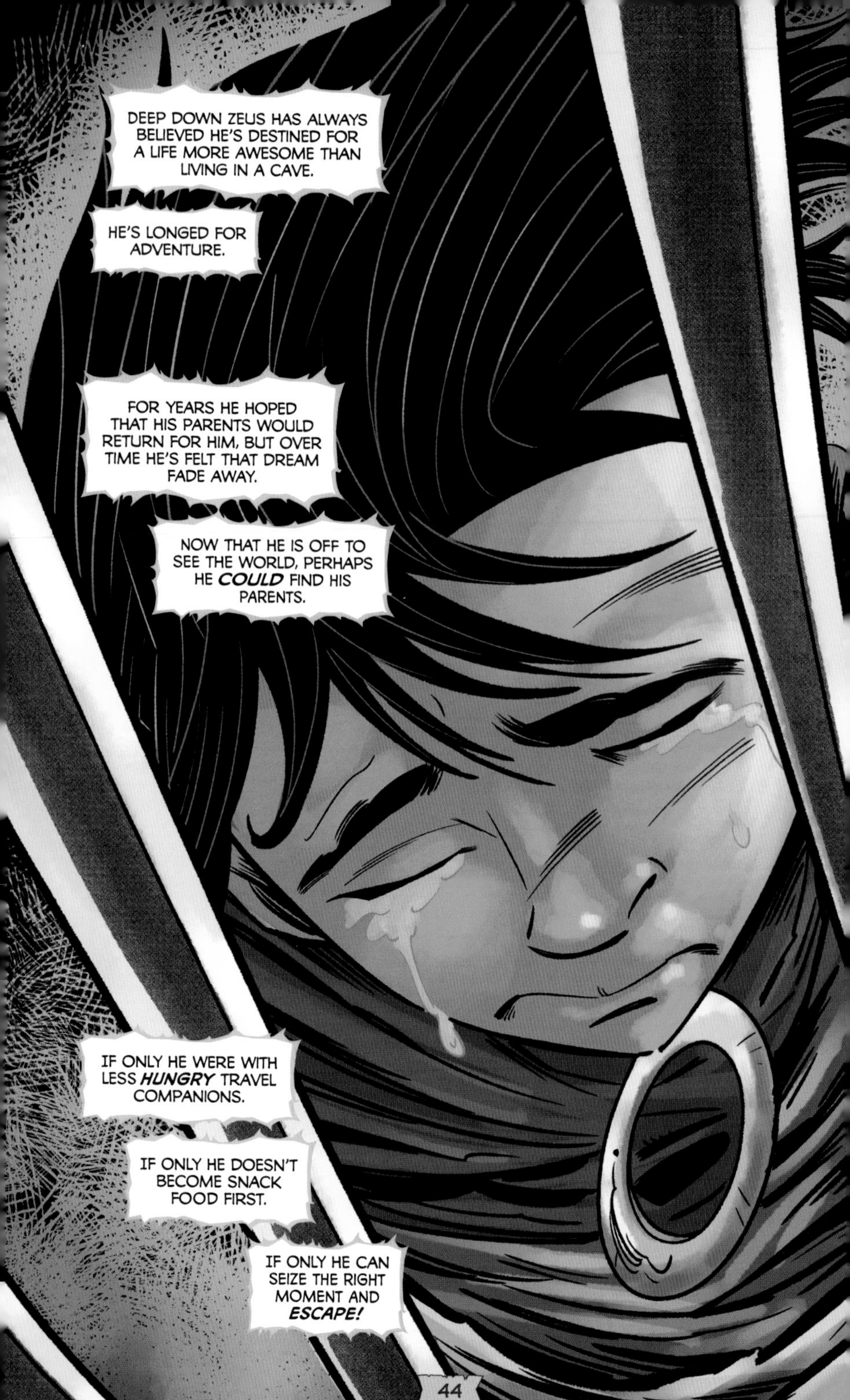
DEEP DOWN ZEUS HAS ALWAYS BELIEVED HE'S DESTINED FOR A LIFE MORE AWESOME THAN LIVING IN A CAVE.
HE'S LONGED FOR ADVENTURE.
FOR YEARS HE HOPED THAT HIS PARENTS WOULD RETURN FOR HIM, BUT OVER TIME HE'S FELT THAT DREAM FADE AWAY.
NOW THAT HE IS OFF TO SEE THE WORLD, PERHAPS HE *COULD* FIND HIS PARENTS.
IF ONLY HE WERE WITH LESS *HUNGRY* TRAVEL COMPANIONS.
IF ONLY HE DOESN'T BECOME SNACK FOOD FIRST.
IF ONLY HE CAN SEIZE THE RIGHT MOMENT AND *ESCAPE!*

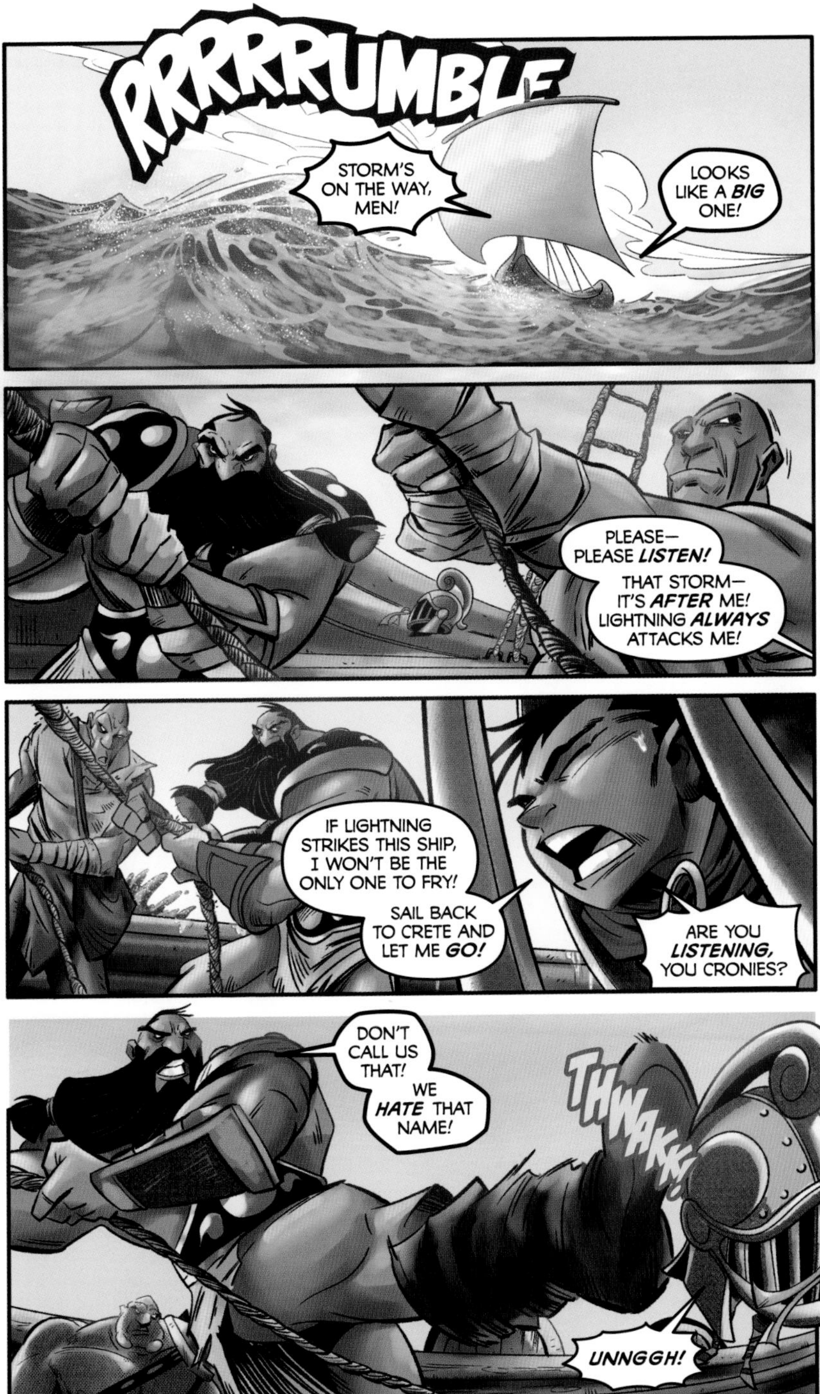
RRRRRUMBLE
STORM'S ON THE WAY, MEN!
LOOKS LIKE A *BIG* ONE!
PLEASE— PLEASE *LISTEN!*
THAT STORM— IT'S *AFTER* ME! LIGHTNING *ALWAYS* ATTACKS ME!
IF LIGHTNING STRIKES THIS SHIP, I WON'T BE THE ONLY ONE TO FRY!
SAIL BACK TO CRETE AND LET ME *GO!*
ARE YOU *LISTENING,* YOU CRONIES?
DON'T CALL US THAT!
WE *HATE* THAT NAME!
THWAKK!
UNNGGH!

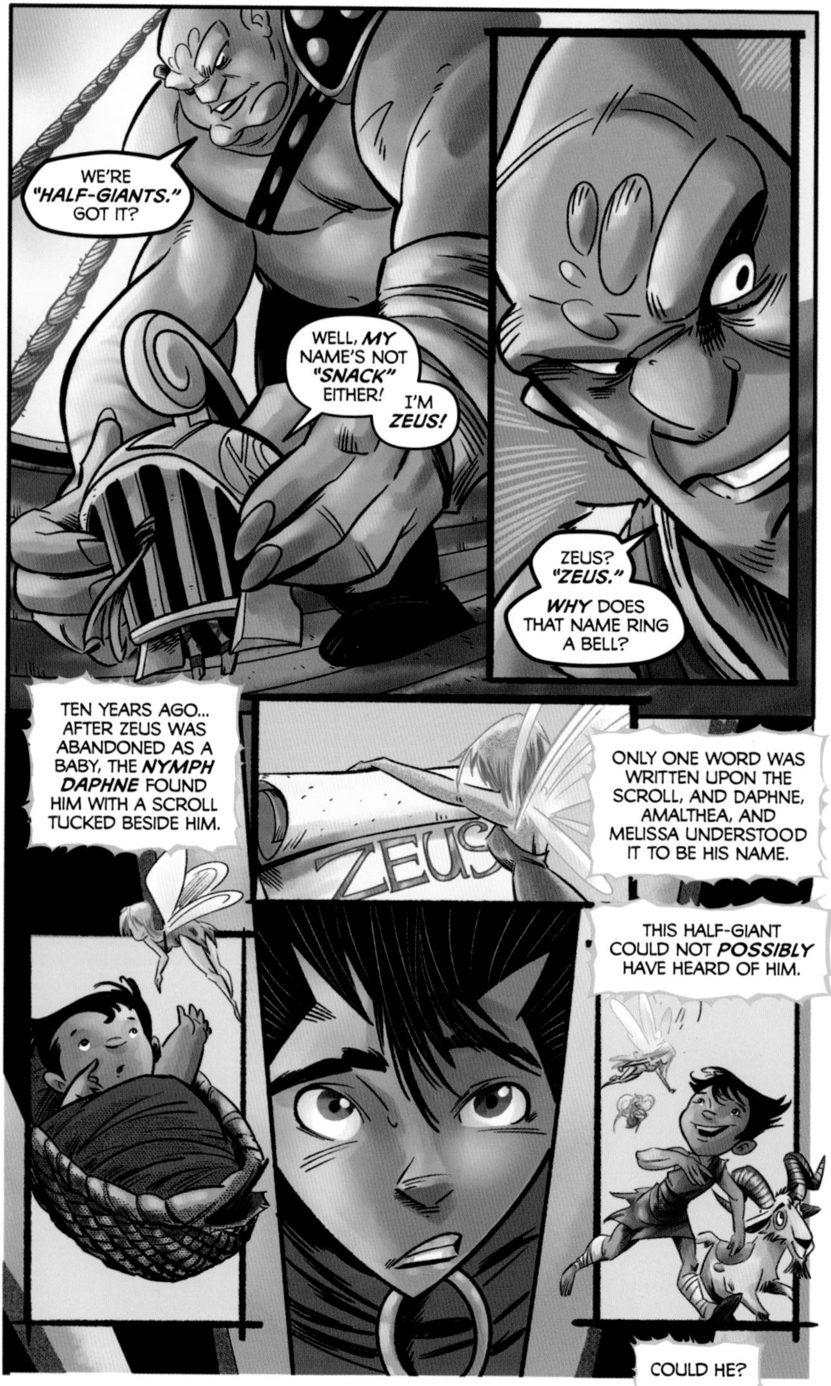
WE'RE "HALF-GIANTS." GOT IT?
WELL, MY NAME'S NOT "SNACK" EITHER!
I'M ZEUS!
ZEUS? "ZEUS."
WHY DOES THAT NAME RING A BELL?
TEN YEARS AGO... AFTER ZEUS WAS ABANDONED AS A BABY, THE NYMPH DAPHNE FOUND HIM WITH A SCROLL TUCKED BESIDE HIM.
ZEUS
ONLY ONE WORD WAS WRITTEN UPON THE SCROLL, AND DAPHNE, AMALTHEA, AND MELISSA UNDERSTOOD IT TO BE HIS NAME.
THIS HALF-GIANT COULD NOT POSSIBLY HAVE HEARD OF HIM.
COULD HE?

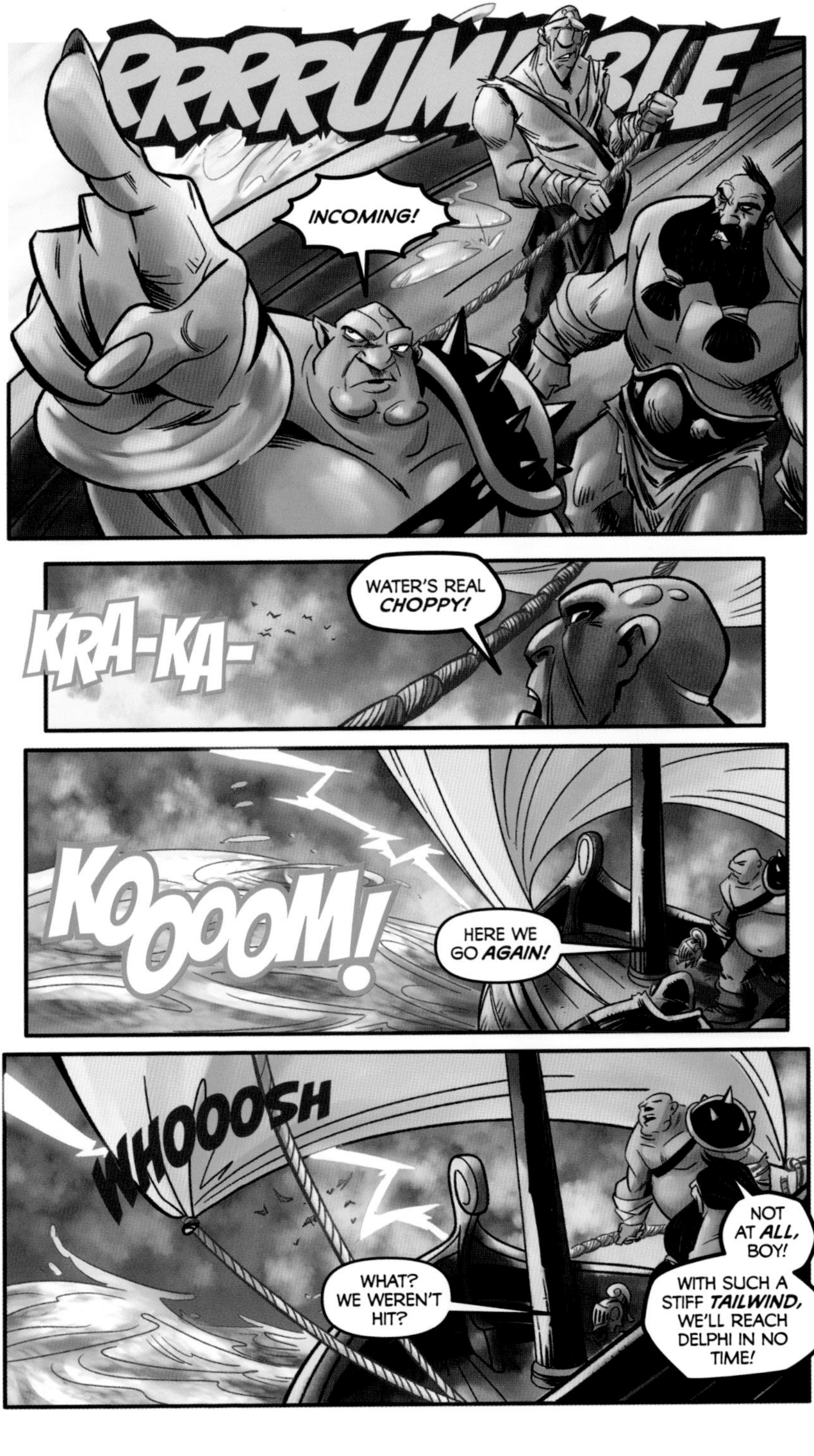
PRRRUMBLE
INCOMING!
KRA-KA-
WATER'S REAL CHOPPY!
KOOOOM!
HERE WE GO AGAIN!
WHOOOSH
WHAT? WE WEREN'T HIT?
NOT AT ALL, BOY!
WITH SUCH A STIFF TAILWIND, WE'LL REACH DELPHI IN NO TIME!

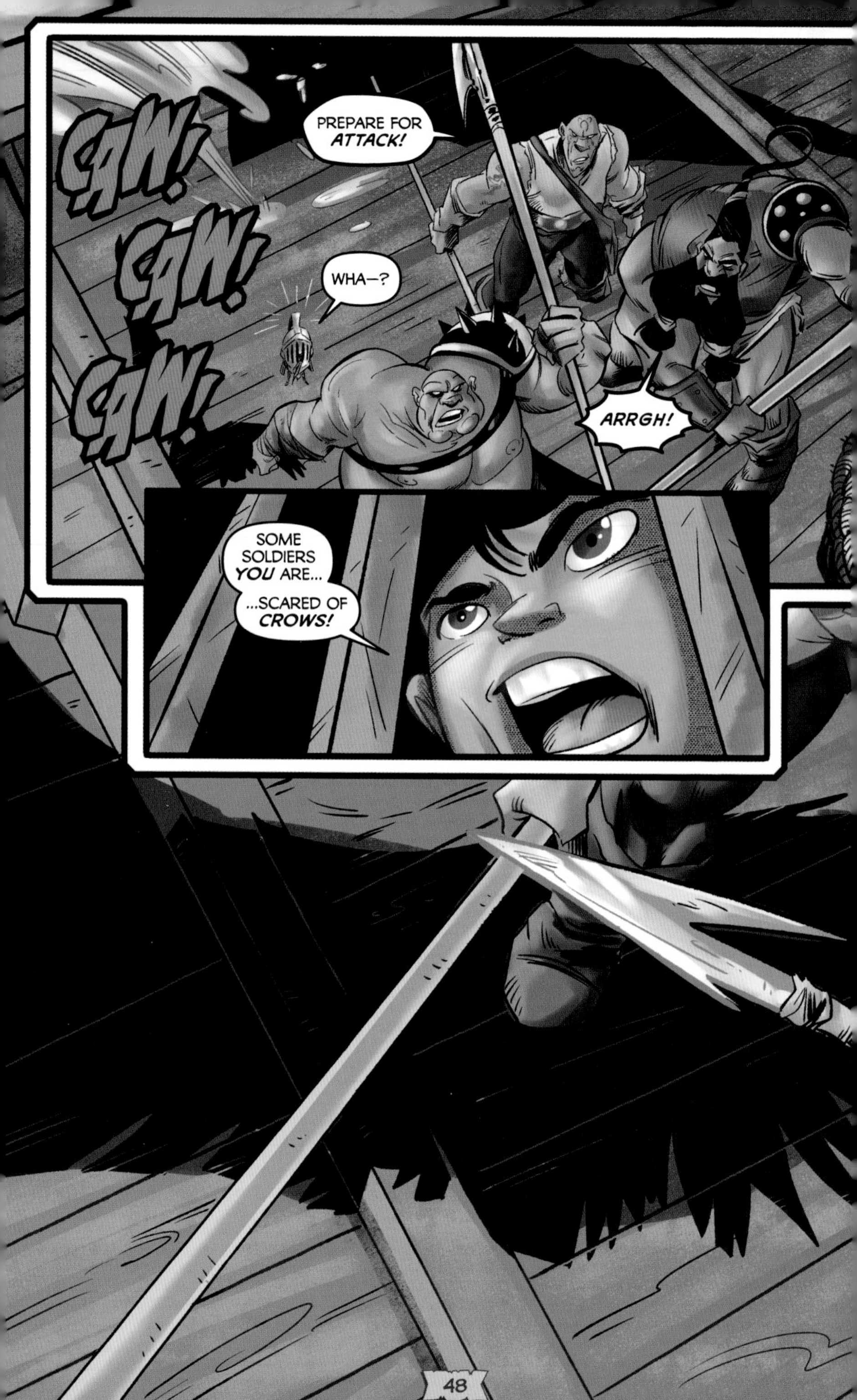
CAW!
CAW!
CAW!
PREPARE FOR ATTACK!
WHA–?
ARRGH!
SOME SOLDIERS YOU ARE...
...SCARED OF CROWS!

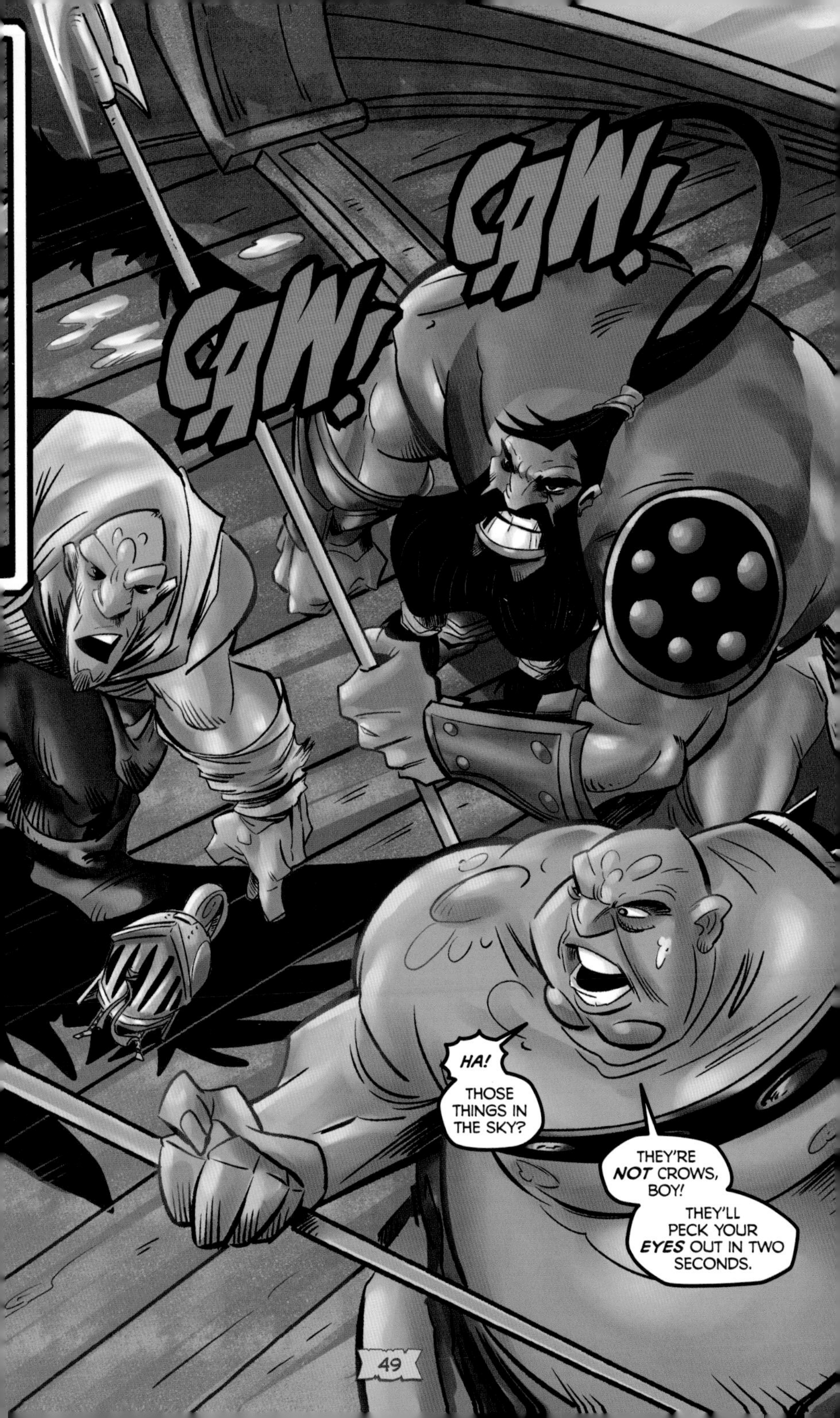
CAW! CAW!
HA!
THOSE THINGS IN THE SKY?
THEY'RE NOT CROWS, BOY!
THEY'LL PECK YOUR EYES OUT IN TWO SECONDS.

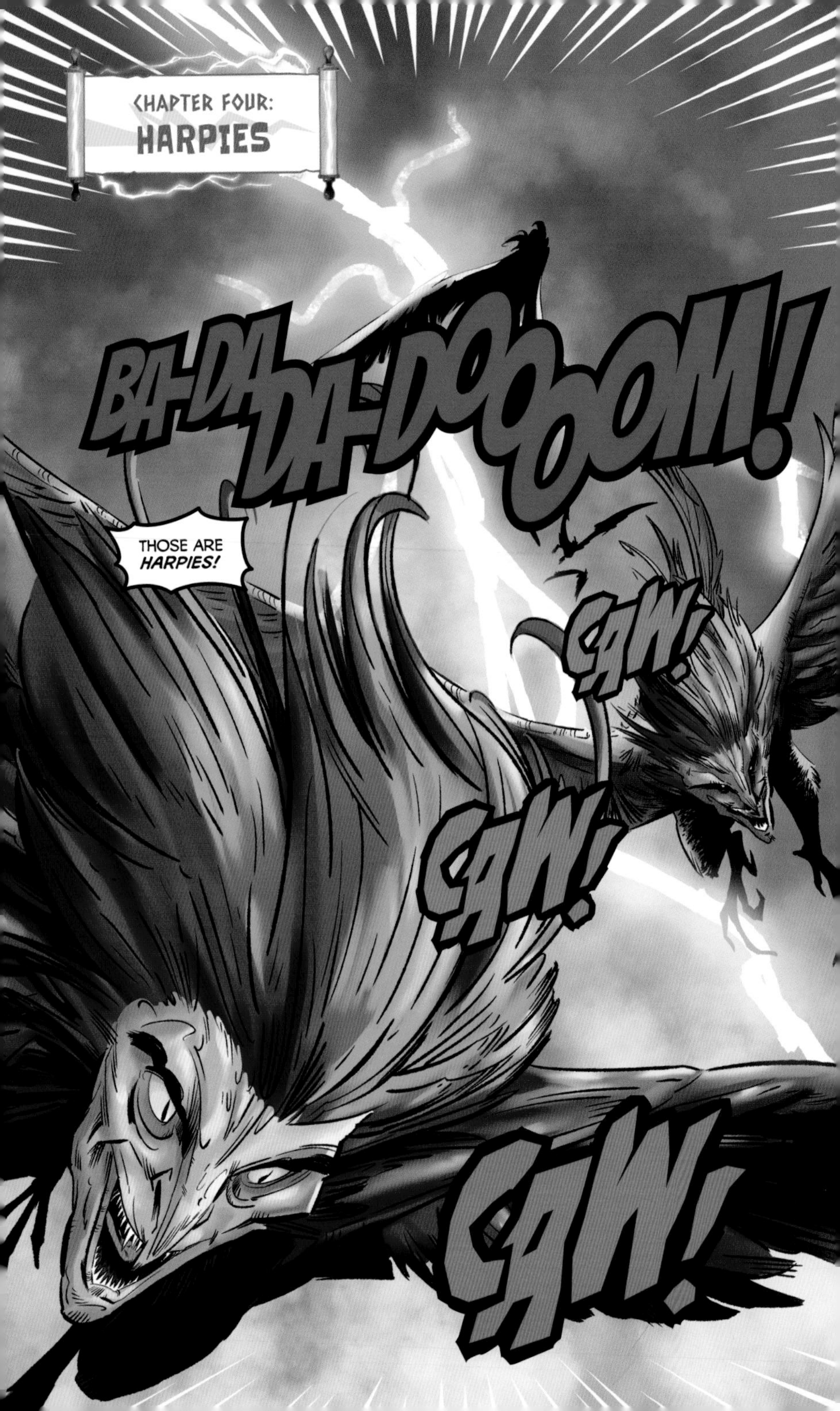
CHAPTER FOUR:
HARPIES
BA-DA DA-DOOOOOM!
THOSE ARE *HARPIES!*
CAW!
CAW!
CAW!

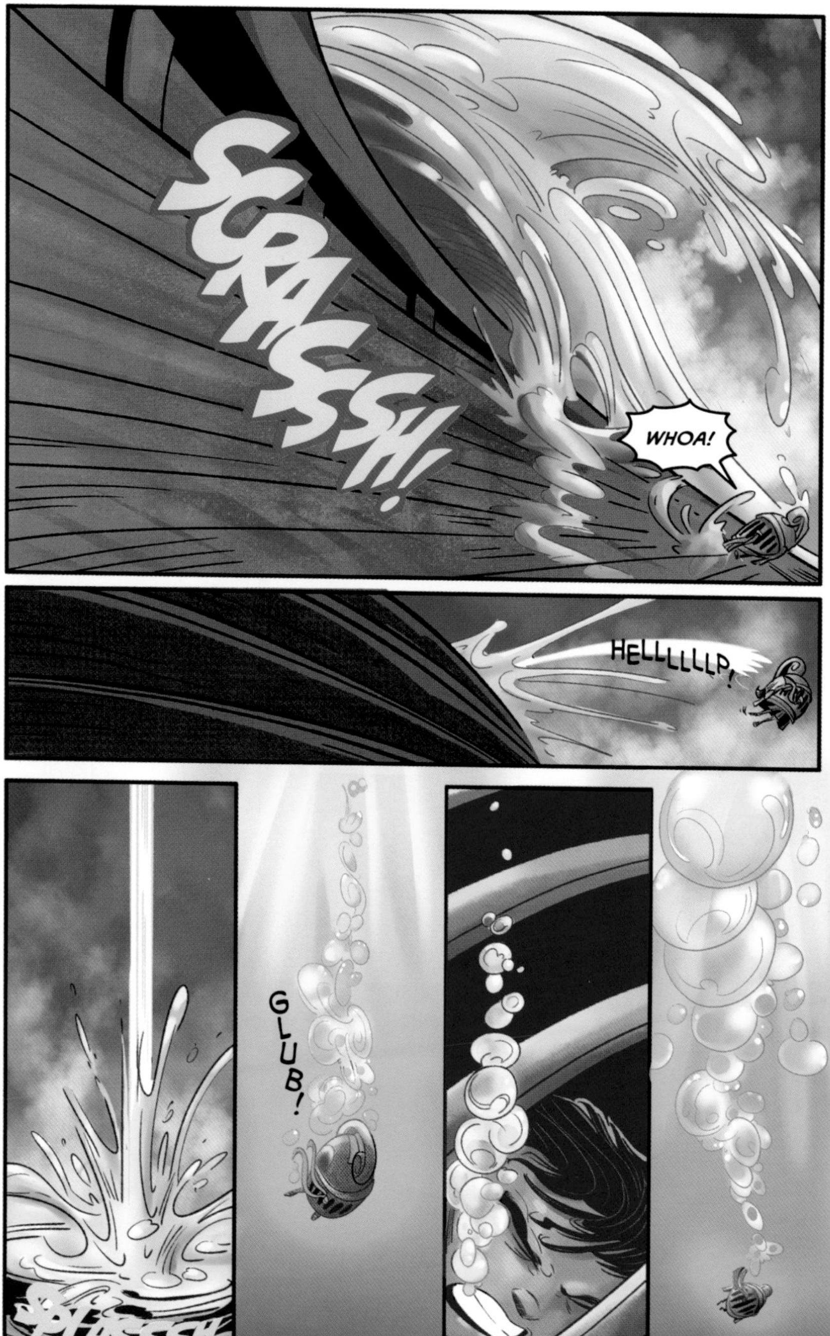
SCRASSH!
WHOA!
HELLLLLLP!
SPLASSSH
GLUB!

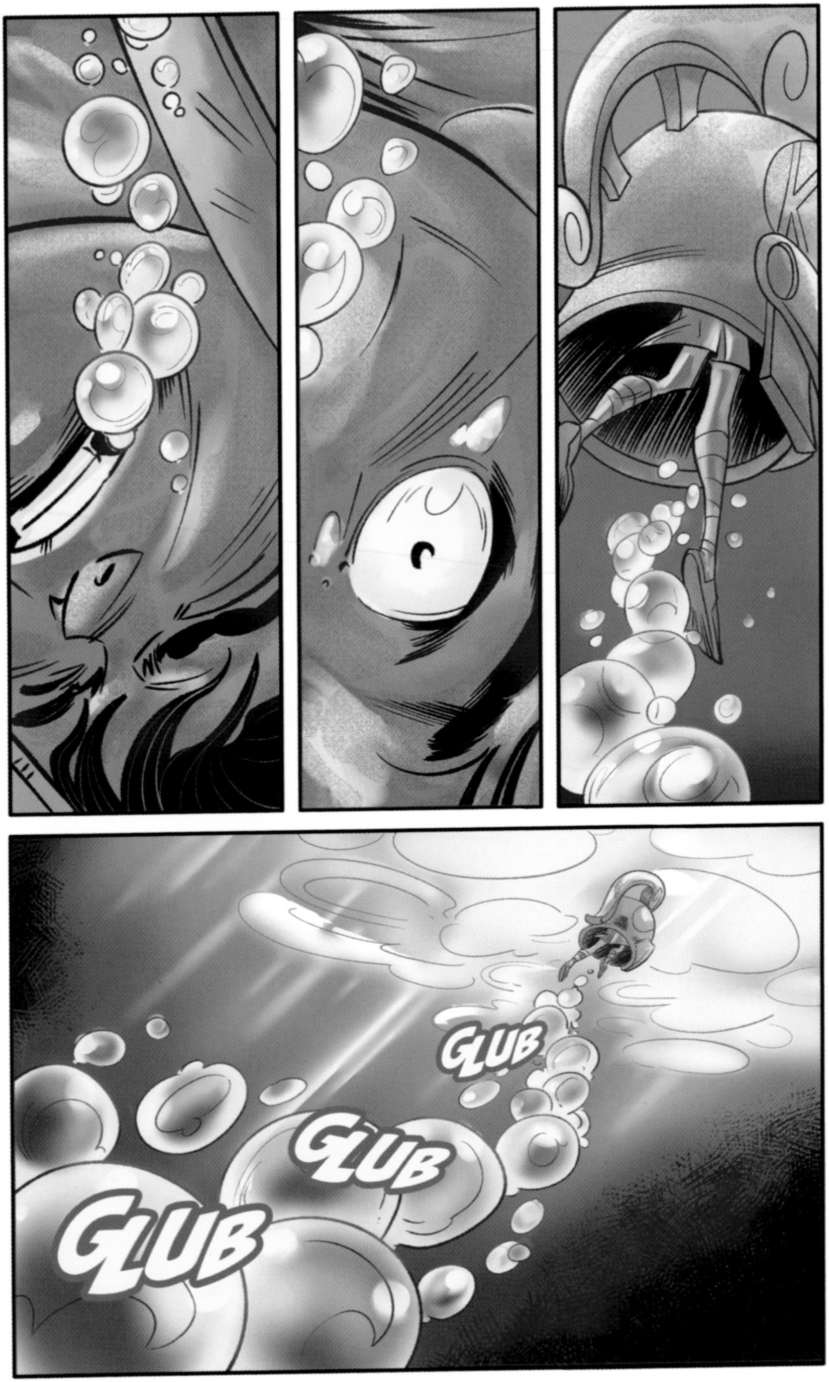
GLUB
GLUB
GLUB

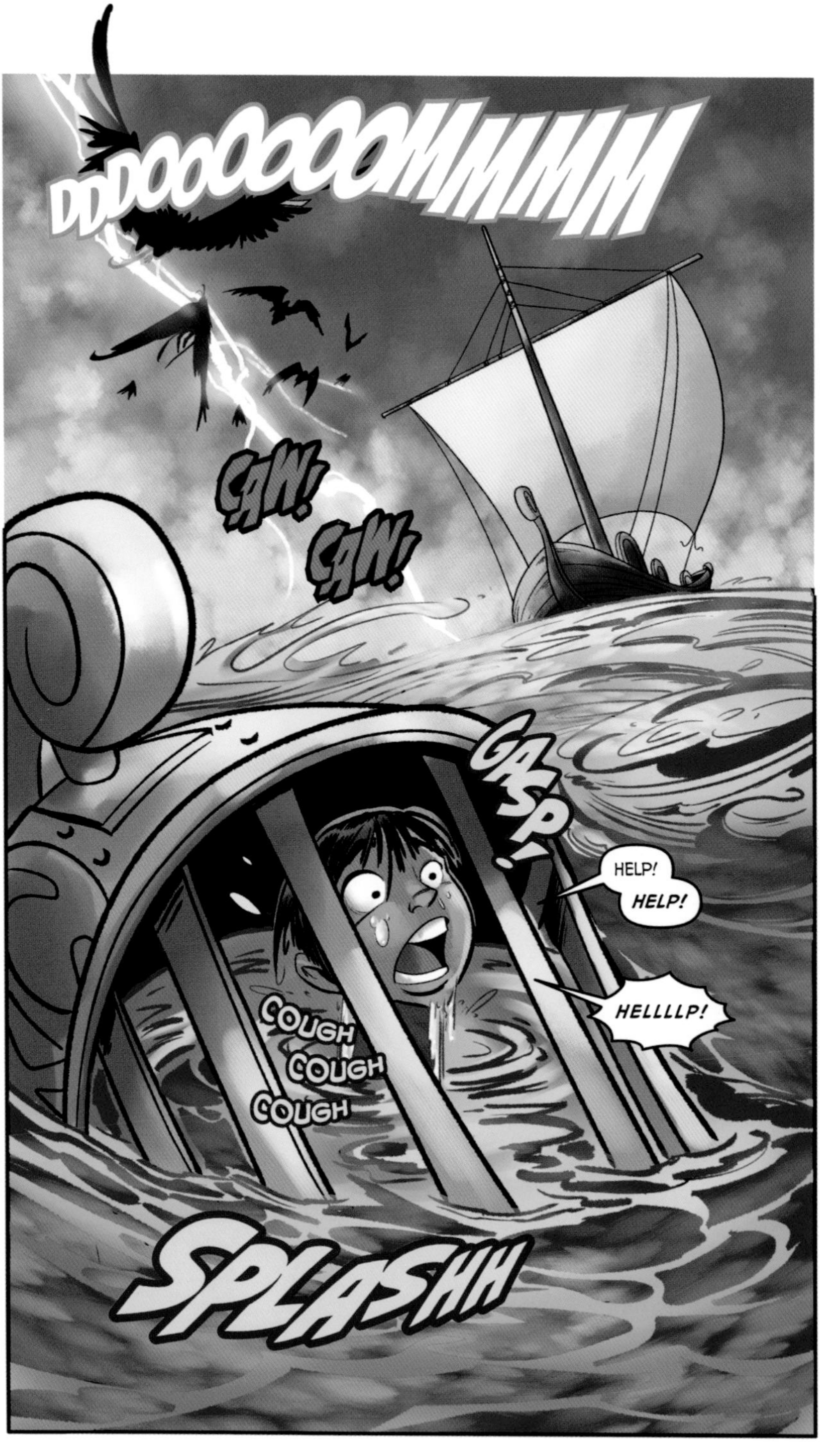
DDDOOOOOOOMMMMM
CAW!
CAW!
GASP!
HELP!
HELP!
HELLLLP!
COUGH
COUGH
COUGH
SPLASHH

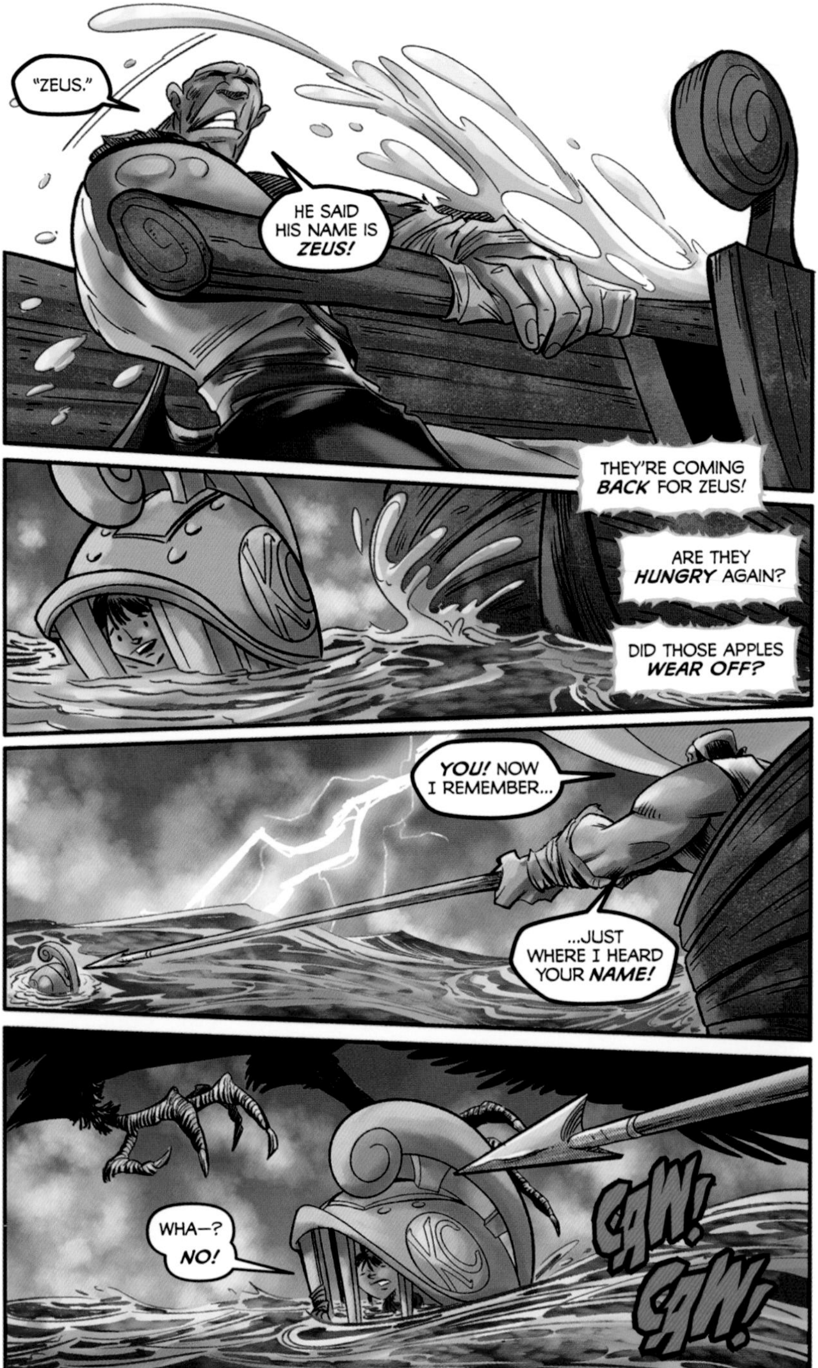
"ZEUS."
HE SAID HIS NAME IS ZEUS!
THEY'RE COMING BACK FOR ZEUS!
ARE THEY HUNGRY AGAIN?
DID THOSE APPLES WEAR OFF?
YOU! NOW I REMEMBER...
...JUST WHERE I HEARD YOUR NAME!
WHA–? NO!
CAW! CAW!

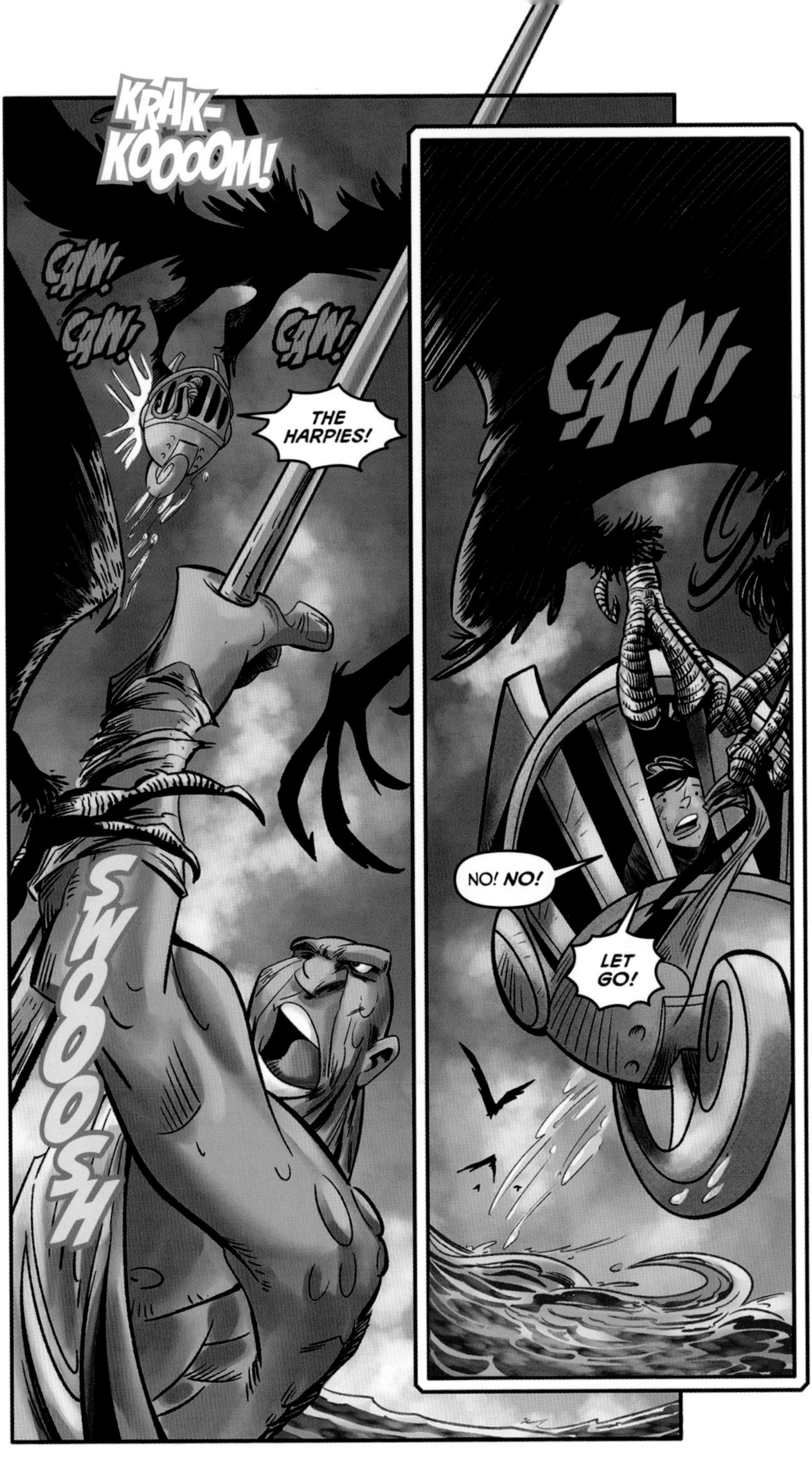
KRAK-KOOOOM!
CAW!
CAW!
CAW!
THE HARPIES!
SWOOOOSH
CAW!
NO! **NO!**
LET GO!

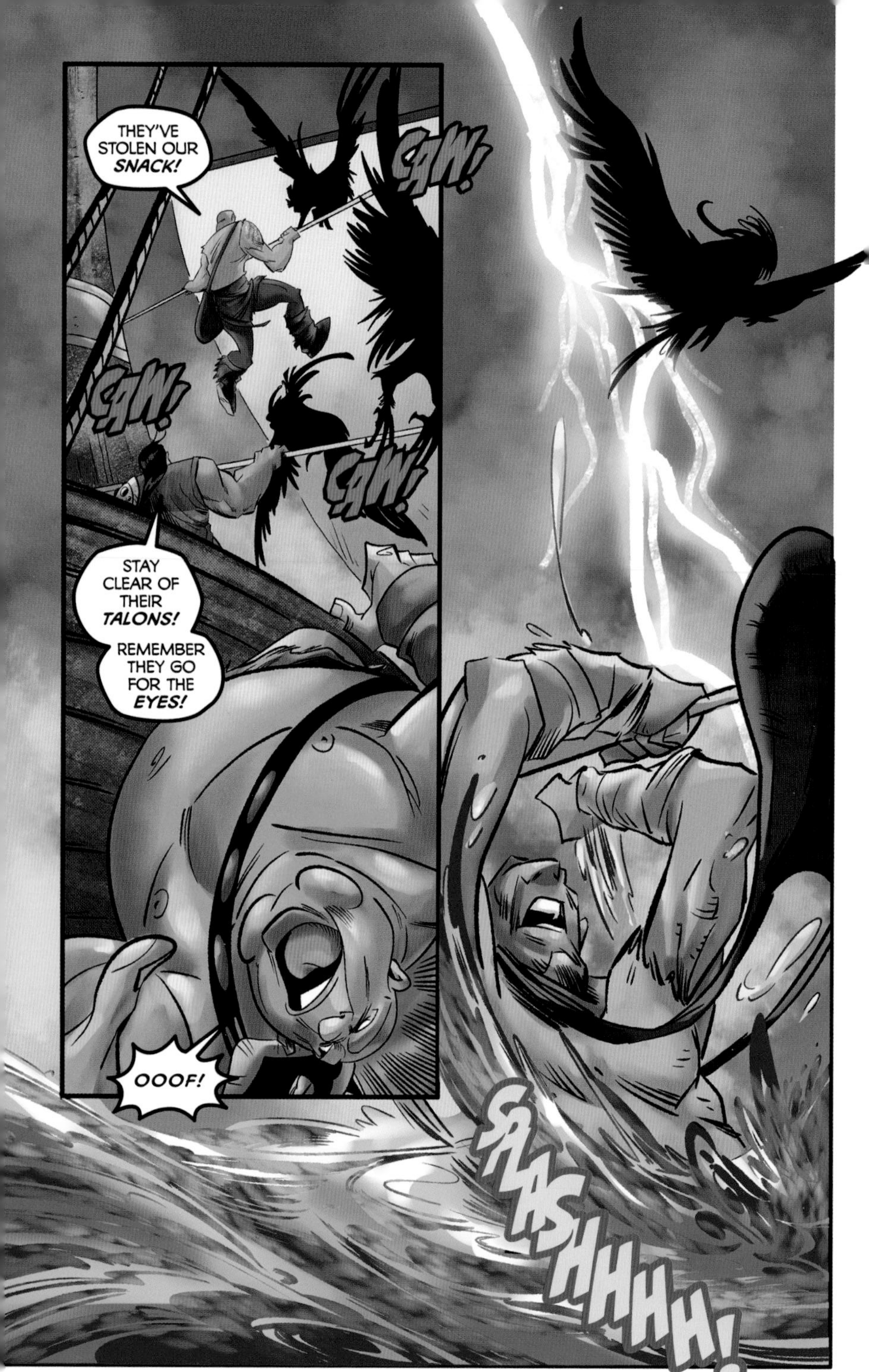
THEY'VE STOLEN OUR SNACK!
CAW!
CAW!
CAW!
STAY CLEAR OF THEIR TALONS!
REMEMBER THEY GO FOR THE EYES!
OOOF!
SPLASHHHHH!

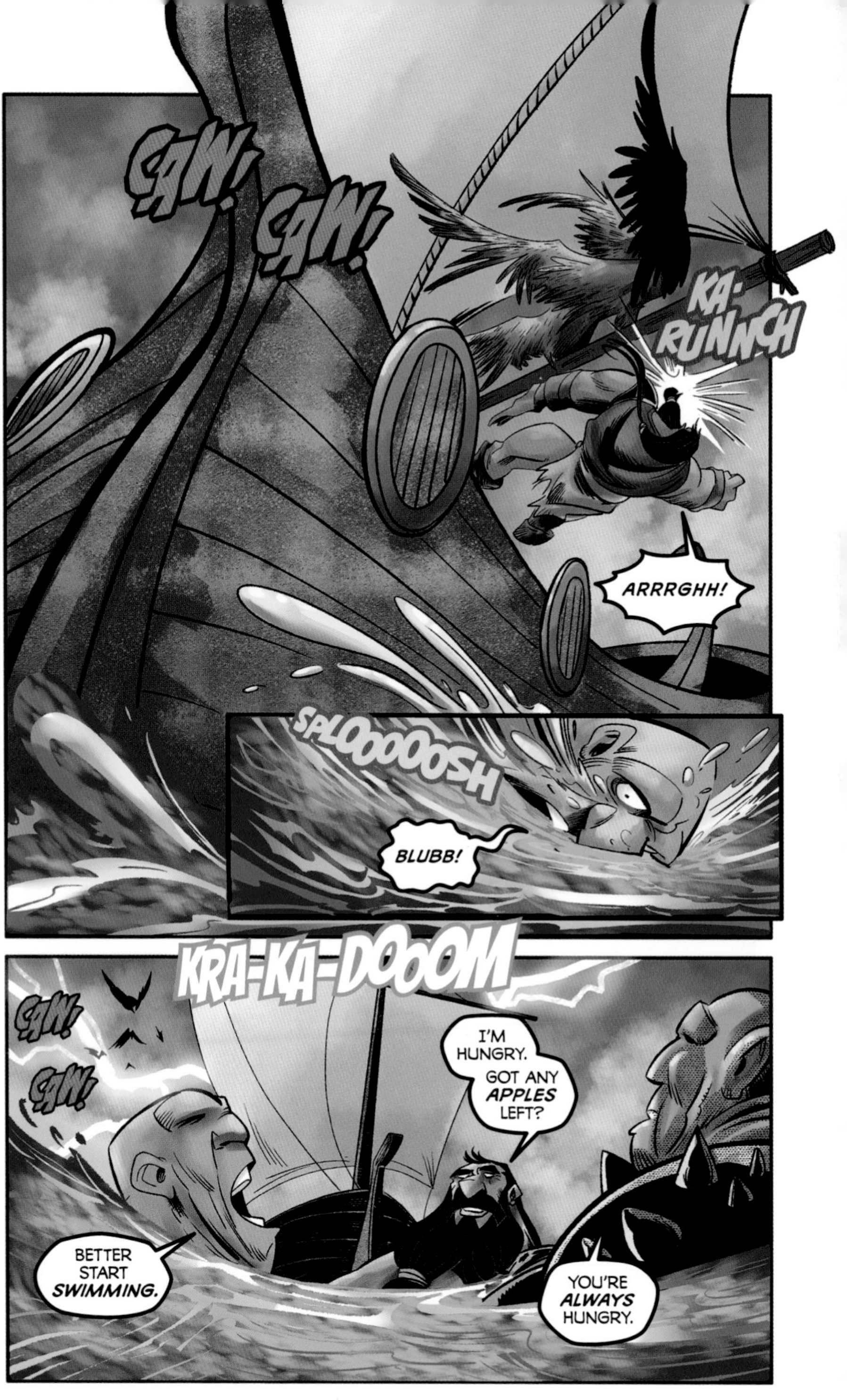
CAW!
CAW!
KA-RUNNCH
ARRRGHH!
SPLOOOOOOSH
BLUBB!
KRA-KA-DOOOM
CAW!
CAW!
I'M HUNGRY. GOT ANY APPLES LEFT?
BETTER START SWIMMING.
YOU'RE ALWAYS HUNGRY.

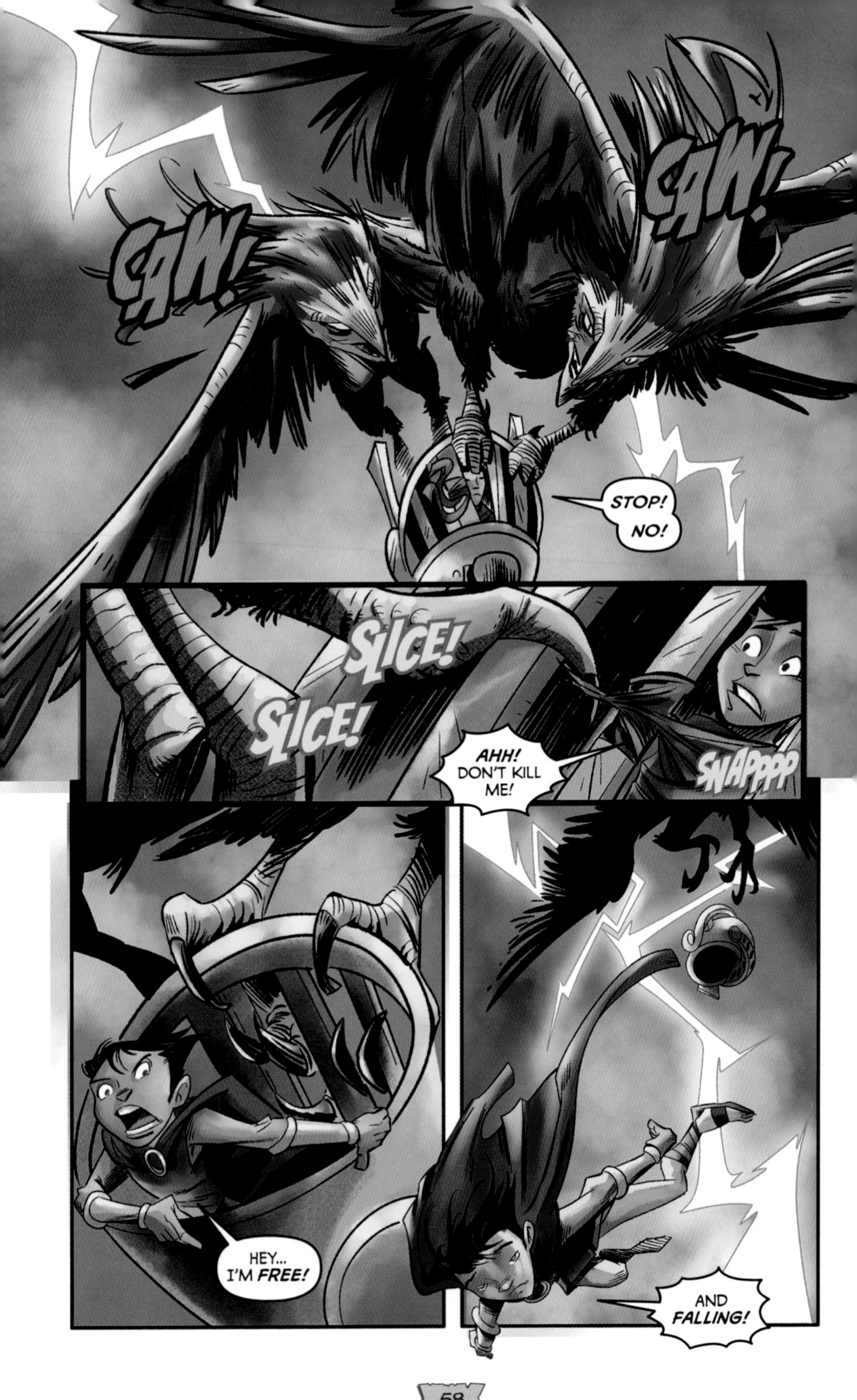
CAW!
CAW!
STOP!
NO!
SLICE!
SLICE!
AHH! DON'T KILL ME!
SNAPPPP
HEY... I'M FREE!
AND FALLING!

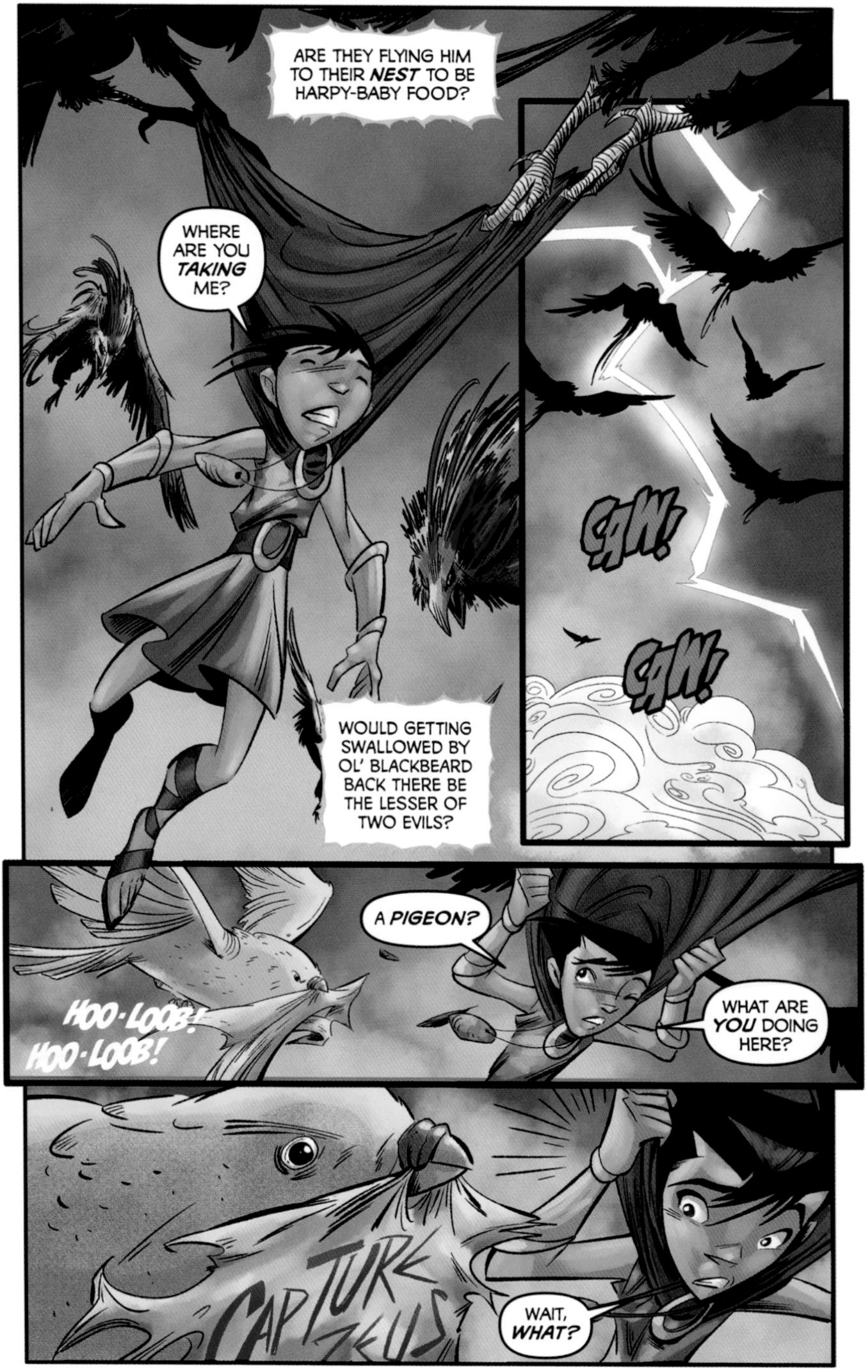
ARE THEY FLYING HIM TO THEIR *NEST* TO BE HARPY-BABY FOOD?
WHERE ARE YOU *TAKING* ME?
CAW!
CAW!
WOULD GETTING SWALLOWED BY OL' BLACKBEARD BACK THERE BE THE LESSER OF TWO EVILS?
A *PIGEON?*
HOO-LOOB! HOO-LOOB!
WHAT ARE *YOU* DOING HERE?
CAPTURE ZEUS
WAIT, *WHAT?*

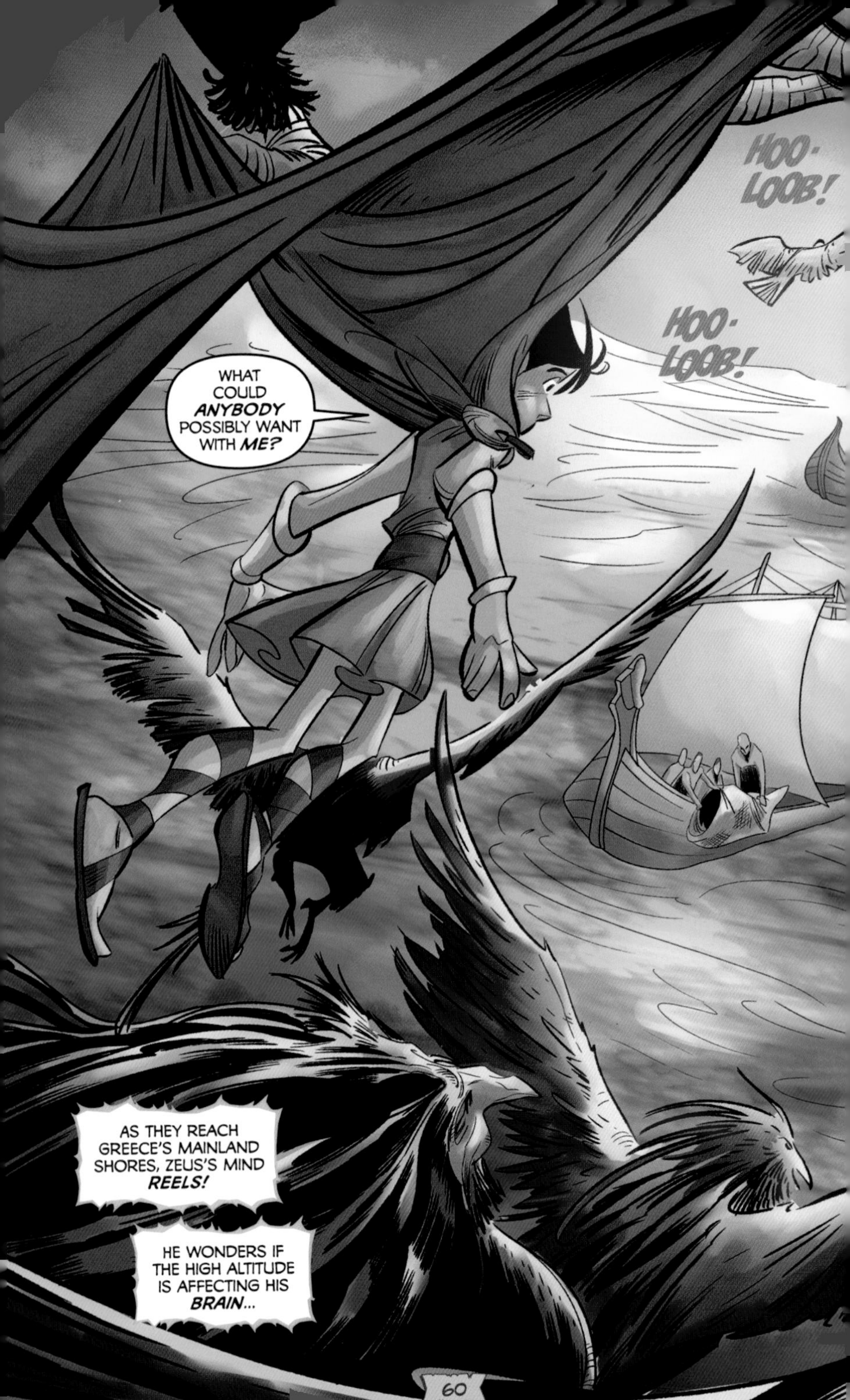
HOO-LOOB!
HOO-LOOB!
WHAT COULD ANYBODY POSSIBLY WANT WITH ME?
AS THEY REACH GREECE'S MAINLAND SHORES, ZEUS'S MIND REELS!
HE WONDERS IF THE HIGH ALTITUDE IS AFFECTING HIS BRAIN...

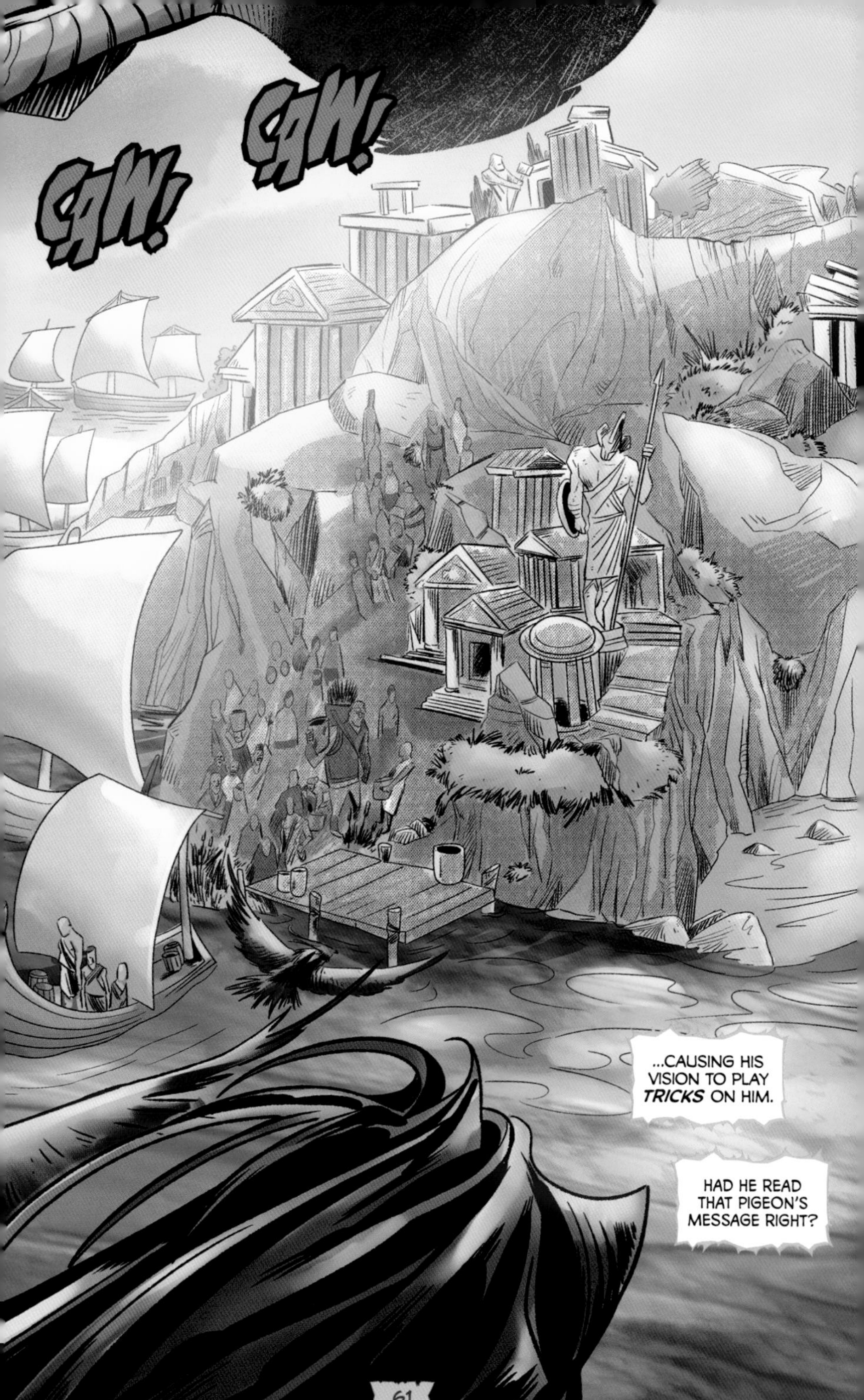
CAW!
CAW!
...CAUSING HIS VISION TO PLAY TRICKS ON HIM.
HAD HE READ THAT PIGEON'S MESSAGE RIGHT?

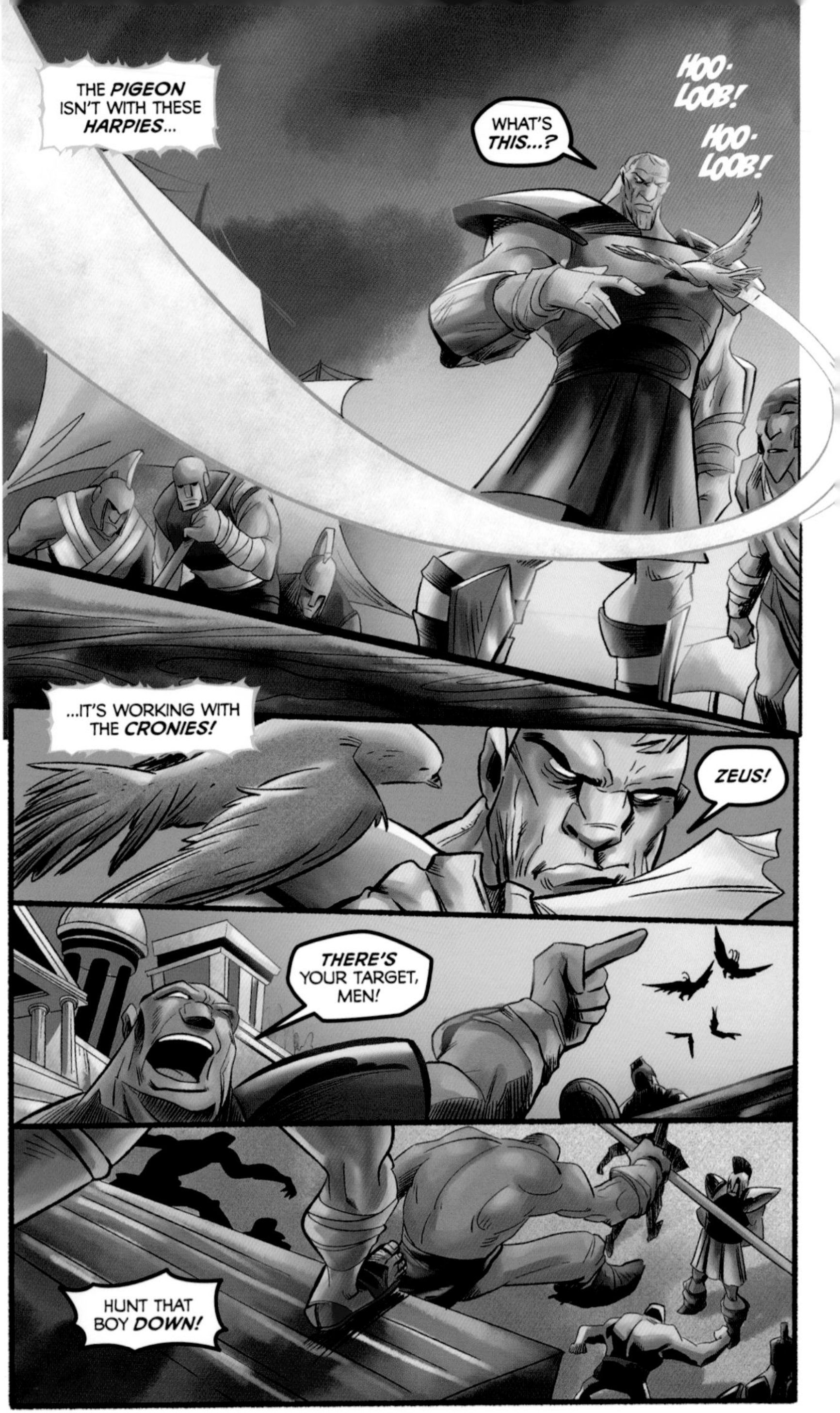
THE PIGEON ISN'T WITH THESE HARPIES...
WHAT'S THIS...?
HOO-LOOB!
HOO-LOOB!
...IT'S WORKING WITH THE CRONIES!
ZEUS!
THERE'S YOUR TARGET, MEN!
HUNT THAT BOY DOWN!

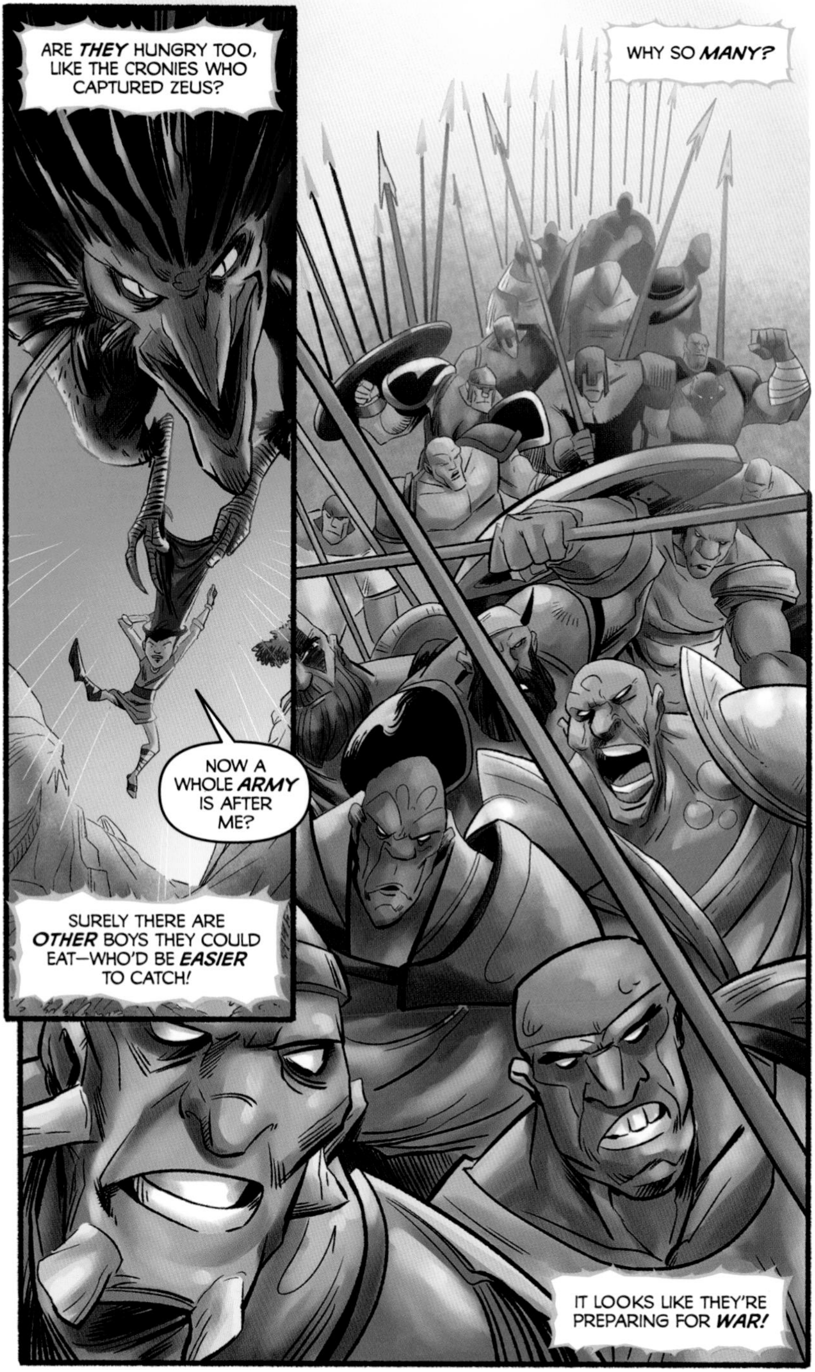
ARE *THEY* HUNGRY TOO, LIKE THE CRONIES WHO CAPTURED ZEUS?
WHY SO *MANY?*
NOW A WHOLE *ARMY* IS AFTER ME?
SURELY THERE ARE *OTHER* BOYS THEY COULD EAT—WHO'D BE *EASIER* TO CATCH!
IT LOOKS LIKE THEY'RE PREPARING FOR *WAR!*

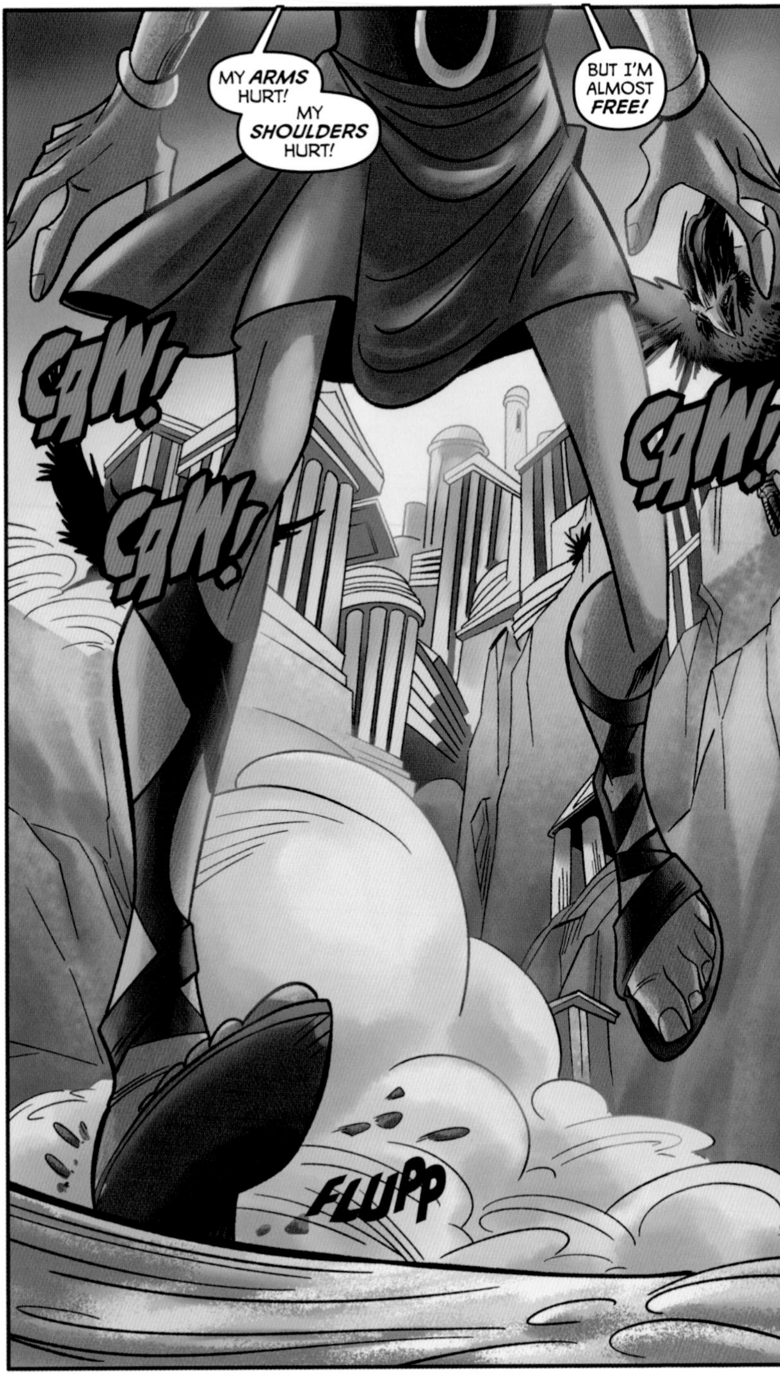
MY ARMS HURT! MY SHOULDERS HURT!
BUT I'M ALMOST FREE!
CAW!
CAW!
CAW!
FLUPP

CHAPTER FIVE: BOLT

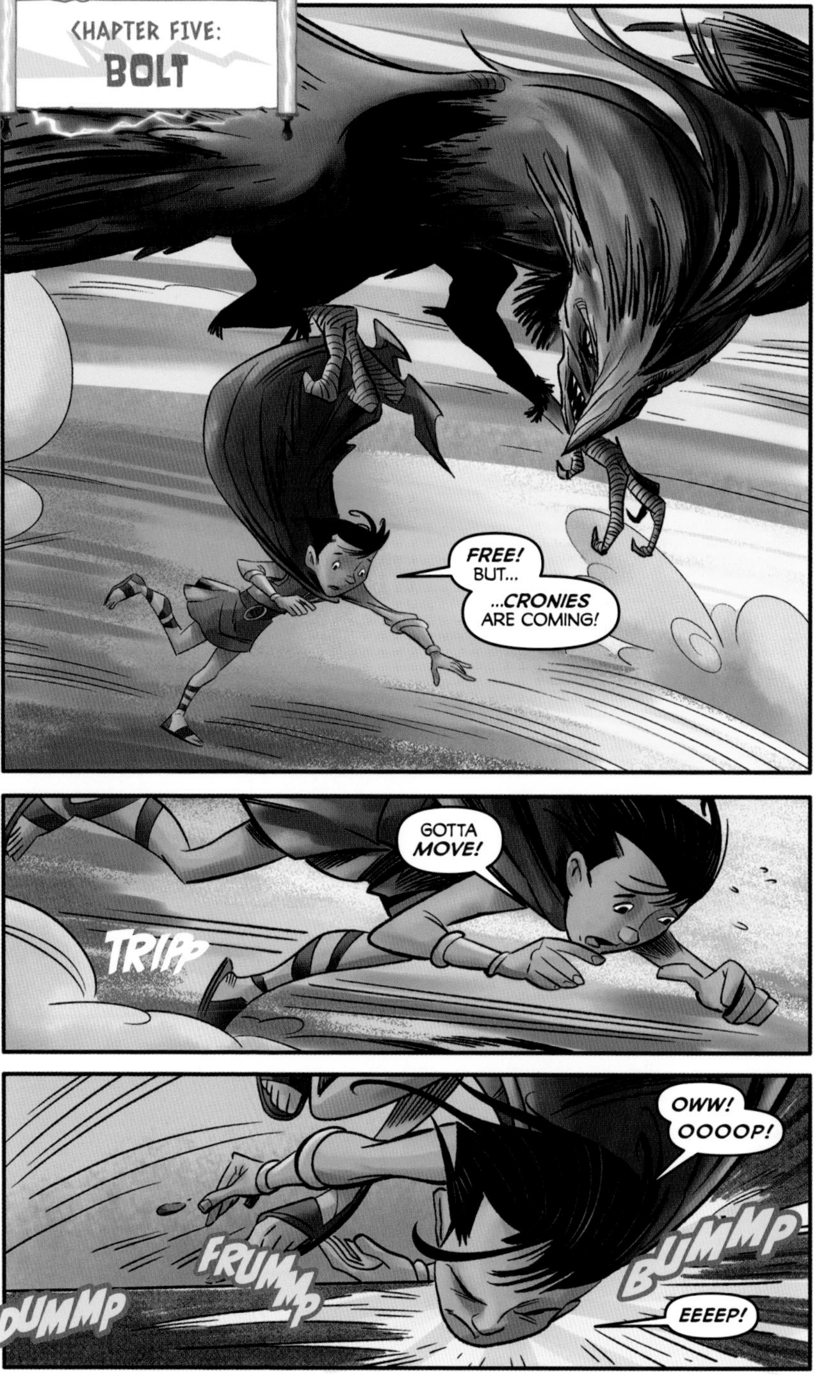
FREE! BUT...
...CRONIES ARE COMING!
GOTTA MOVE!
TRIPP
OWW! OOOOP!
FRUMMP
DUMMP
BUMMP
EEEEP!

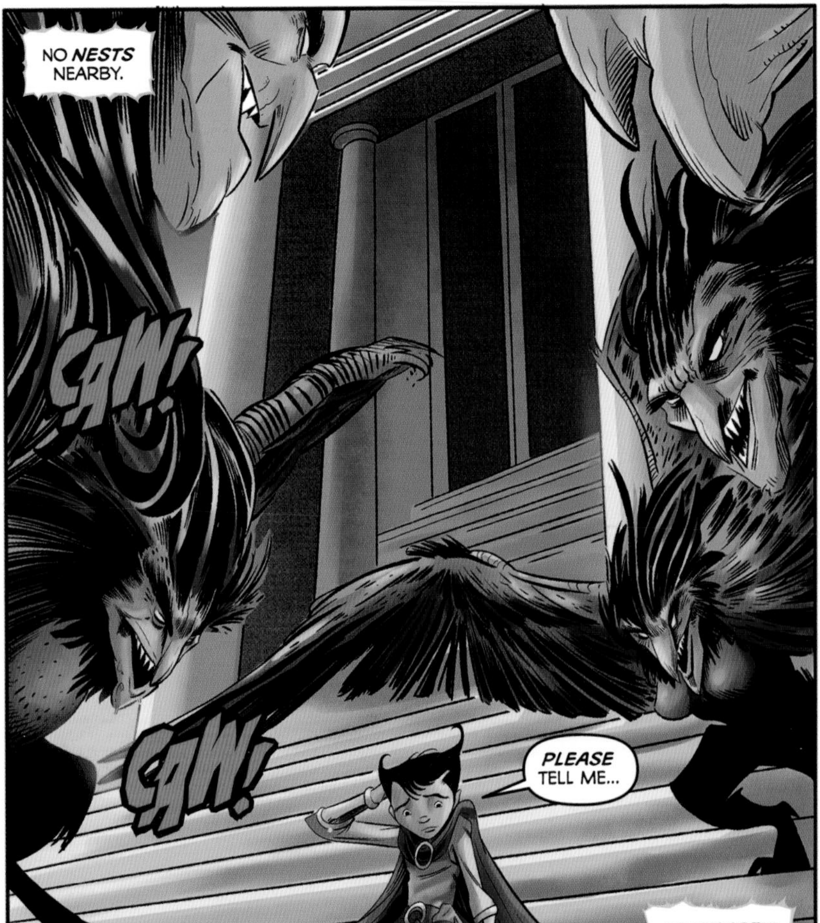
NO *NESTS* NEARBY.
CAW!
CAW!
PLEASE TELL ME...
NO *HUNGRY* BABY BIRDS.

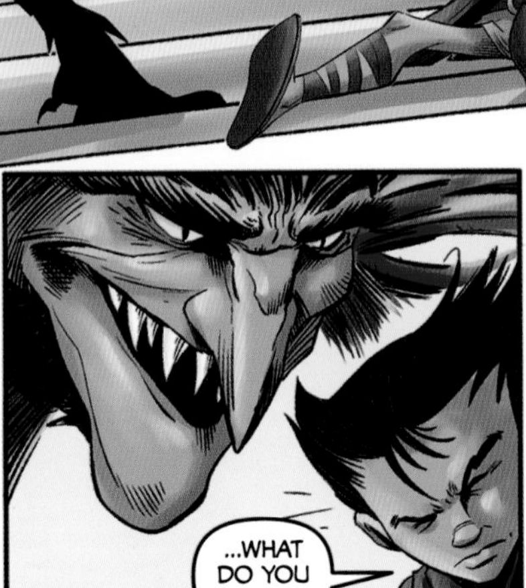
...WHAT DO YOU *WANT?*

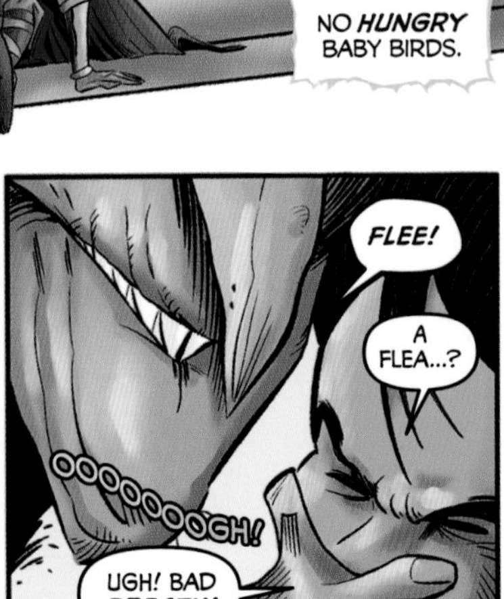
FLEE!
A FLEA...?
OOOOOOOOOGH!
UGH! BAD *BREATH!*

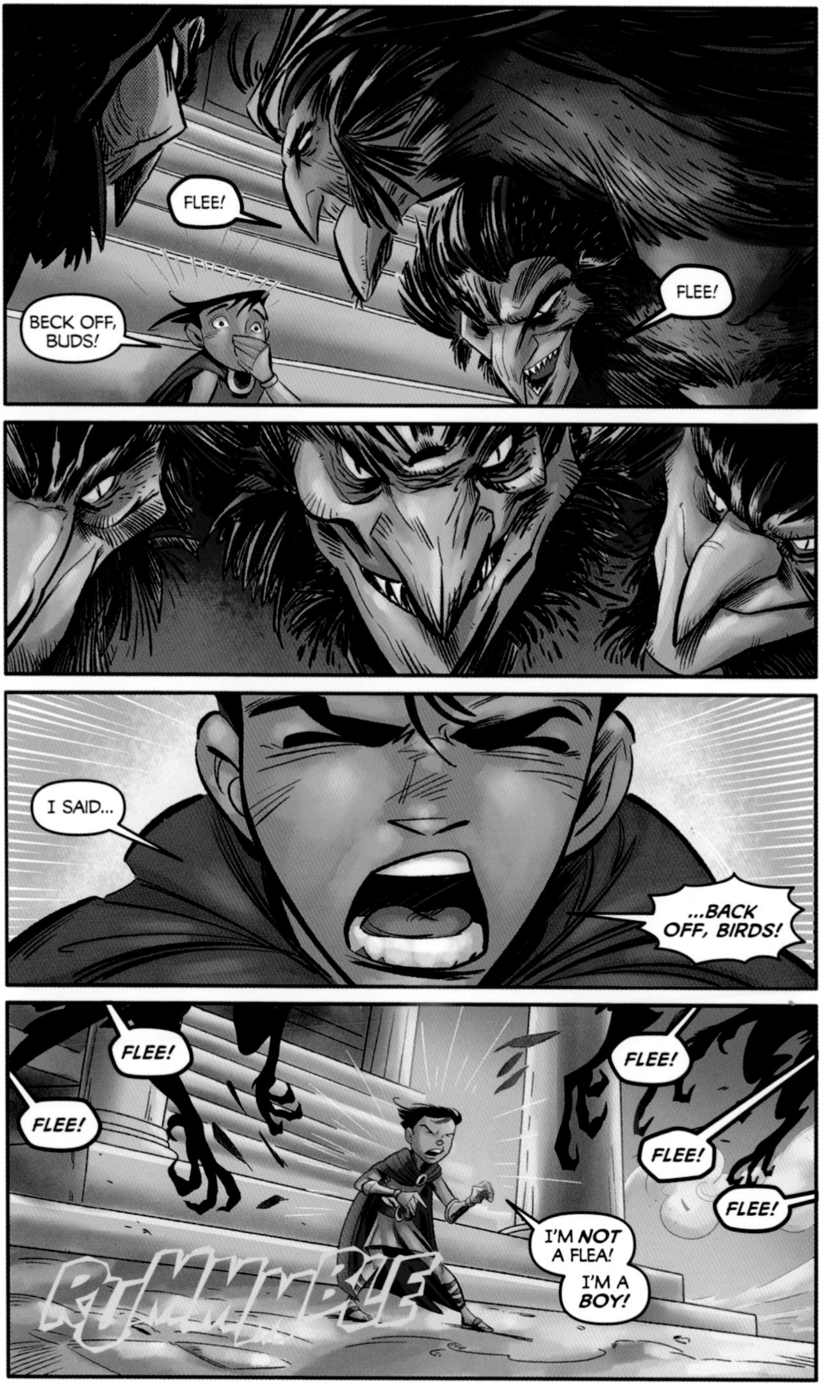
FLEE!
BECK OFF, BUDS!
FLEE!
I SAID...
...BACK OFF, BIRDS!
FLEE!
FLEE!
FLEE!
FLEE!
FLEE!
I'M *NOT* A FLEA!
I'M A *BOY!*
RUMMMMBLE

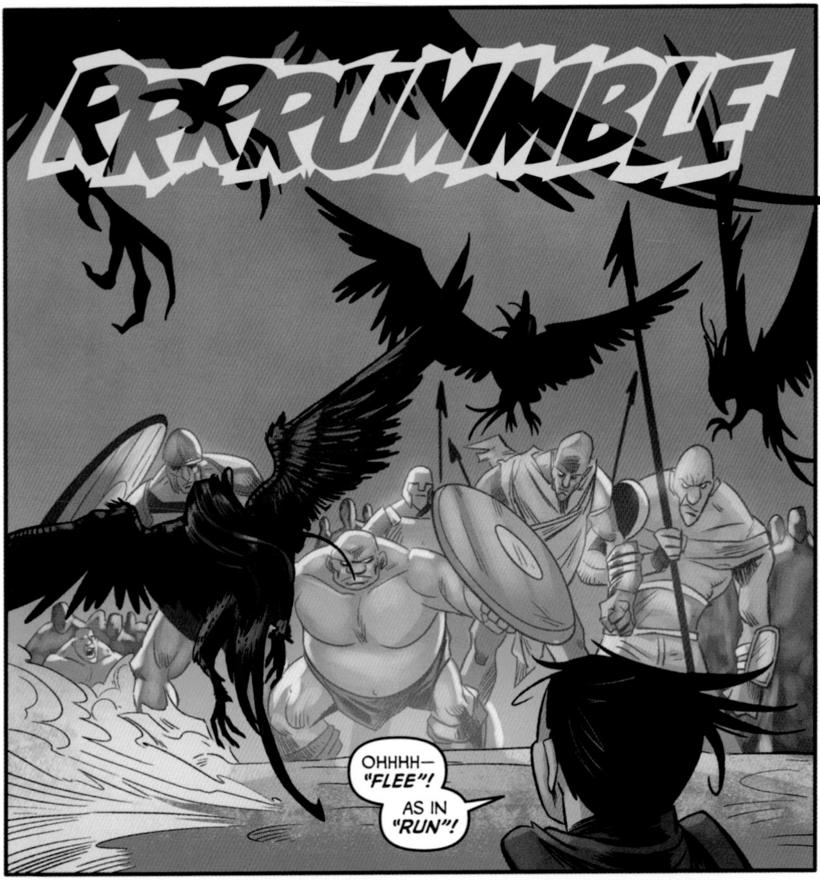
RRRRUMMBLE
OHHHH—"FLEE"!
AS IN "RUN"!

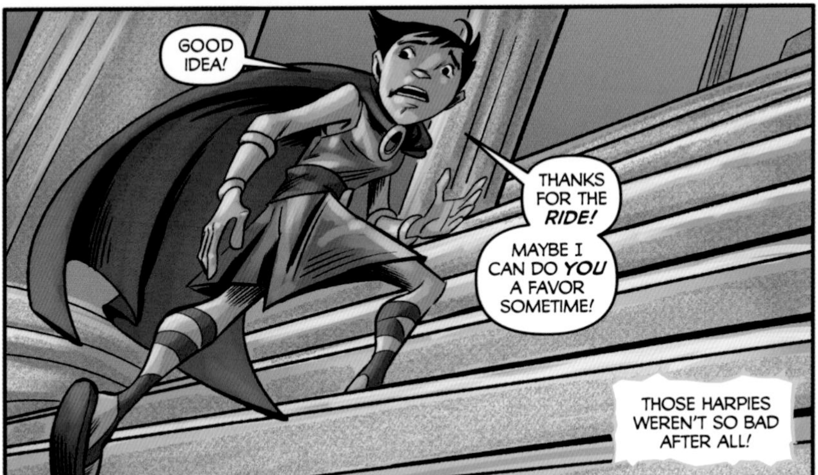
GOOD IDEA!
THANKS FOR THE RIDE!
MAYBE I CAN DO YOU A FAVOR SOMETIME!
THOSE HARPIES WEREN'T SO BAD AFTER ALL!

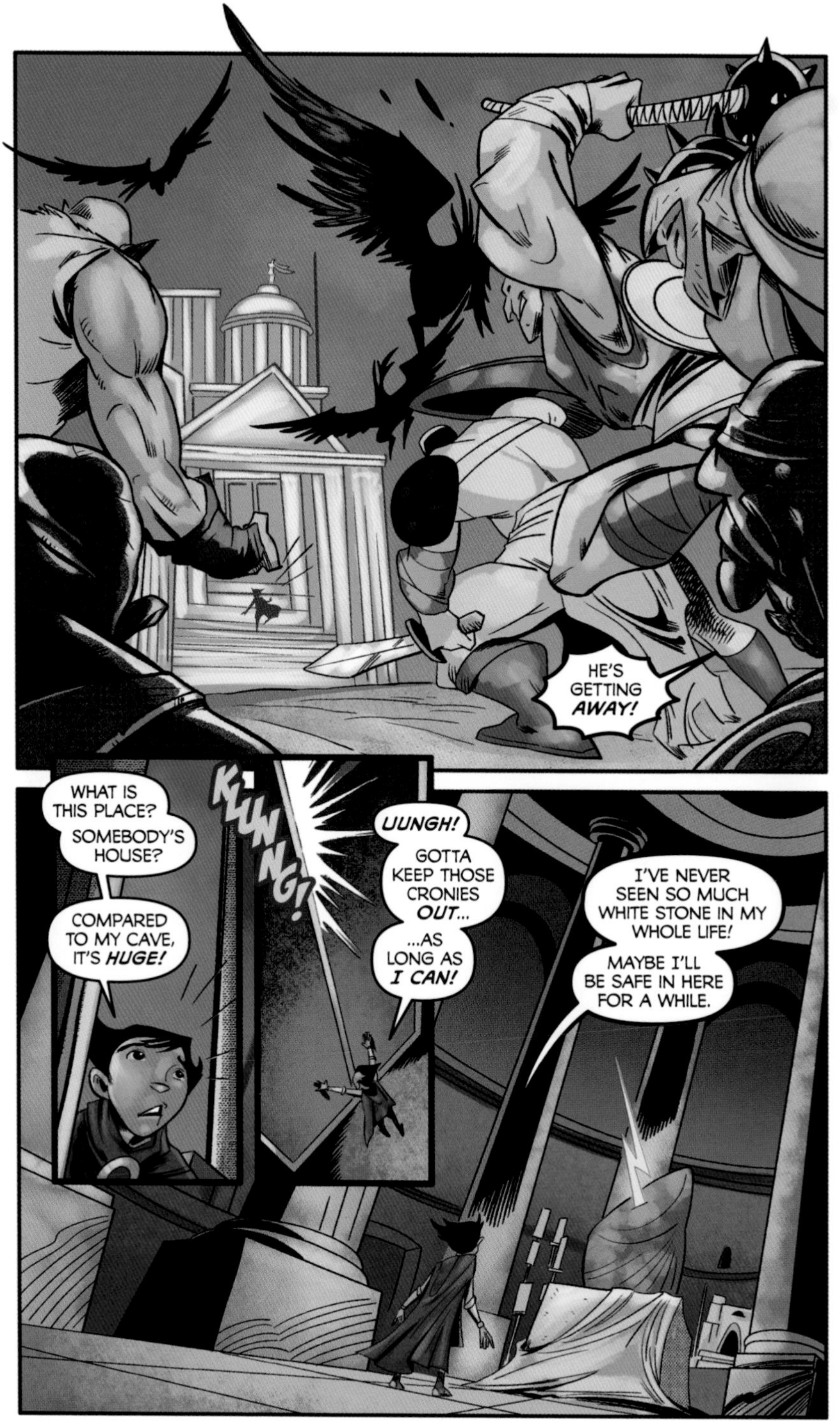
HE'S GETTING *AWAY!*
WHAT IS THIS PLACE?
SOMEBODY'S HOUSE?
COMPARED TO MY CAVE, IT'S *HUGE!*
KLUNNG!
UUNGH!
GOTTA KEEP THOSE CRONIES *OUT*...
...AS LONG AS *I CAN!*
I'VE NEVER SEEN SO MUCH WHITE STONE IN MY WHOLE LIFE!
MAYBE I'LL BE SAFE IN HERE FOR A WHILE.

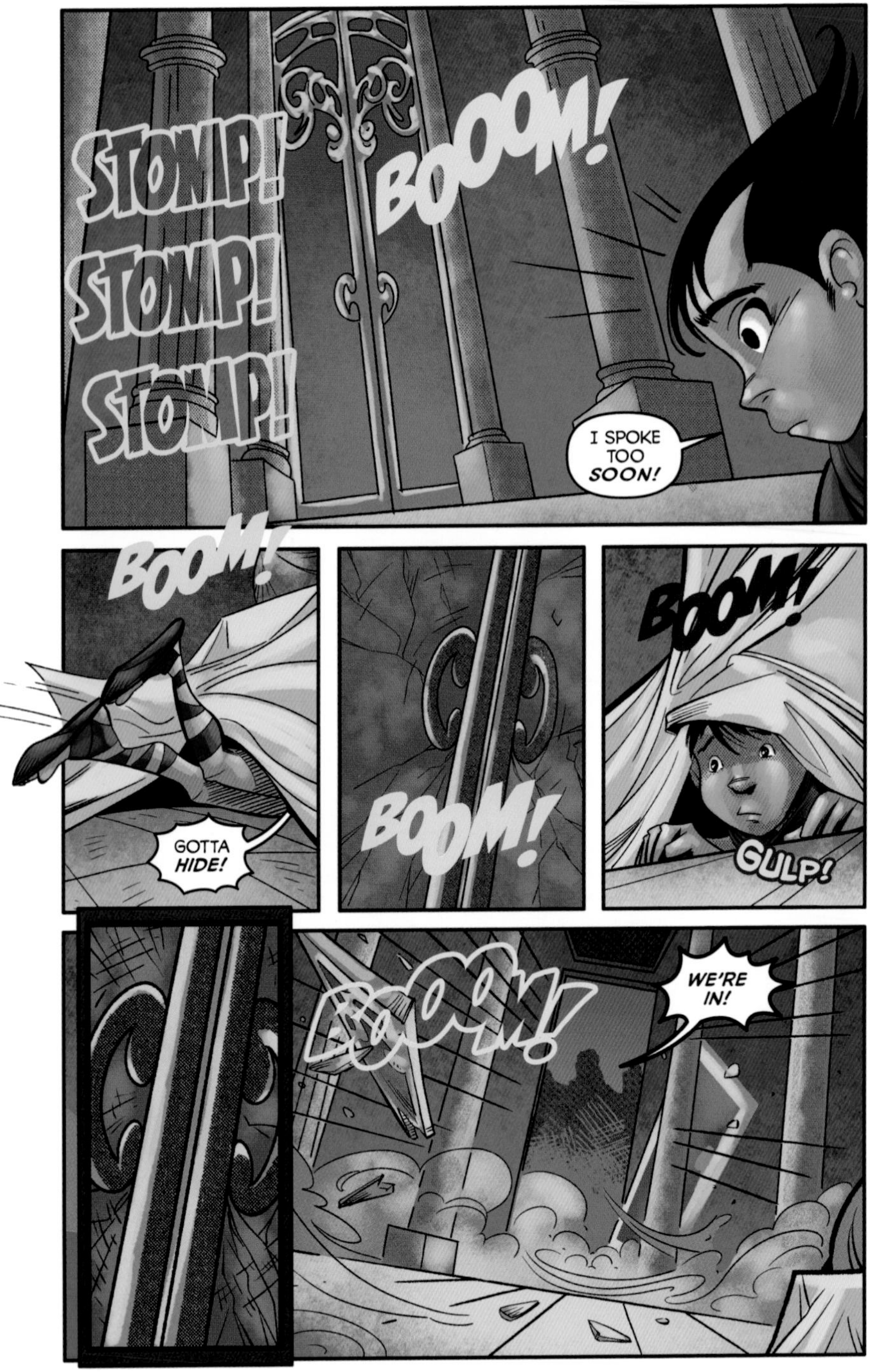
STOMP!
STOMP!
STOMP!
BOOOM!
I SPOKE TOO SOON!
BOOM!
GOTTA HIDE!
BOOM!
BOOM!
GULP!
BOOOM!
WE'RE IN!

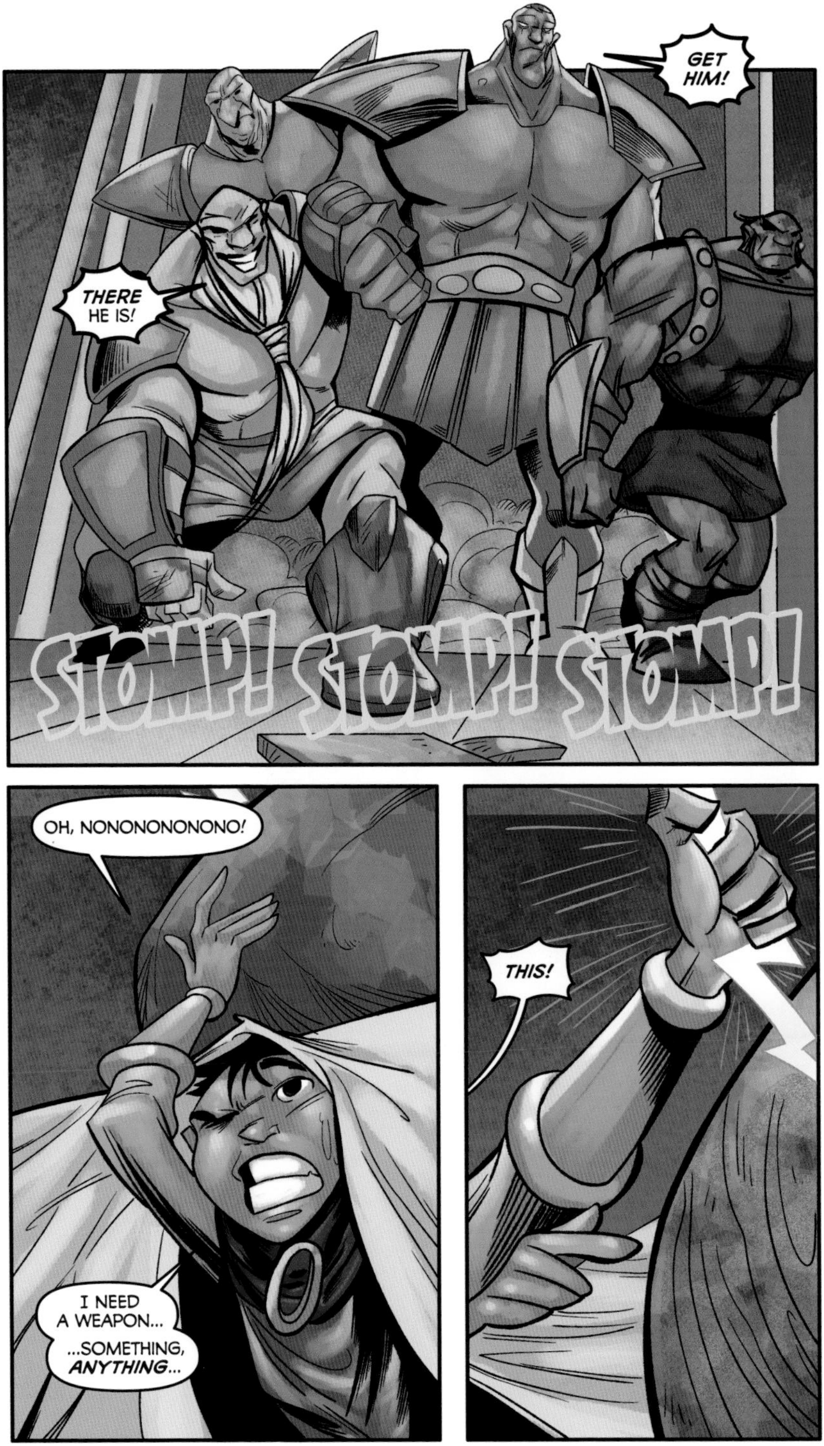
GET HIM!
THERE HE IS!
STOMP! STOMP! STOMP!
OH, NONONONONONO!
I NEED A WEAPON...
...SOMETHING, ANYTHING...
THIS!

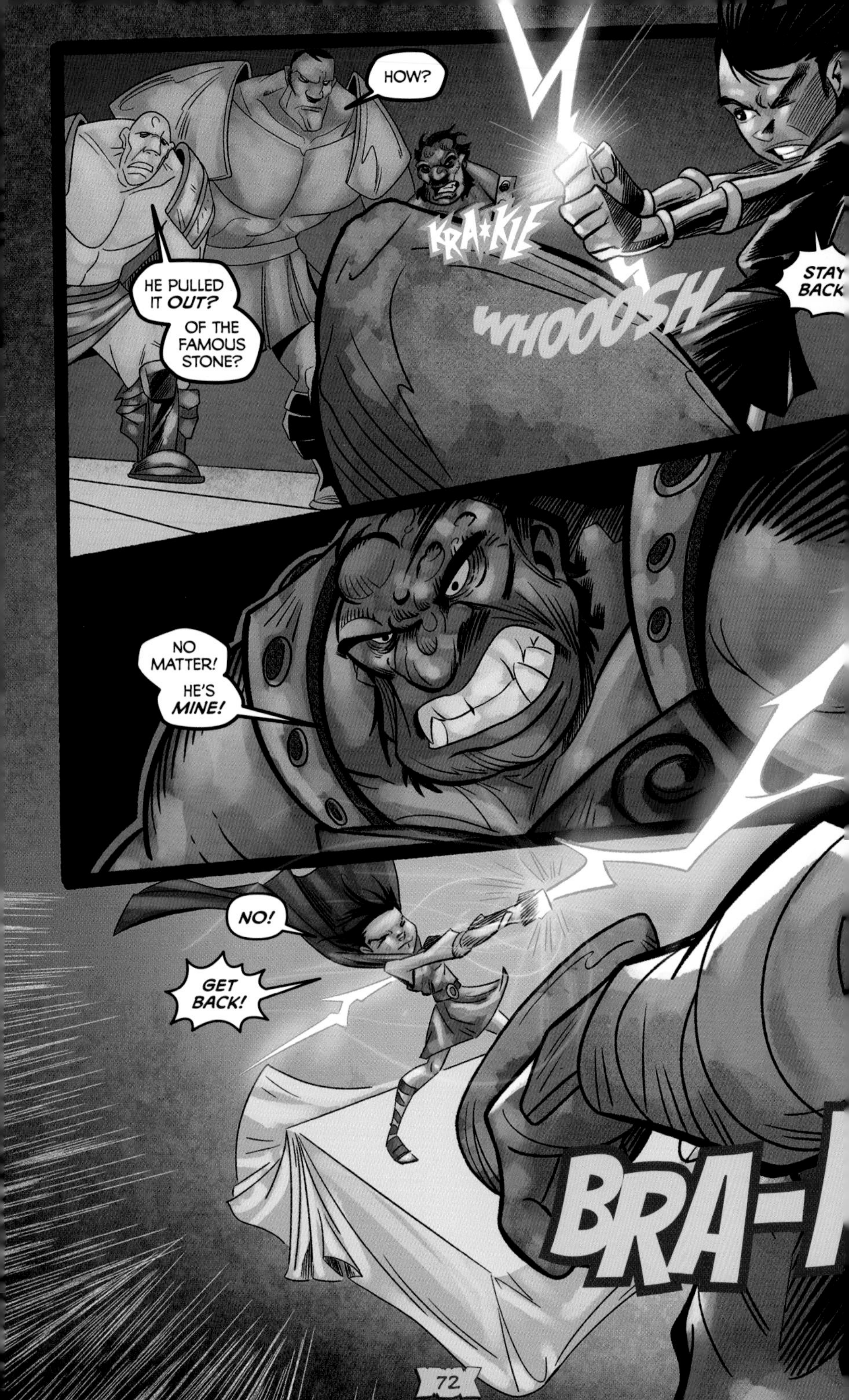

HOW?
KRA*KLE
HE PULLED IT OUT?
OF THE FAMOUS STONE?
WHOOOSH
STAY BACK
NO MATTER!
HE'S MINE!
NO!
GET BACK!
BRA-

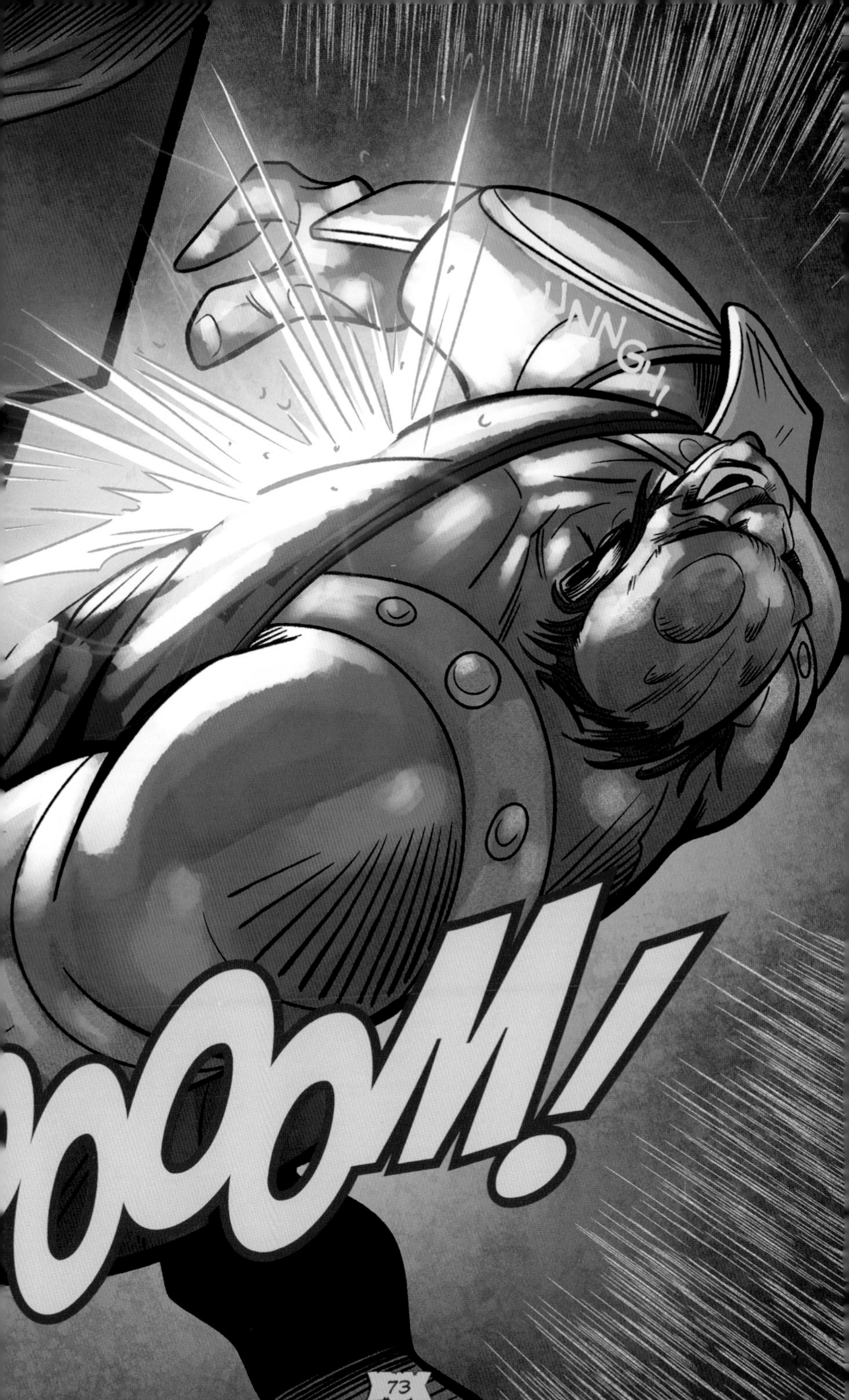
UNNGH!
OOOM!

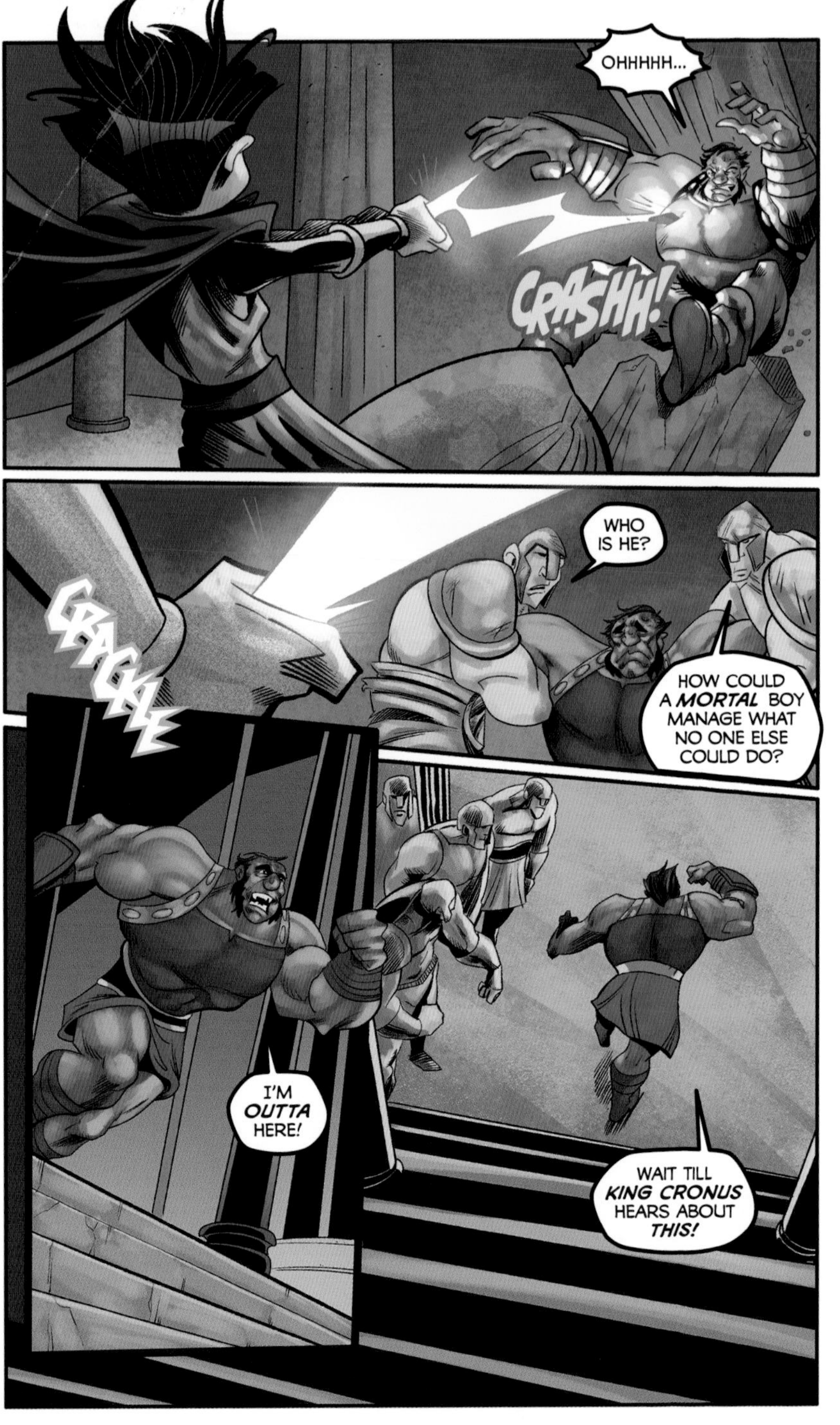
OHHHHH...
CRASHH!
WHO IS HE?
HOW COULD A MORTAL BOY MANAGE WHAT NO ONE ELSE COULD DO?
CRACKLE
I'M OUTTA HERE!
WAIT TILL KING CRONUS HEARS ABOUT THIS!

CHAPTER SIX:
THE WOMAN IN THE MIST

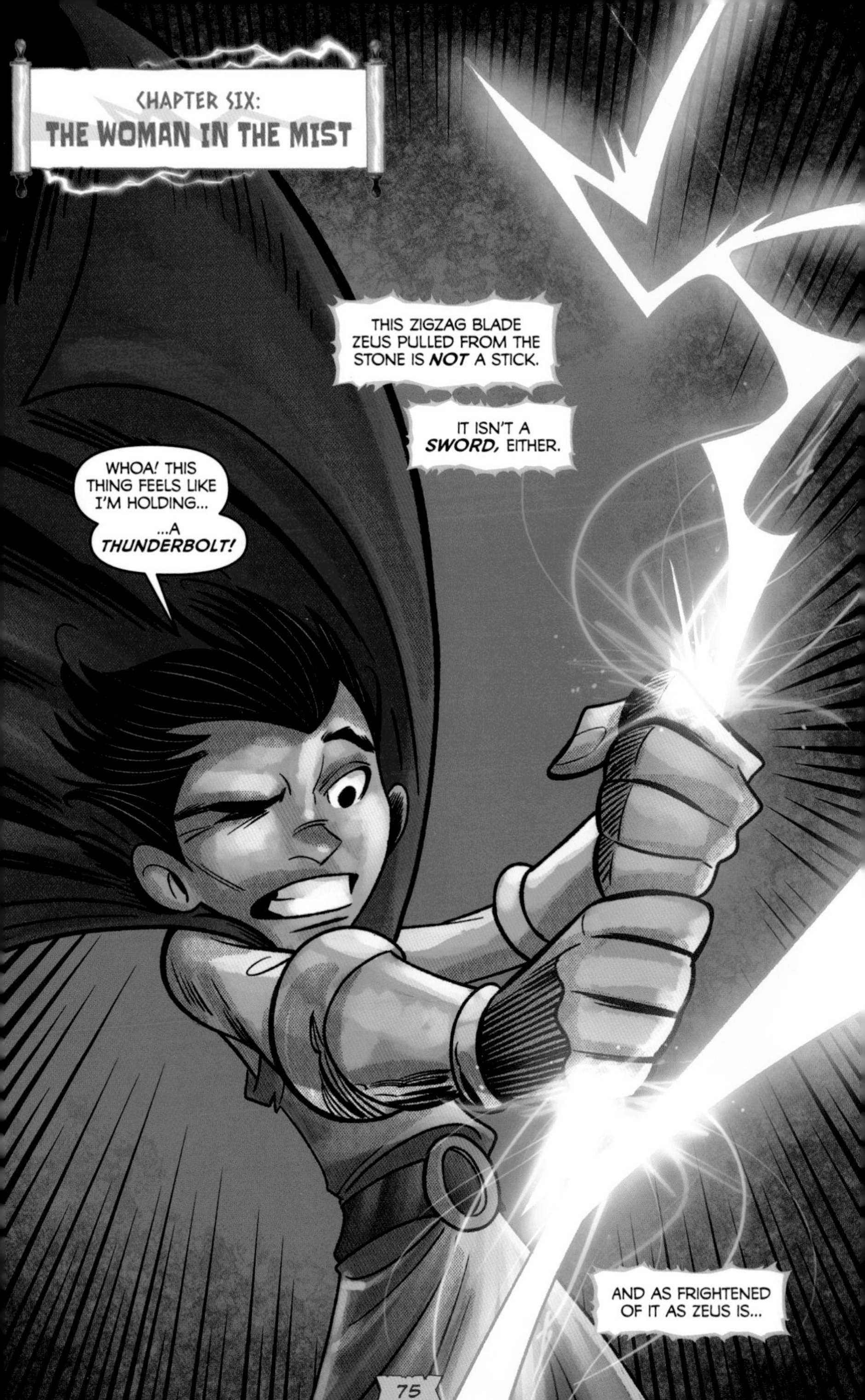
THIS ZIGZAG BLADE ZEUS PULLED FROM THE STONE IS NOT A STICK.
IT ISN'T A SWORD, EITHER.
WHOA! THIS THING FEELS LIKE I'M HOLDING... ...A THUNDERBOLT!
AND AS FRIGHTENED OF IT AS ZEUS IS...

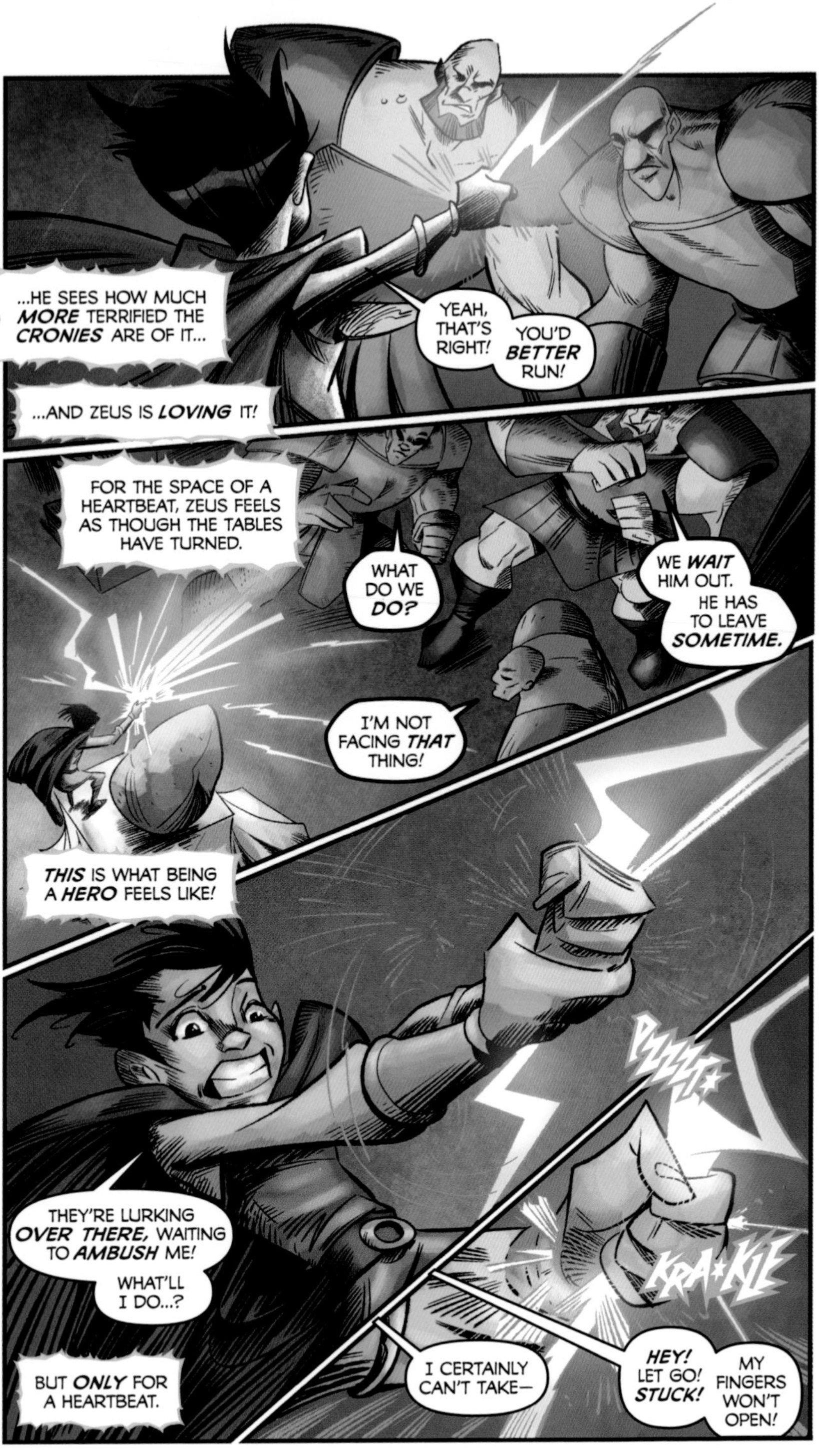

...HE SEES HOW MUCH MORE TERRIFIED THE CRONIES ARE OF IT...
YEAH, THAT'S RIGHT!
YOU'D BETTER RUN!
...AND ZEUS IS LOVING IT!
FOR THE SPACE OF A HEARTBEAT, ZEUS FEELS AS THOUGH THE TABLES HAVE TURNED.
WHAT DO WE DO?
WE WAIT HIM OUT.
HE HAS TO LEAVE SOMETIME.
I'M NOT FACING THAT THING!
THIS IS WHAT BEING A HERO FEELS LIKE!
THEY'RE LURKING OVER THERE, WAITING TO AMBUSH ME!
WHAT'LL I DO...?
BUT ONLY FOR A HEARTBEAT.
I CERTAINLY CAN'T TAKE—
KRA*KLE
HEY! LET GO! STUCK!
MY FINGERS WON'T OPEN!

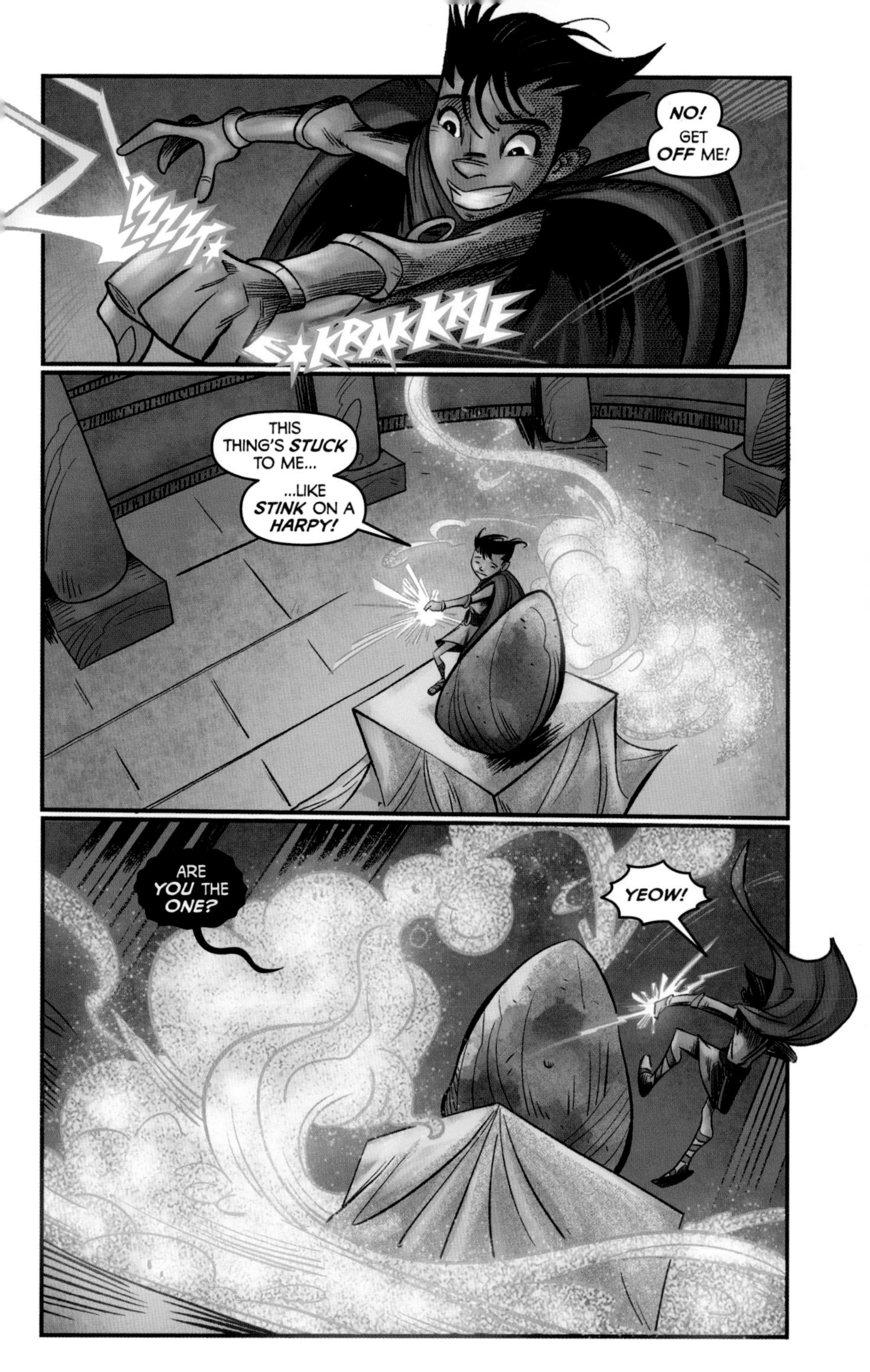
NO! GET OFF ME!
THIS THING'S STUCK TO ME...
...LIKE STINK ON A HARPY!
ARE YOU THE ONE?
YEOW!

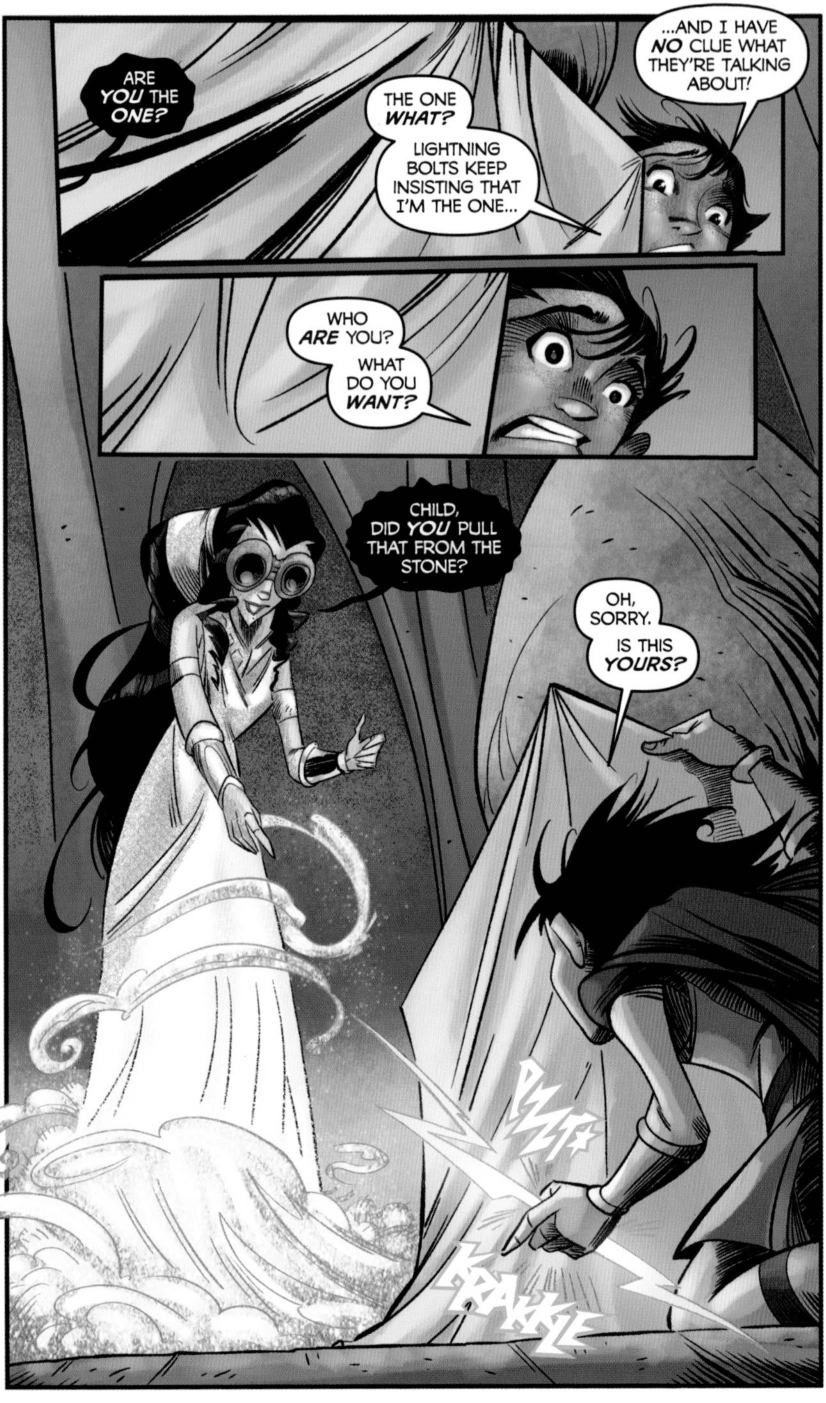
ARE YOU THE ONE?
THE ONE WHAT?
LIGHTNING BOLTS KEEP INSISTING THAT I'M THE ONE...
...AND I HAVE NO CLUE WHAT THEY'RE TALKING ABOUT!
WHO ARE YOU?
WHAT DO YOU WANT?
CHILD, DID YOU PULL THAT FROM THE STONE?
OH, SORRY.
IS THIS YOURS?
PZZT
KRAKKLE

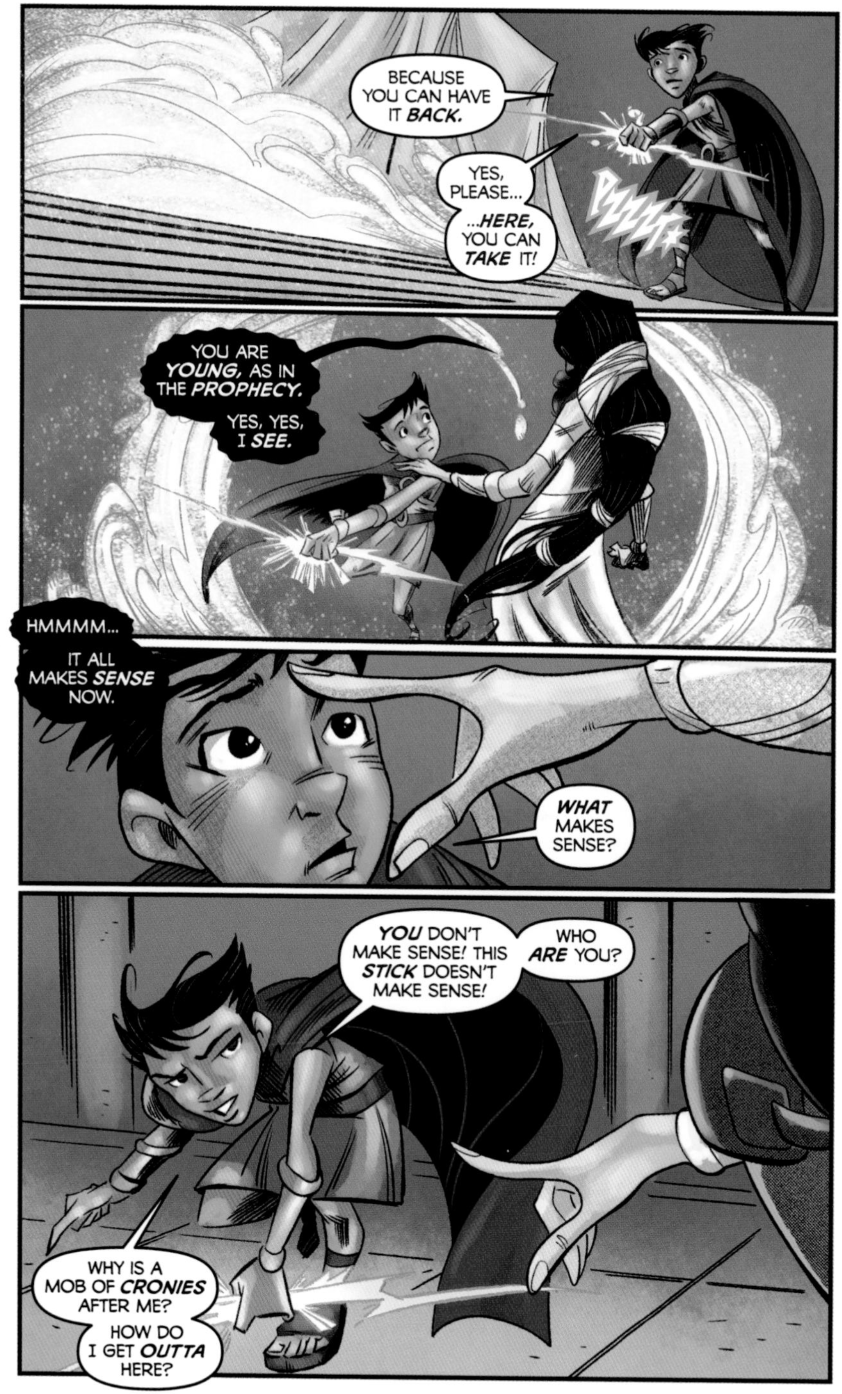
BECAUSE YOU CAN HAVE IT *BACK.*
YES, PLEASE...
...*HERE,* YOU CAN *TAKE* IT!
BZZZT
YOU ARE *YOUNG,* AS IN THE *PROPHECY.*
YES, YES, I *SEE.*
HMMMM...
IT ALL MAKES *SENSE* NOW.
WHAT MAKES SENSE?
YOU DON'T MAKE SENSE! THIS *STICK* DOESN'T MAKE SENSE!
WHO *ARE* YOU?
WHY IS A MOB OF *CRONIES* AFTER ME?
HOW DO I GET *OUTTA* HERE?

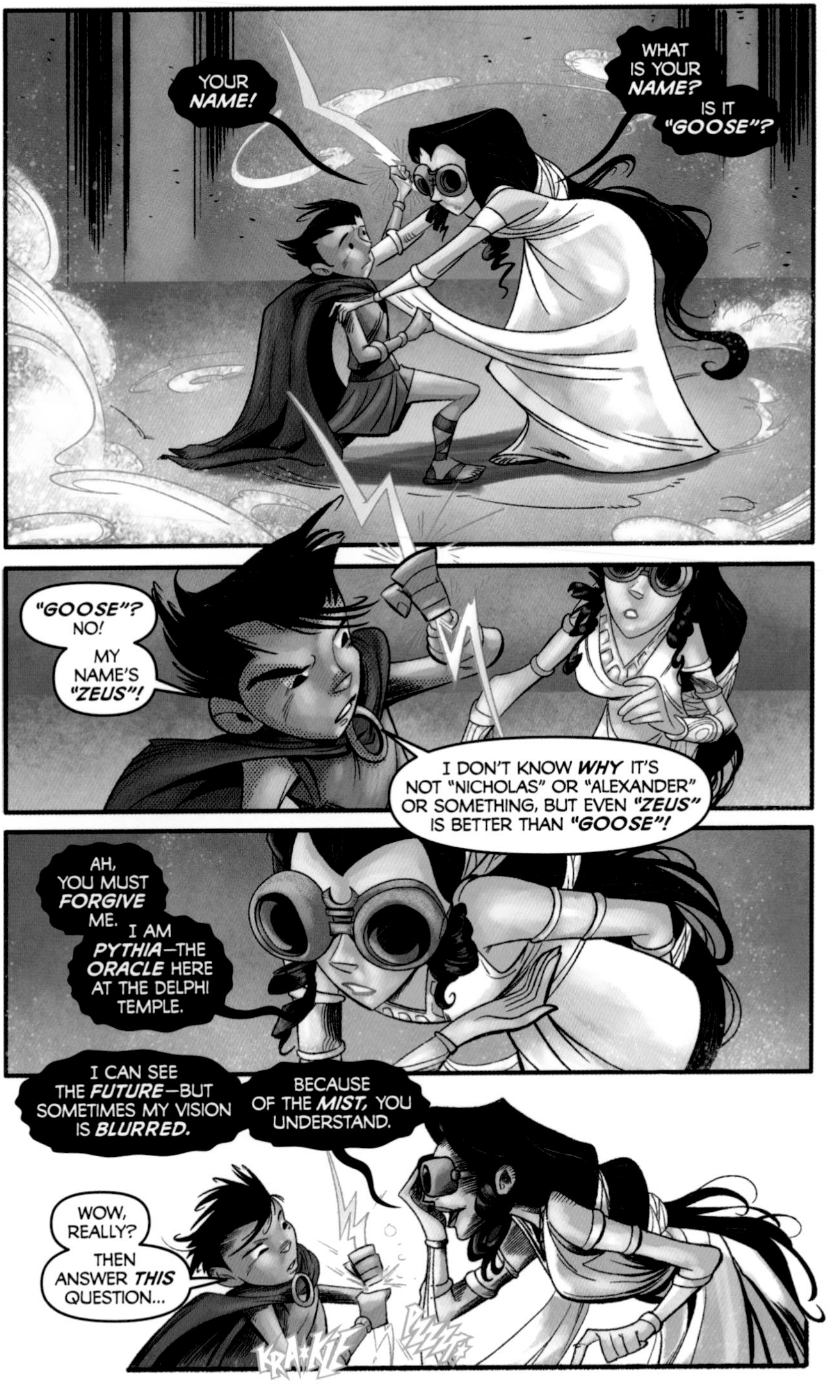

YOUR NAME!
WHAT IS YOUR NAME? IS IT "GOOSE"?
"GOOSE"? NO! MY NAME'S "ZEUS"!
I DON'T KNOW WHY IT'S NOT "NICHOLAS" OR "ALEXANDER" OR SOMETHING, BUT EVEN "ZEUS" IS BETTER THAN "GOOSE"!
AH, YOU MUST FORGIVE ME. I AM PYTHIA—THE ORACLE HERE AT THE DELPHI TEMPLE.
I CAN SEE THE FUTURE—BUT SOMETIMES MY VISION IS BLURRED.
BECAUSE OF THE MIST, YOU UNDERSTAND.
WOW, REALLY? THEN ANSWER THIS QUESTION...

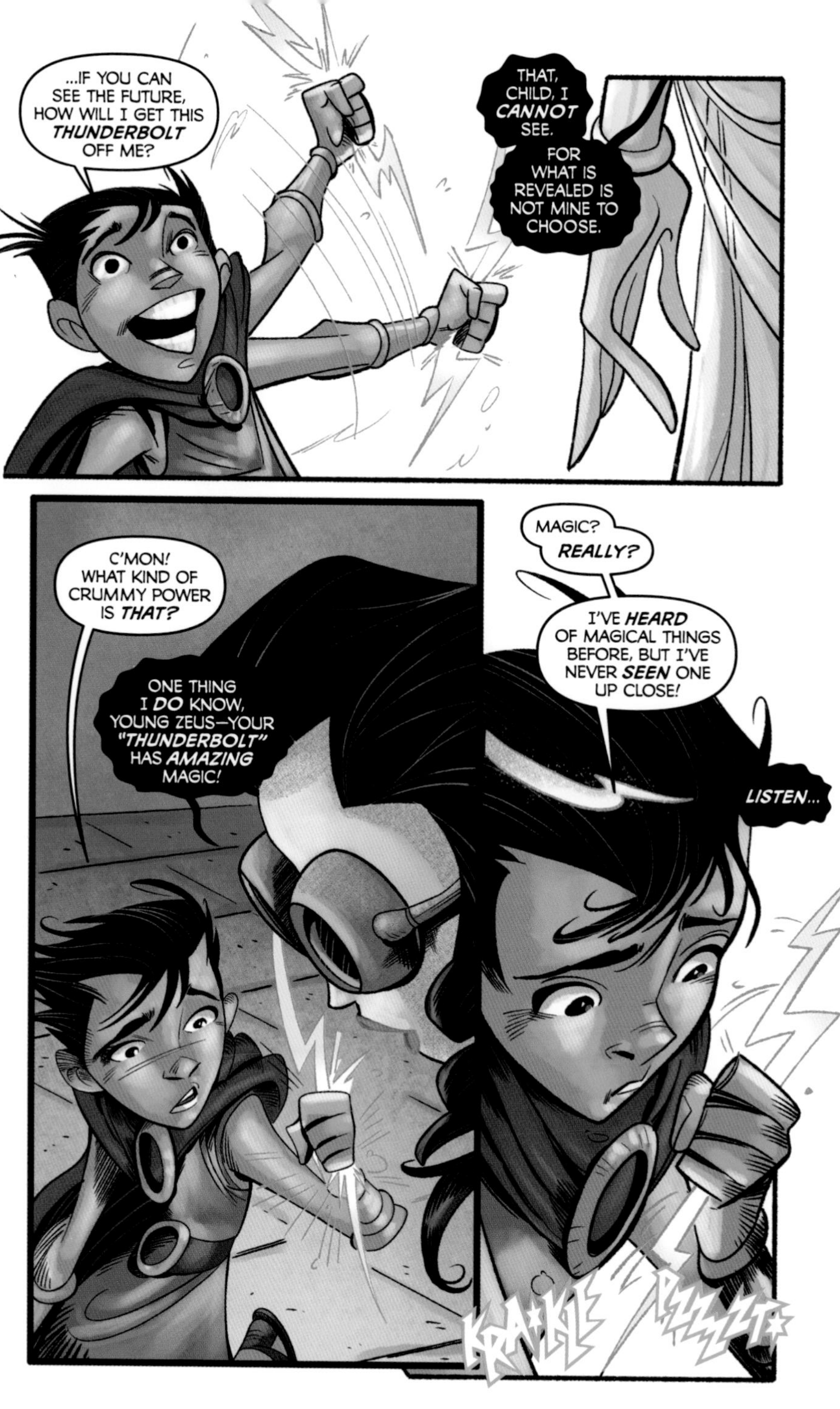
...IF YOU CAN SEE THE FUTURE, HOW WILL I GET THIS THUNDERBOLT OFF ME?
THAT, CHILD, I CANNOT SEE.
FOR WHAT IS REVEALED IS NOT MINE TO CHOOSE.
C'MON! WHAT KIND OF CRUMMY POWER IS THAT?
ONE THING I DO KNOW, YOUNG ZEUS—YOUR "THUNDERBOLT" HAS AMAZING MAGIC!
MAGIC? REALLY?
I'VE HEARD OF MAGICAL THINGS BEFORE, BUT I'VE NEVER SEEN ONE UP CLOSE!
LISTEN...
KRAKLE PZZZT

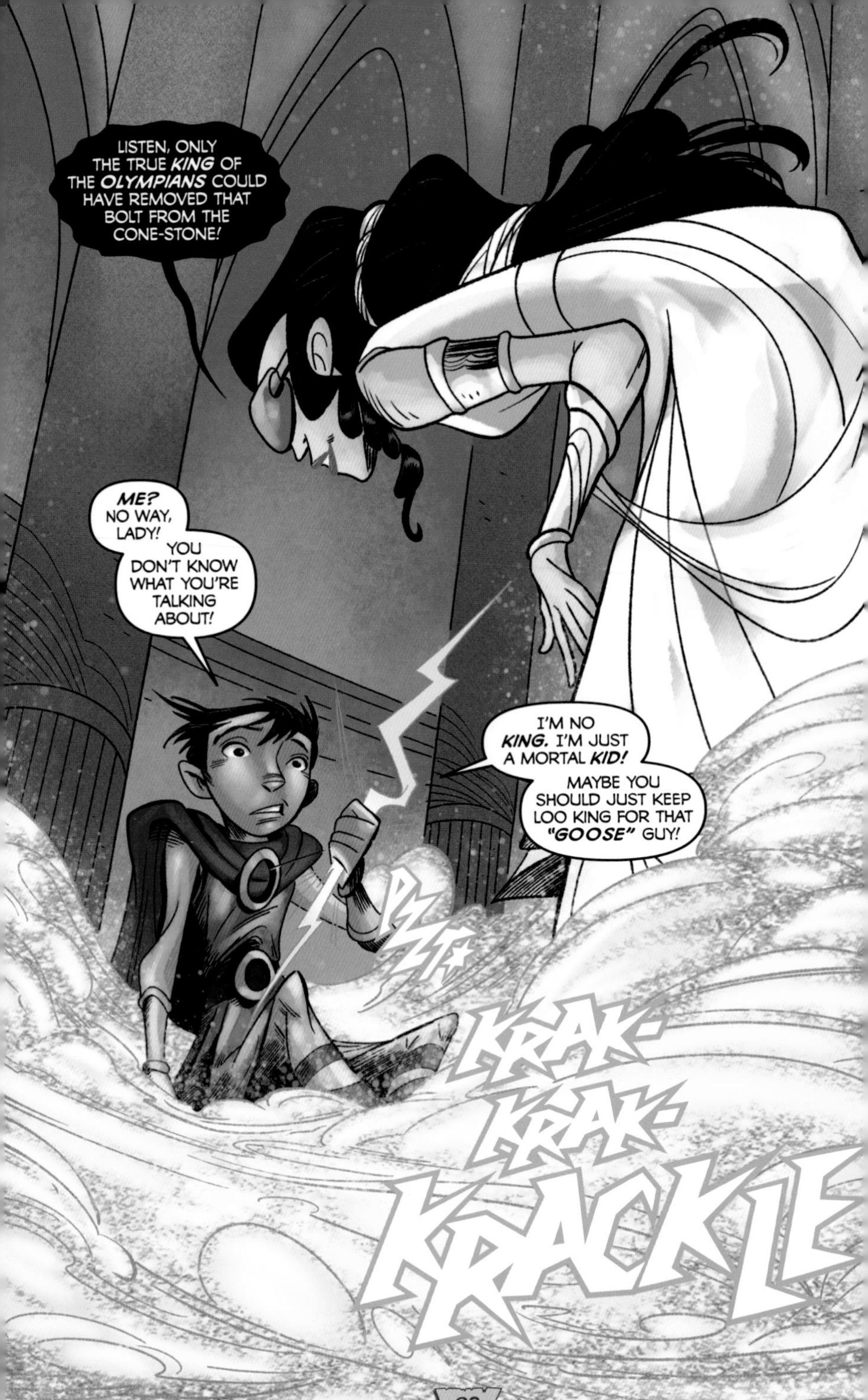
LISTEN, ONLY THE TRUE KING OF THE OLYMPIANS COULD HAVE REMOVED THAT BOLT FROM THE CONE-STONE!
ME? NO WAY, LADY!
YOU DON'T KNOW WHAT YOU'RE TALKING ABOUT!
I'M NO KING. I'M JUST A MORTAL KID!
MAYBE YOU SHOULD JUST KEEP LOO KING FOR THAT "GOOSE" GUY!
KRAK-KRAK-KRACKLE

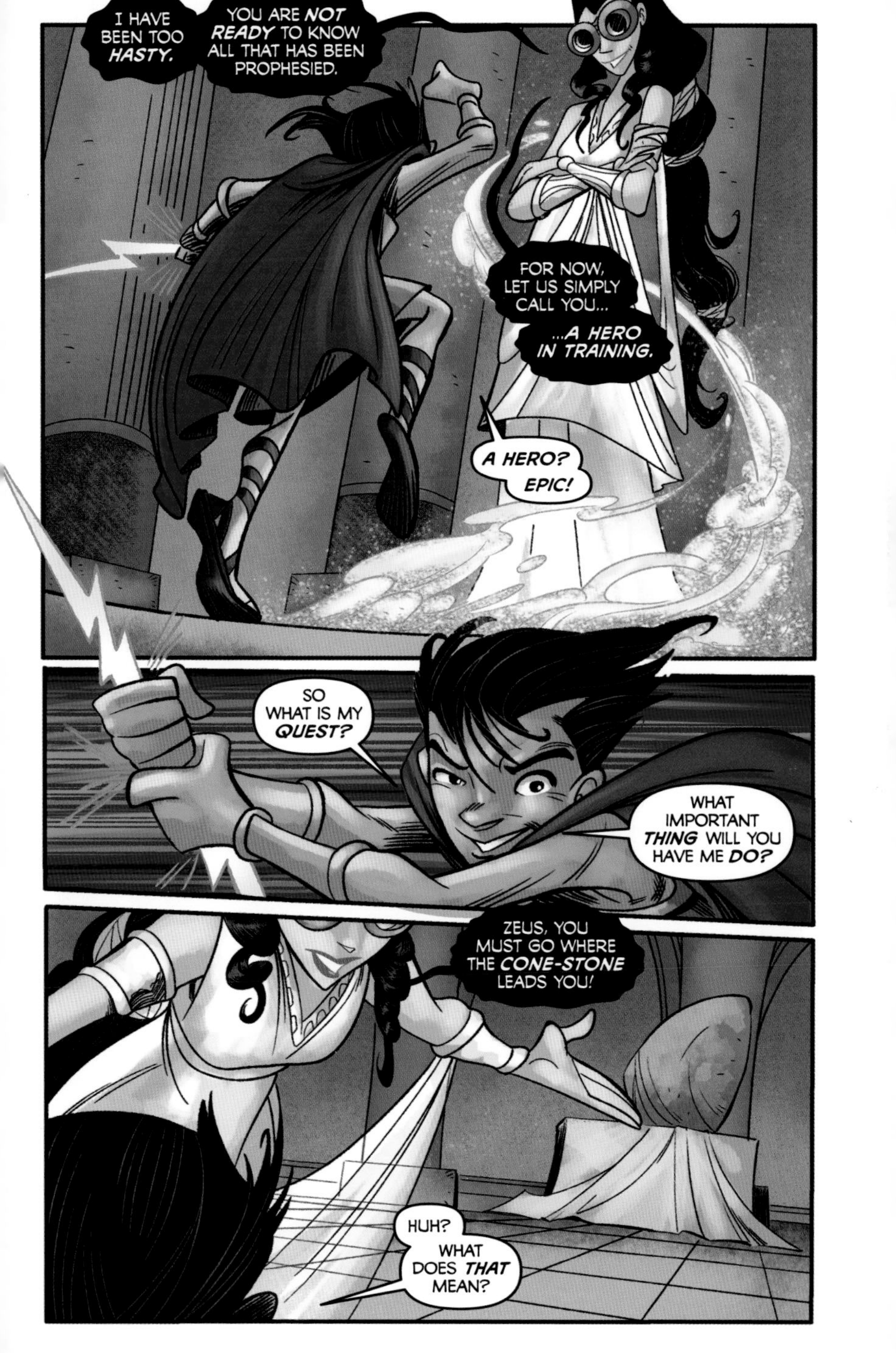
I HAVE BEEN TOO *HASTY.*
YOU ARE ***NOT READY*** TO KNOW ALL THAT HAS BEEN PROPHESIED.
FOR NOW, LET US SIMPLY CALL YOU...
...***A HERO IN TRAINING.***
A HERO? EPIC!
SO WHAT IS MY ***QUEST?***
WHAT IMPORTANT ***THING*** WILL YOU HAVE ME ***DO?***
ZEUS, YOU MUST GO WHERE THE ***CONE-STONE*** LEADS YOU!
HUH?
WHAT DOES ***THAT*** MEAN?

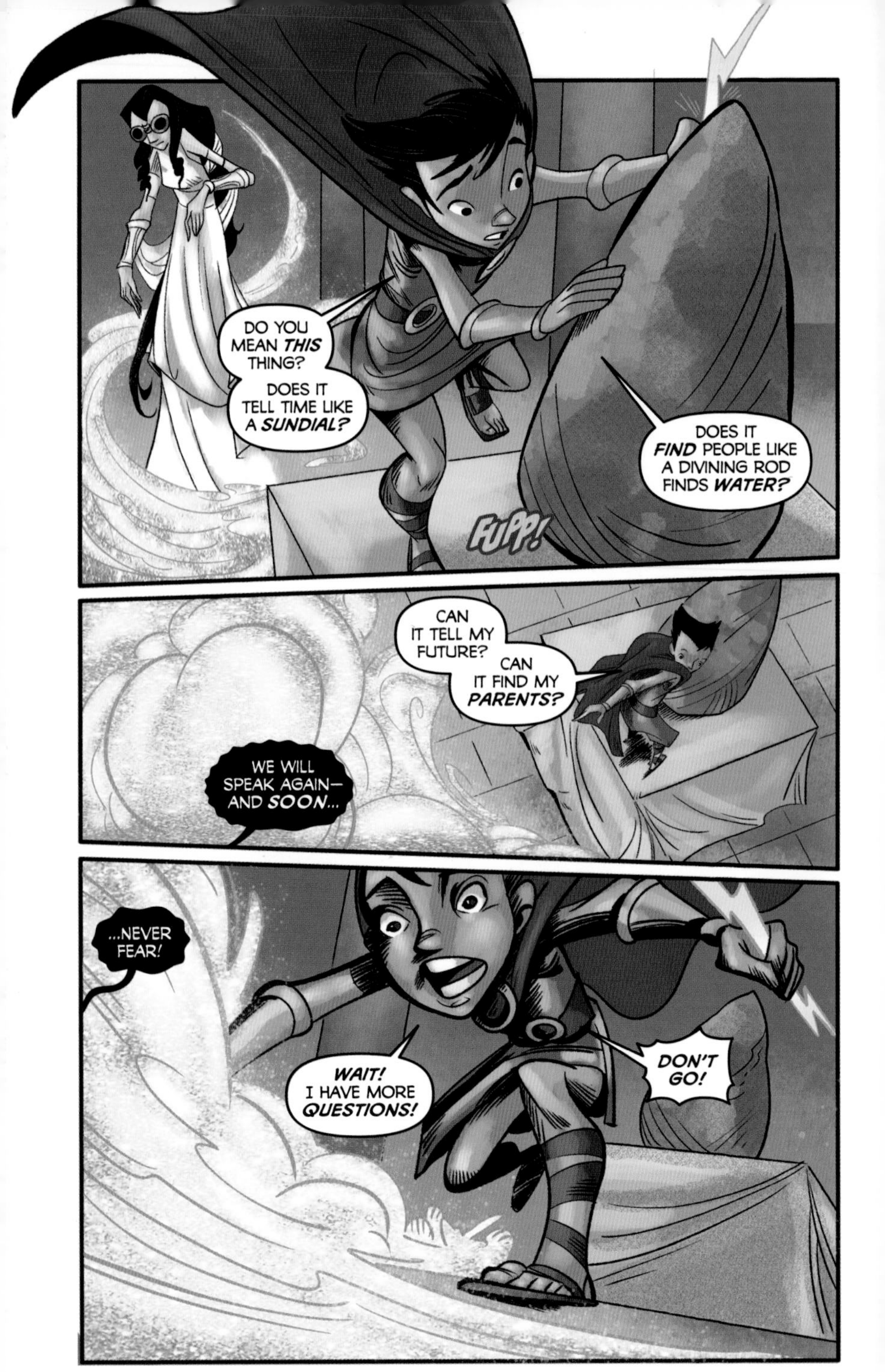
DO YOU MEAN *THIS* THING?
DOES IT TELL TIME LIKE A *SUNDIAL?*
DOES IT *FIND* PEOPLE LIKE A DIVINING ROD FINDS *WATER?*
FUPP!
CAN IT TELL MY FUTURE?
CAN IT FIND MY *PARENTS?*
WE WILL SPEAK AGAIN— AND *SOON*...
...NEVER FEAR!
WAIT! I HAVE MORE *QUESTIONS!*
DON'T GO!

CHAPTER SEVEN: MYSTERIOUS SYMBOLS

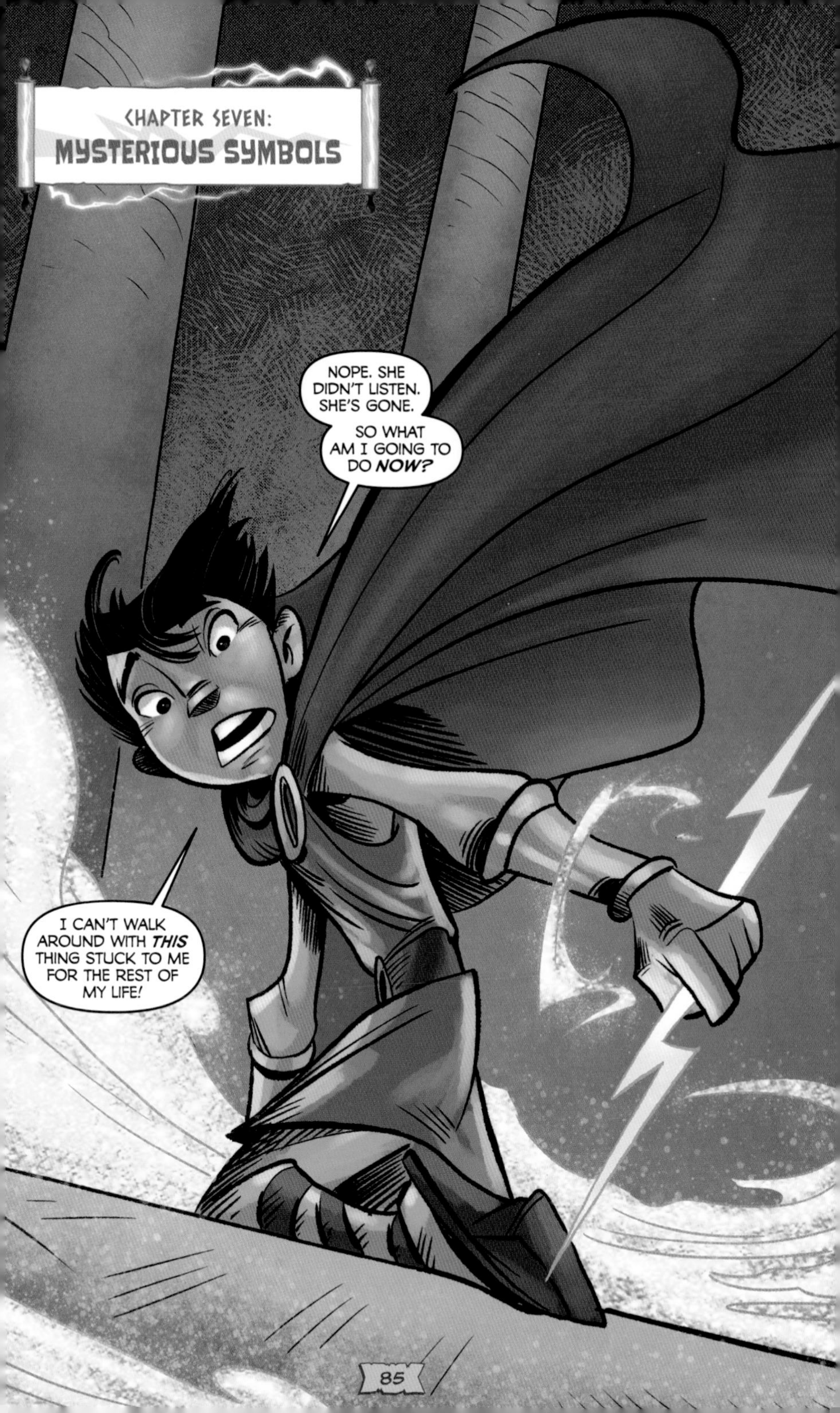
NOPE. SHE DIDN'T LISTEN. SHE'S GONE.
SO WHAT AM I GOING TO DO *NOW?*
I CAN'T WALK AROUND WITH *THIS* THING STUCK TO ME FOR THE REST OF MY LIFE!

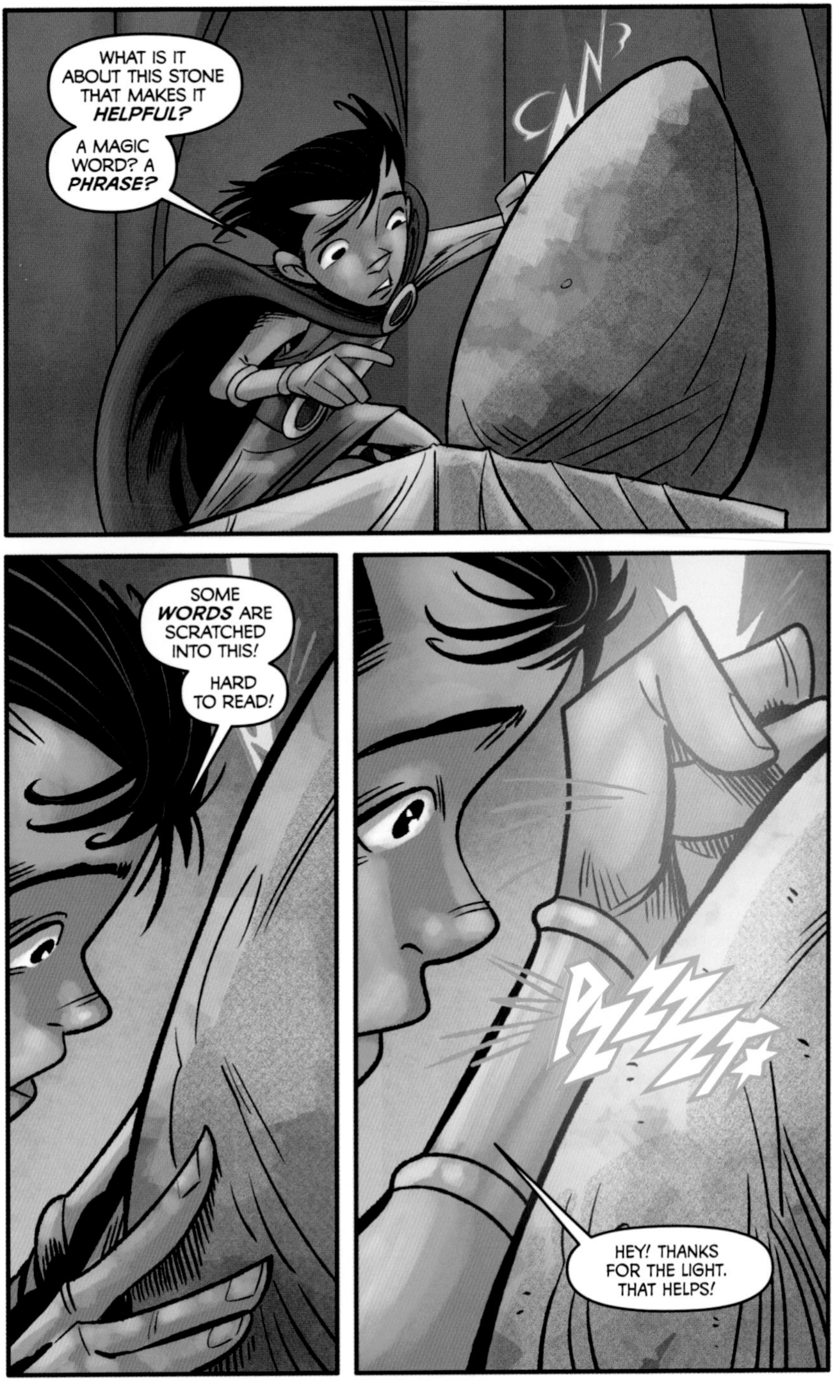
WHAT IS IT ABOUT THIS STONE THAT MAKES IT HELPFUL?
A MAGIC WORD? A PHRASE?
SOME WORDS ARE SCRATCHED INTO THIS!
HARD TO READ!
HEY! THANKS FOR THE LIGHT. THAT HELPS!

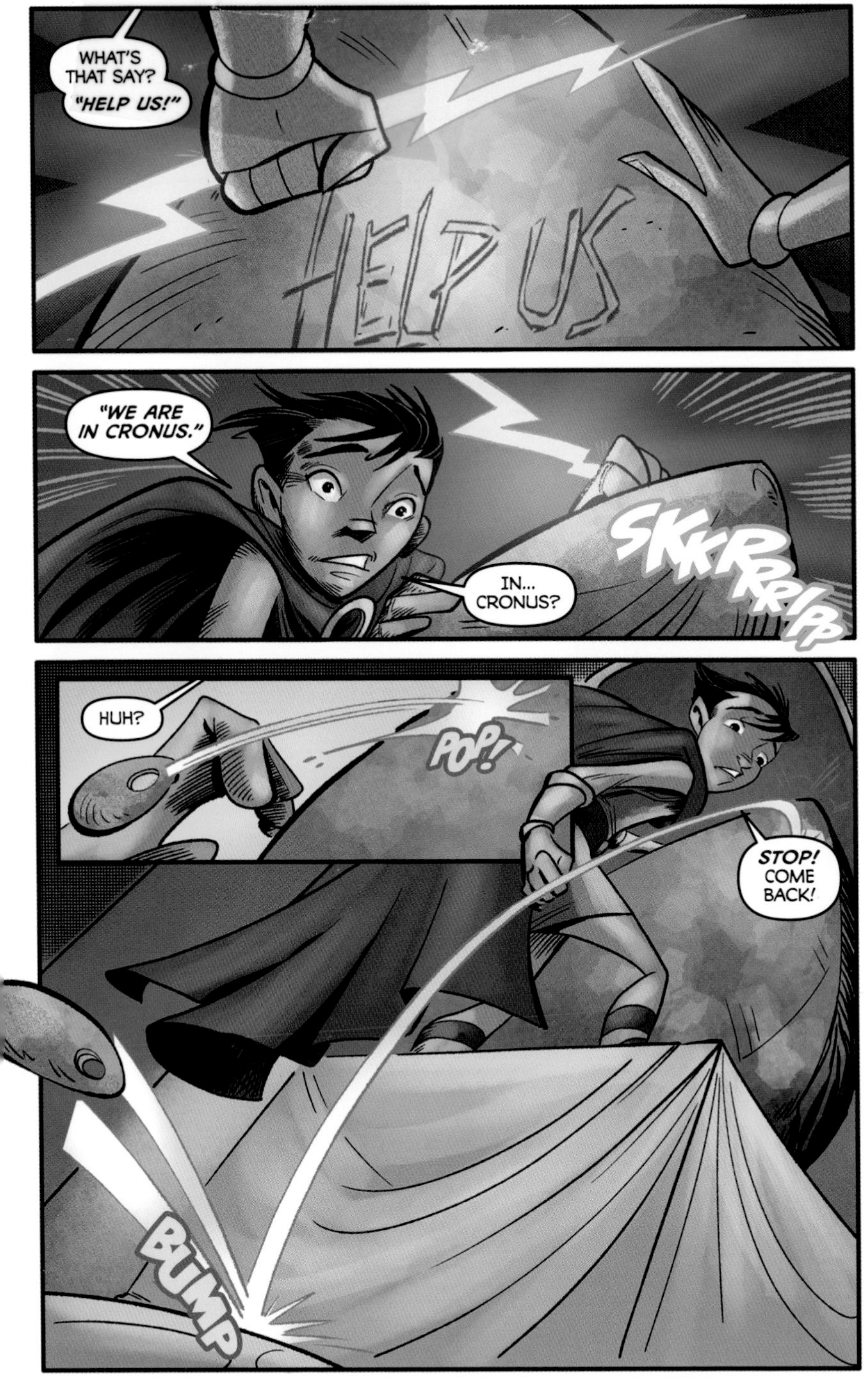
WHAT'S THAT SAY? "HELP US!"
HELP US
"WE ARE IN CRONUS."
IN... CRONUS?
SKKRRRIPP
HUH?
POP!
STOP! COME BACK!
BUMP

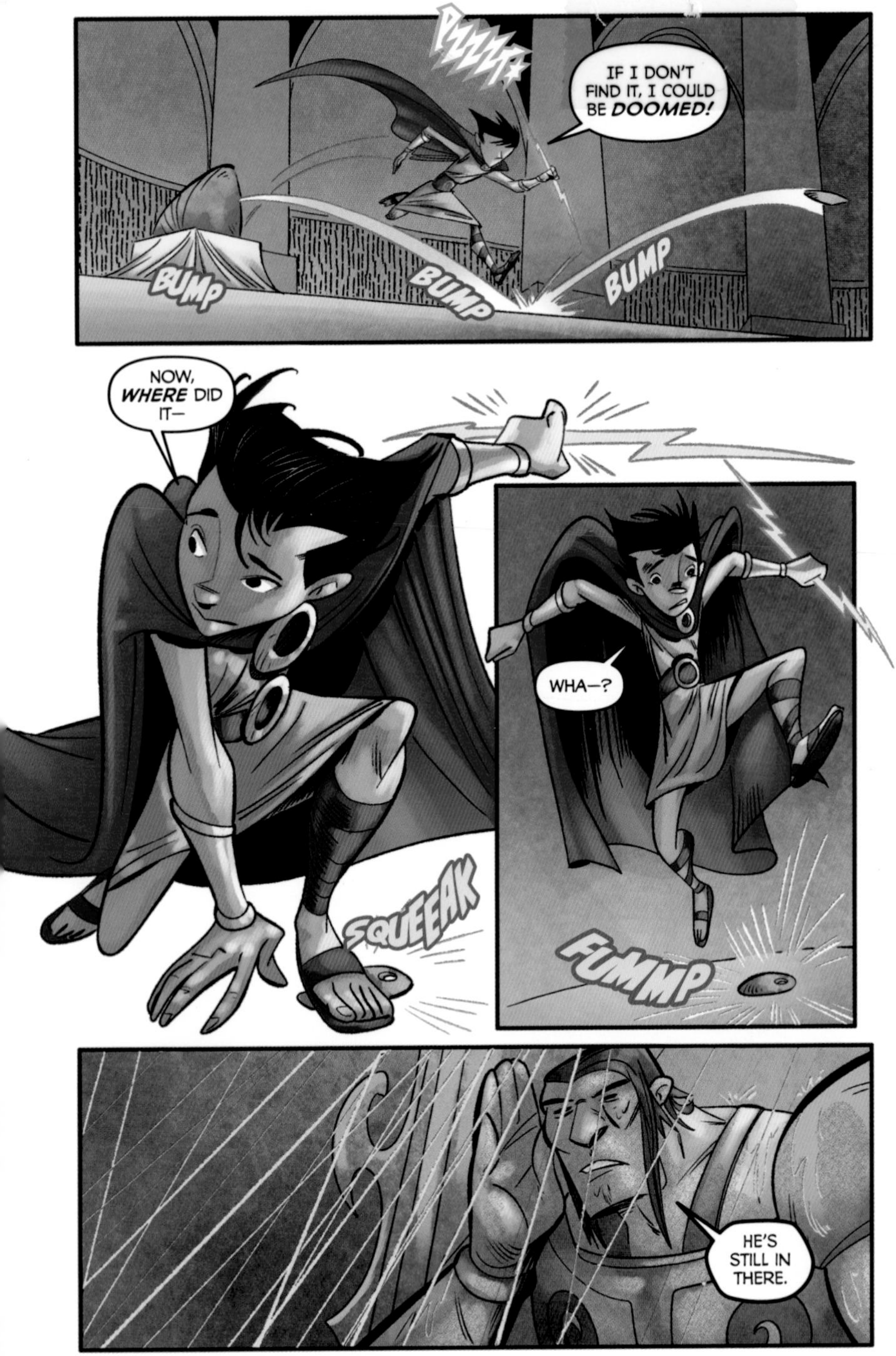
BZZZT
IF I DON'T FIND IT, I COULD BE DOOMED!
BUMP
BUMP
BUMP
NOW, WHERE DID IT—
SQUEEAK
WHA—?
FUMMP
HE'S STILL IN THERE.

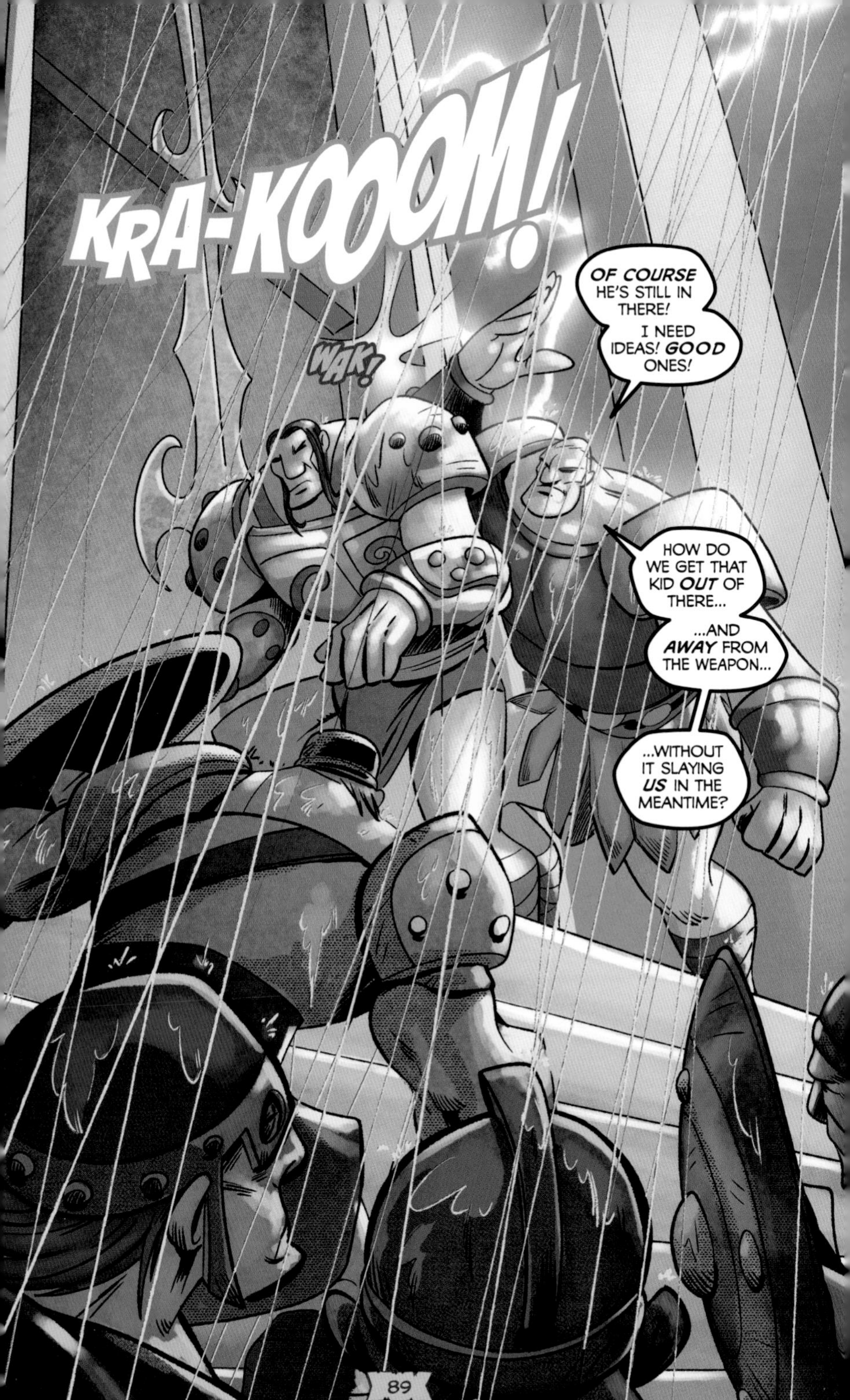
KRA-KOOOM!
WAK!
OF COURSE HE'S STILL IN THERE!
I NEED IDEAS! GOOD ONES!
HOW DO WE GET THAT KID OUT OF THERE...
...AND AWAY FROM THE WEAPON...
...WITHOUT IT SLAYING US IN THE MEANTIME?

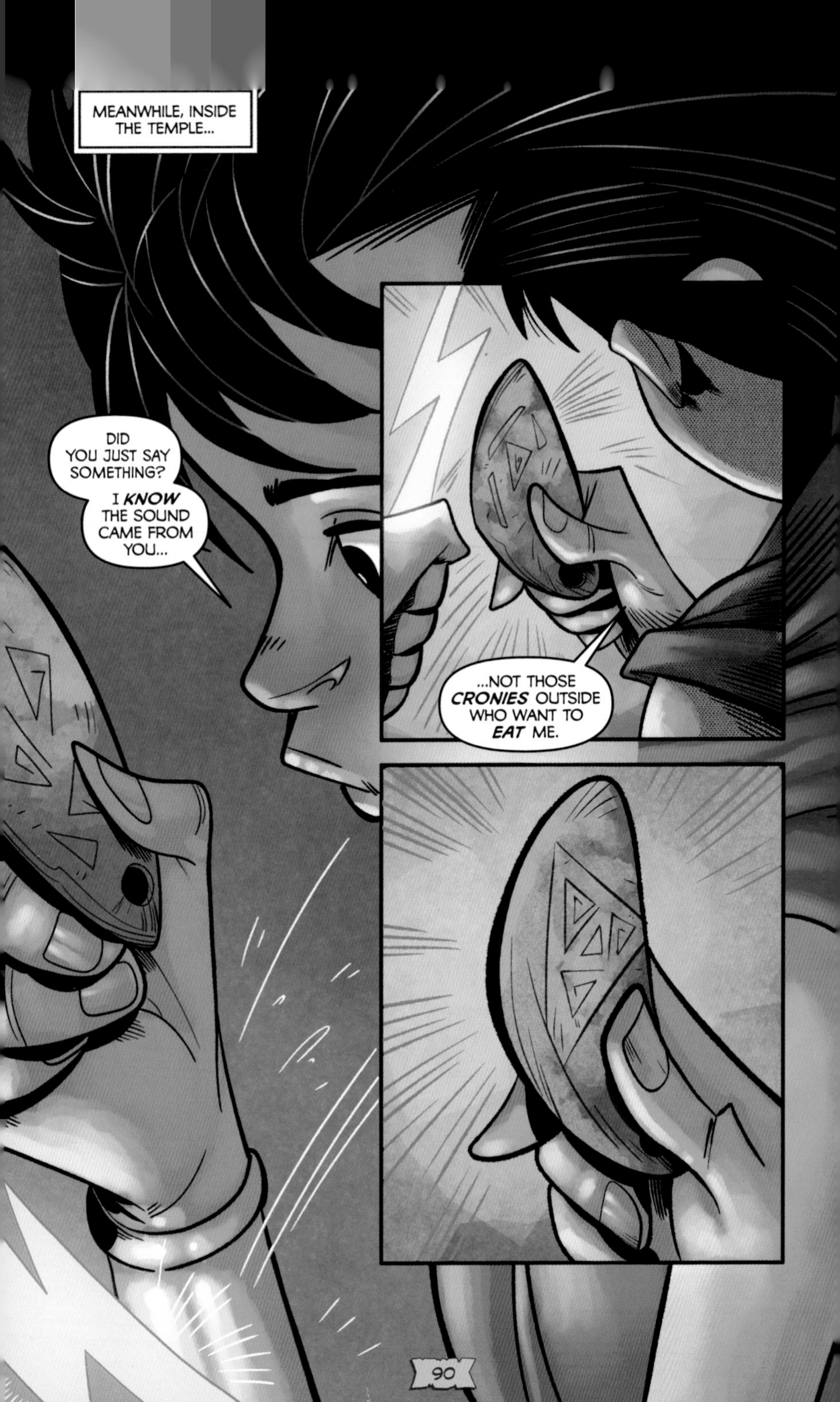
MEANWHILE, INSIDE THE TEMPLE...
DID YOU JUST SAY SOMETHING?
I KNOW THE SOUND CAME FROM YOU...
...NOT THOSE CRONIES OUTSIDE WHO WANT TO EAT ME.

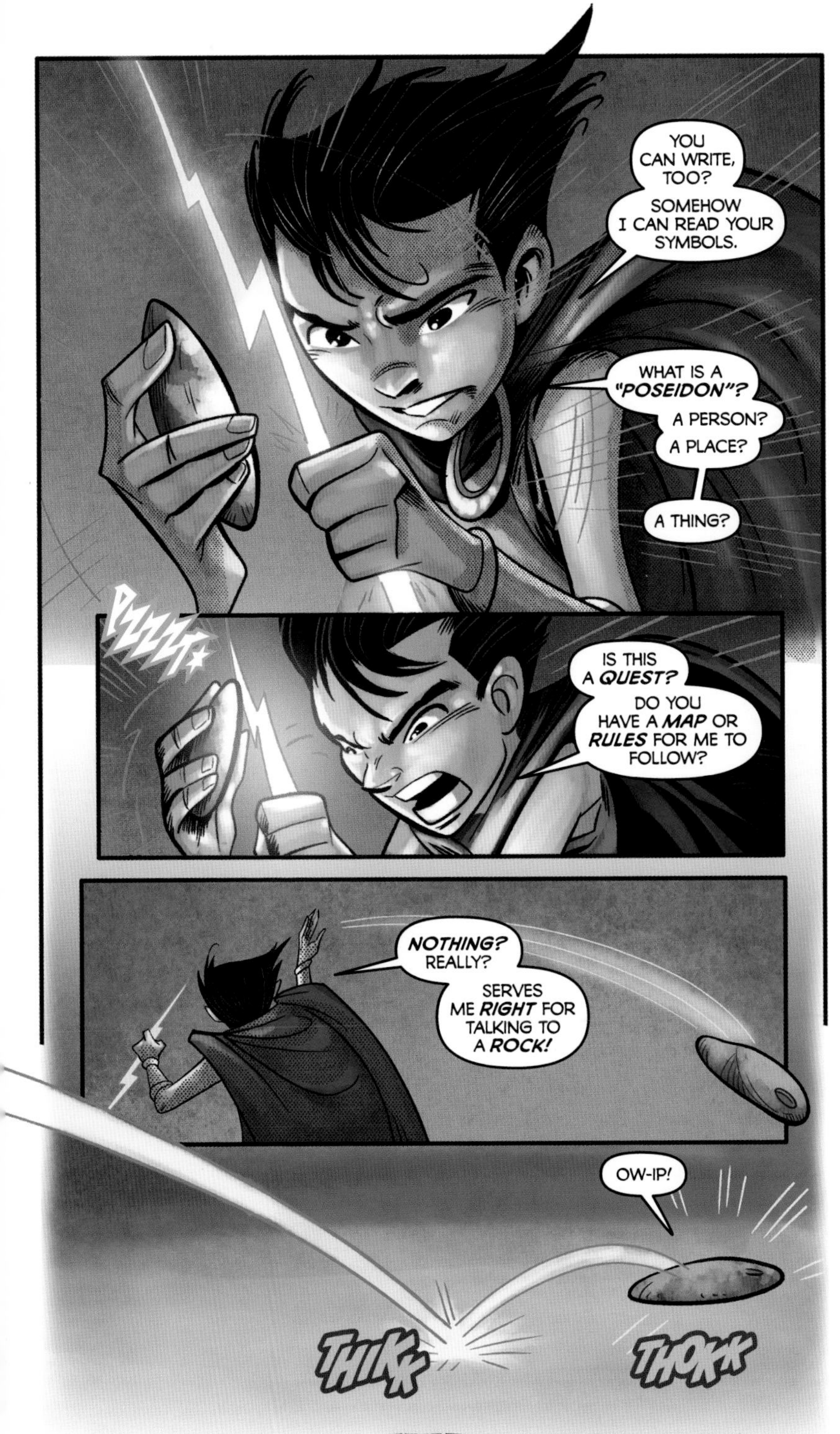
YOU CAN WRITE, TOO?
SOMEHOW I CAN READ YOUR SYMBOLS.
WHAT IS A "POSEIDON"?
A PERSON?
A PLACE?
A THING?
BZZZT!
IS THIS A QUEST?
DO YOU HAVE A MAP OR RULES FOR ME TO FOLLOW?
NOTHING? REALLY?
SERVES ME RIGHT FOR TALKING TO A ROCK!
OW-IP!
THIKK
THOKK

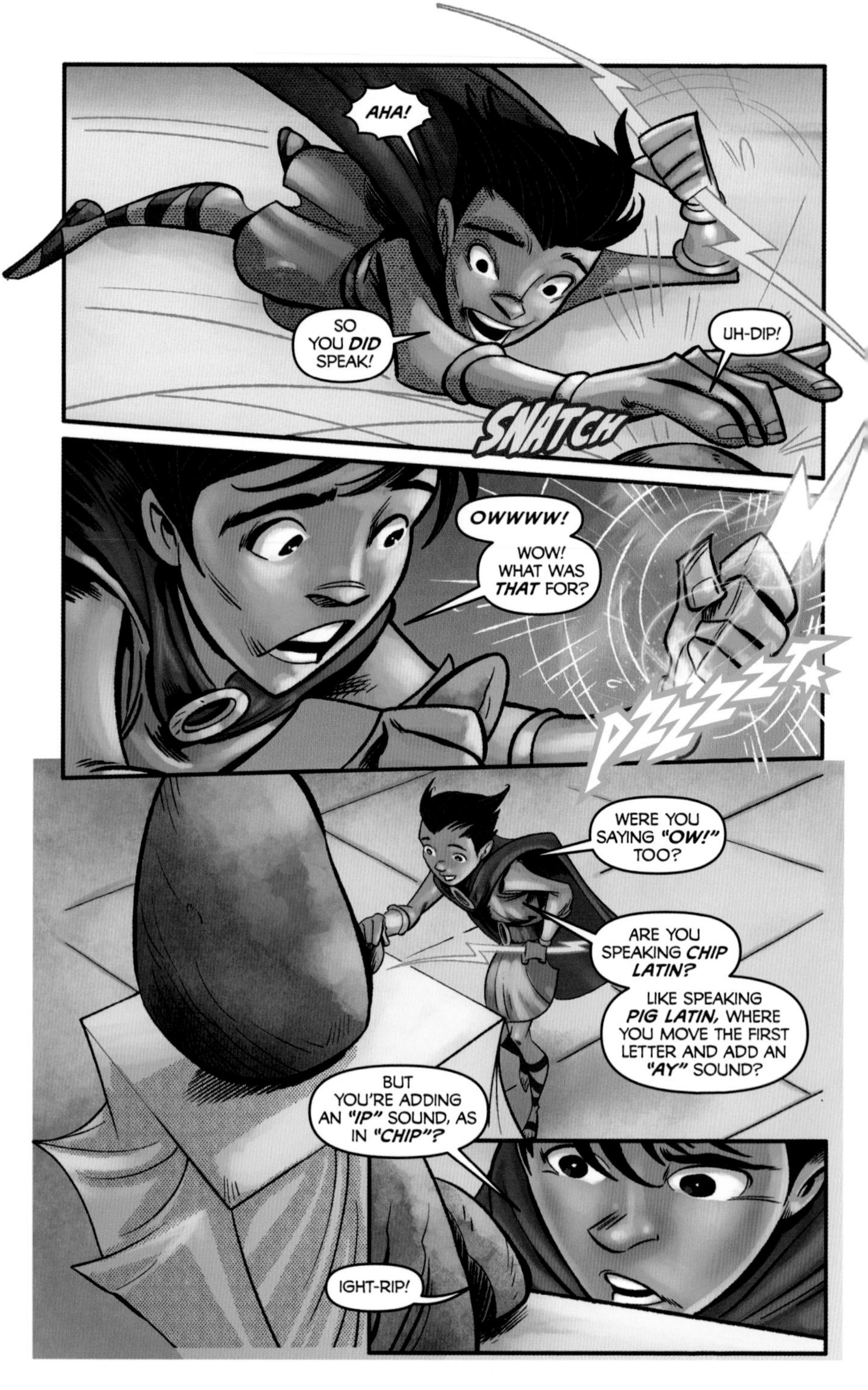
AHA!
SO YOU *DID* SPEAK!
UH-DIP!
SNATCH
OWWWW!
WOW! WHAT WAS *THAT* FOR?
PZZZZT
WERE YOU SAYING *"OW!"* TOO?
ARE YOU SPEAKING *CHIP LATIN?*
LIKE SPEAKING *PIG LATIN,* WHERE YOU MOVE THE FIRST LETTER AND ADD AN *"AY"* SOUND?
BUT YOU'RE ADDING AN *"IP"* SOUND, AS IN *"CHIP"?*
IGHT-RIP!

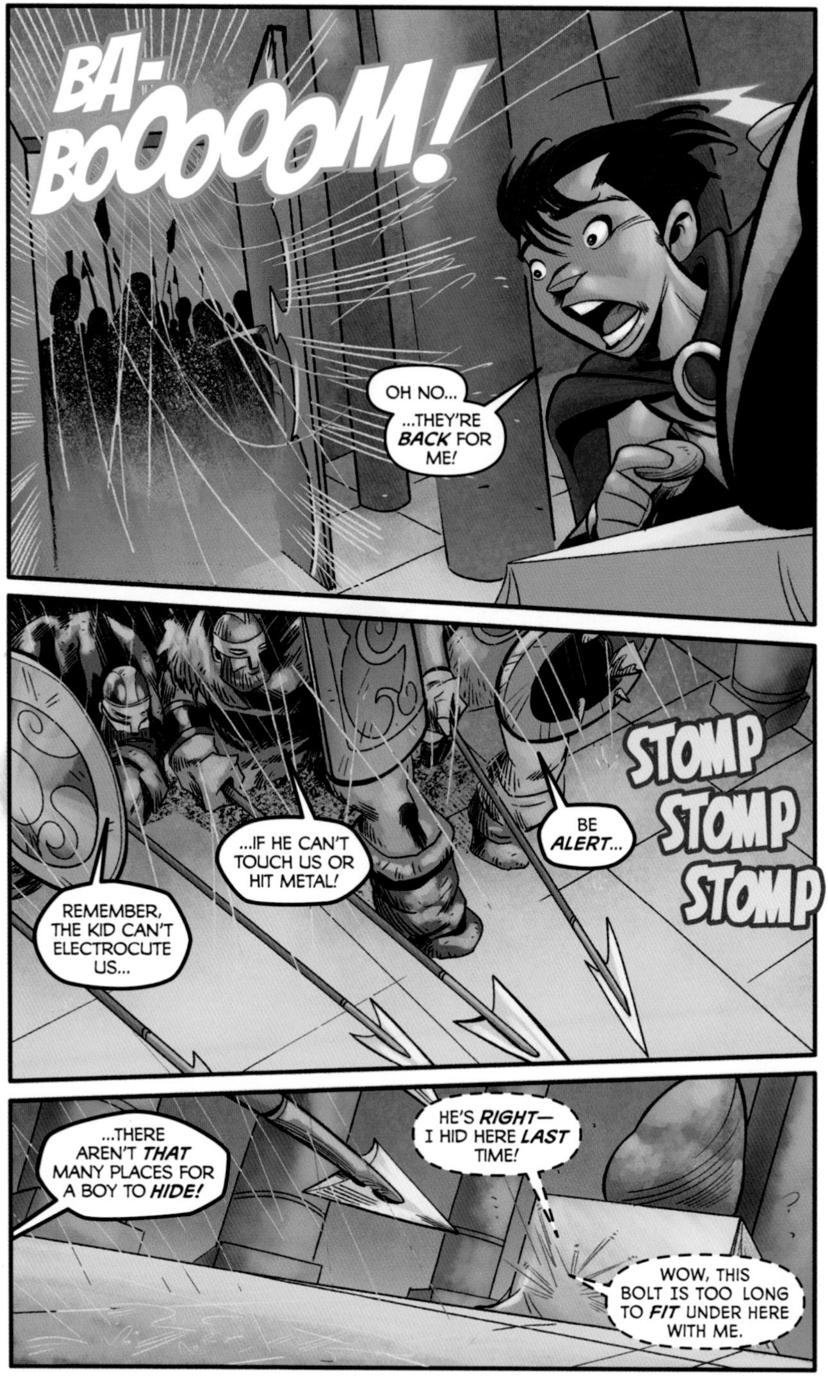
BA-BOOOOOM!
OH NO... ...THEY'RE BACK FOR ME!
STOMP STOMP STOMP
BE ALERT...
...IF HE CAN'T TOUCH US OR HIT METAL!
REMEMBER, THE KID CAN'T ELECTROCUTE US...
...THERE AREN'T THAT MANY PLACES FOR A BOY TO HIDE!
HE'S RIGHT— I HID HERE LAST TIME!
WOW, THIS BOLT IS TOO LONG TO FIT UNDER HERE WITH ME.

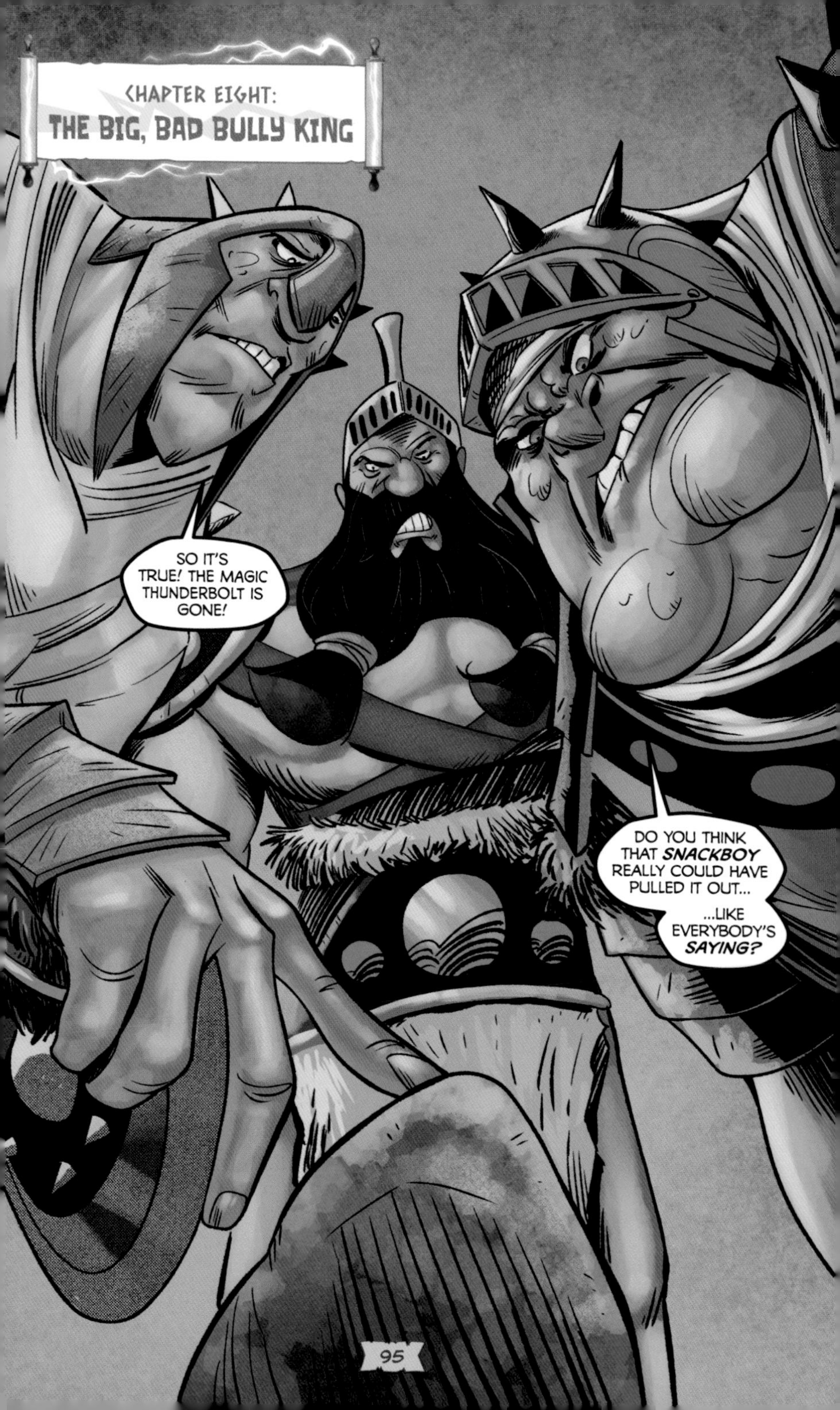

CHAPTER EIGHT:
THE BIG, BAD BULLY KING
SO IT'S TRUE! THE MAGIC THUNDERBOLT IS GONE!
DO YOU THINK THAT SNACKBOY REALLY COULD HAVE PULLED IT OUT...
...LIKE EVERYBODY'S SAYING?

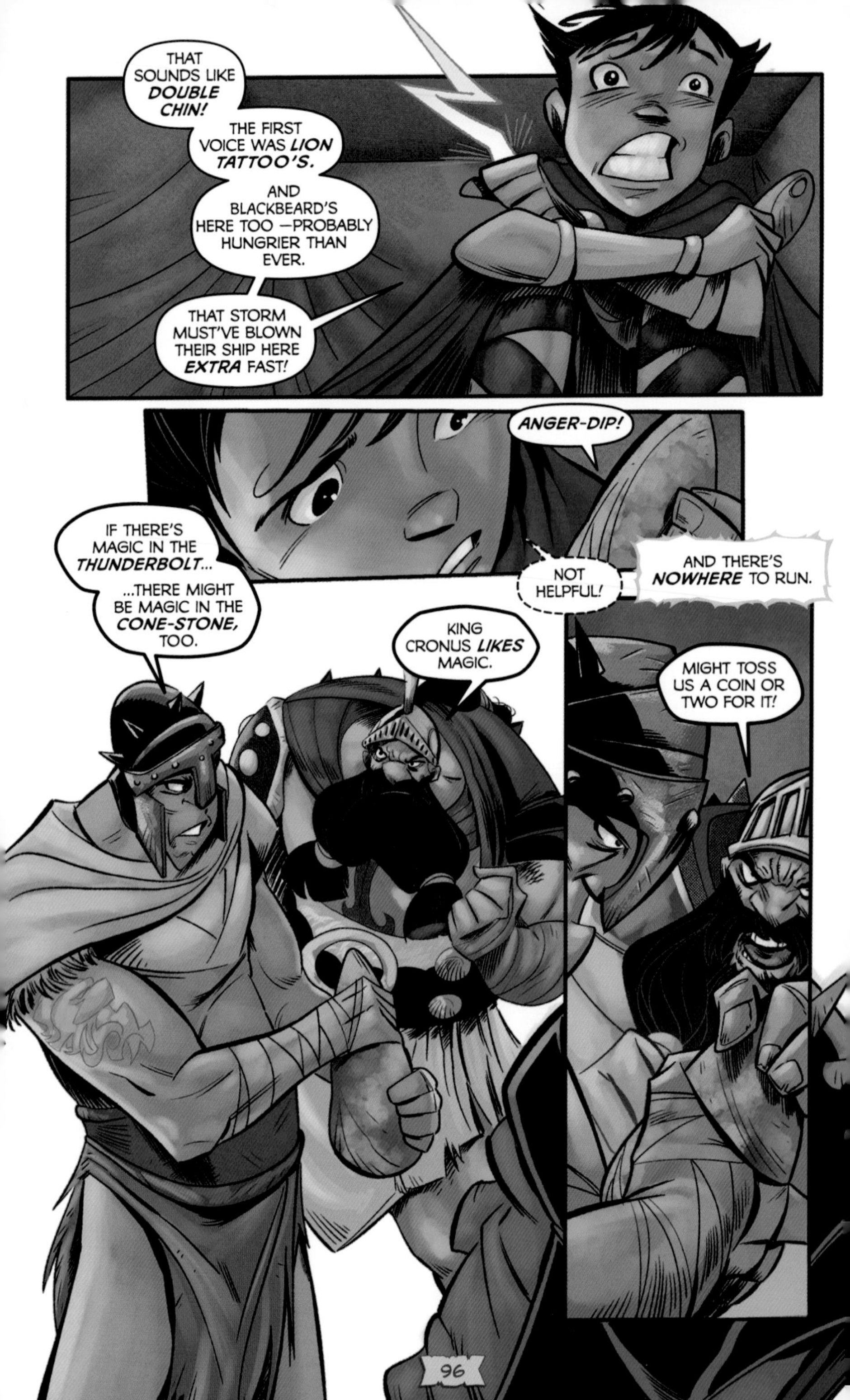

THAT SOUNDS LIKE DOUBLE CHIN!
THE FIRST VOICE WAS LION TATTOO'S.
AND BLACKBEARD'S HERE TOO —PROBABLY HUNGRIER THAN EVER.
THAT STORM MUST'VE BLOWN THEIR SHIP HERE EXTRA FAST!
ANGER-DIP!
NOT HELPFUL!
AND THERE'S NOWHERE TO RUN.
IF THERE'S MAGIC IN THE THUNDERBOLT...
...THERE MIGHT BE MAGIC IN THE CONE-STONE, TOO.
KING CRONUS LIKES MAGIC.
MIGHT TOSS US A COIN OR TWO FOR IT!

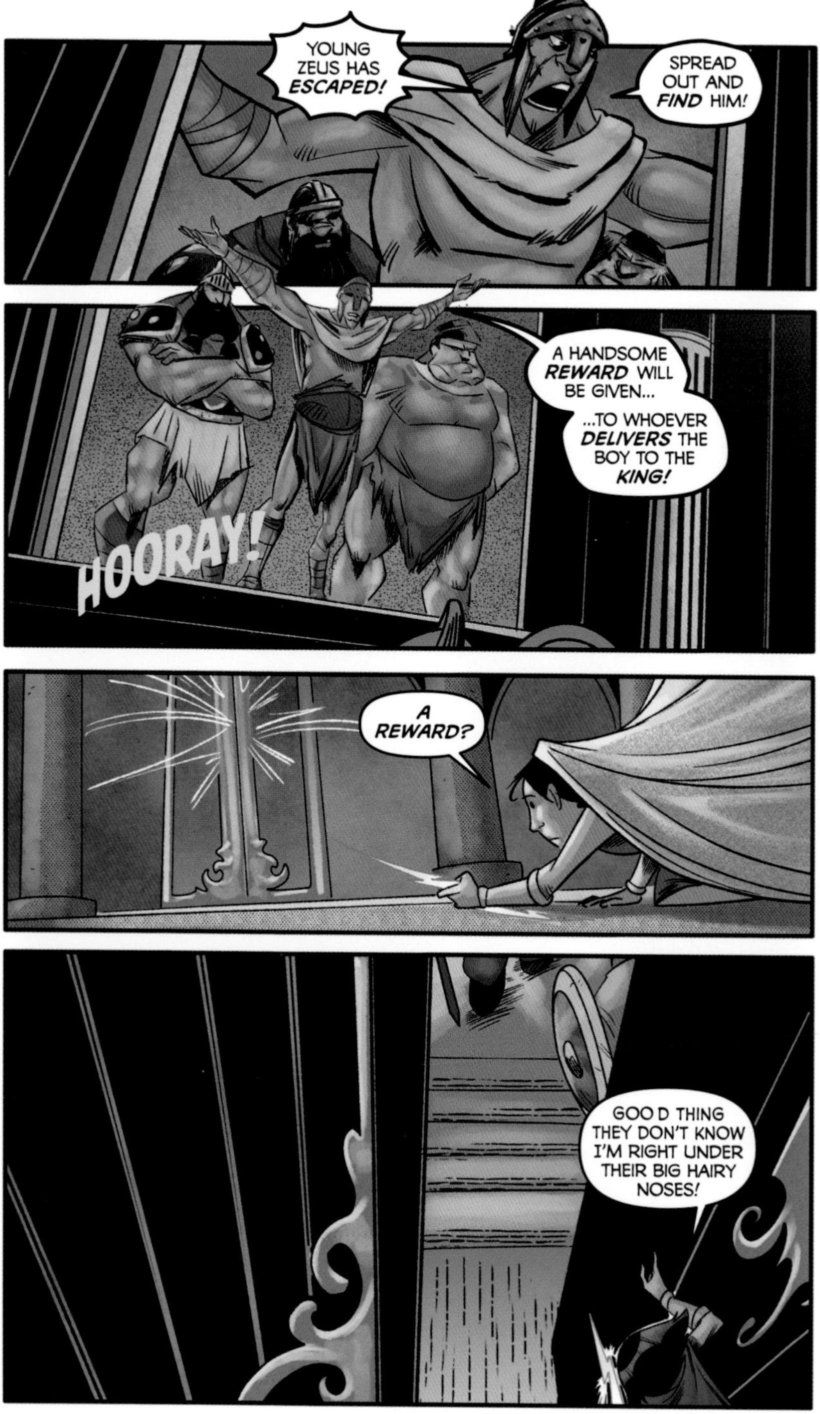
YOUNG ZEUS HAS *ESCAPED!*
SPREAD OUT AND *FIND* HIM!
A HANDSOME *REWARD* WILL BE GIVEN...
...TO WHOEVER *DELIVERS* THE BOY TO THE *KING!*
HOORAY!
A REWARD?
GOO D THING THEY DON'T KNOW I'M RIGHT UNDER THEIR BIG HAIRY NOSES!

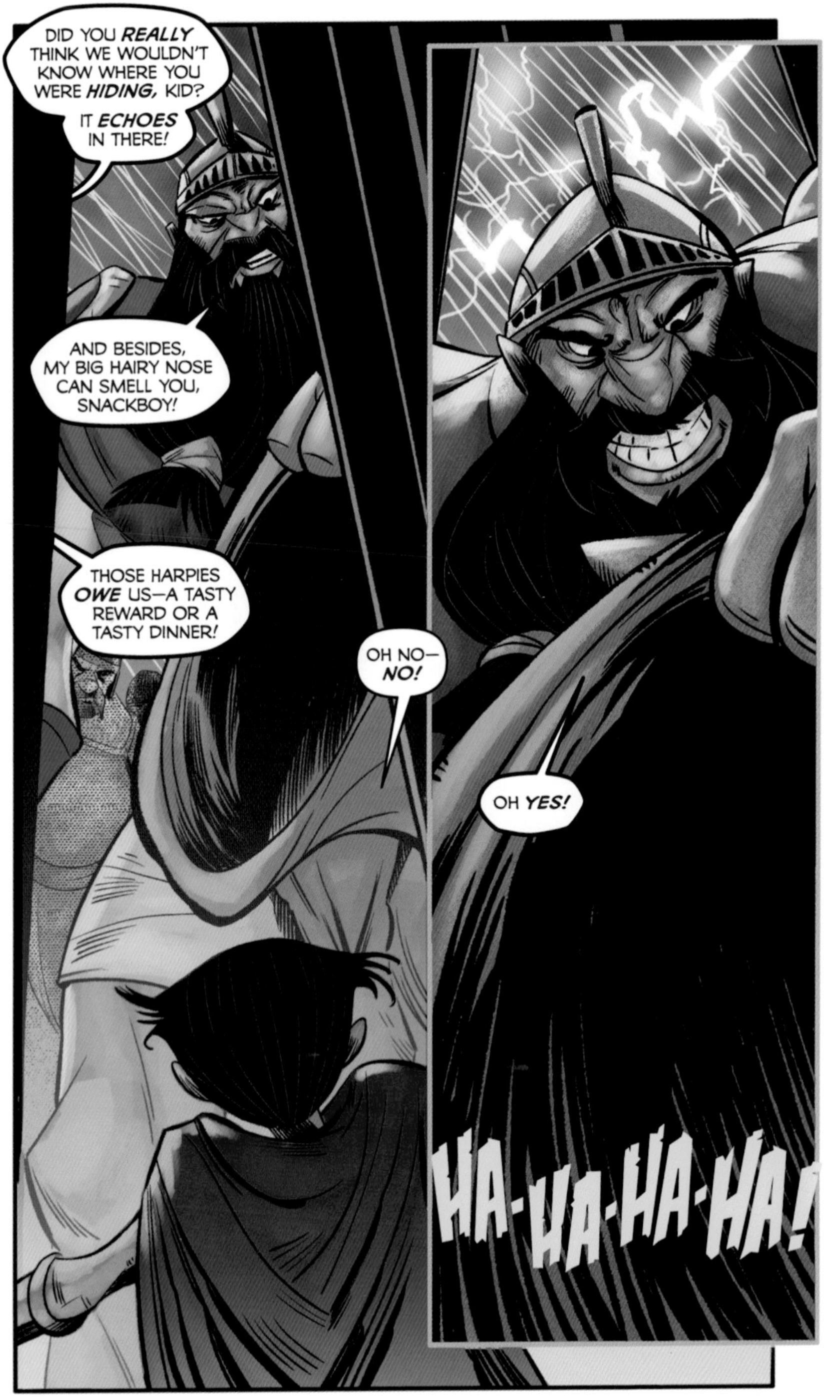
DID YOU *REALLY* THINK WE WOULDN'T KNOW WHERE YOU WERE *HIDING,* KID?
IT *ECHOES* IN THERE!
AND BESIDES, MY BIG HAIRY NOSE CAN SMELL YOU, SNACKBOY!
THOSE HARPIES *OWE* US—A TASTY REWARD OR A TASTY DINNER!
OH NO—*NO!*
OH *YES!*
HA-HA-HA-HA!

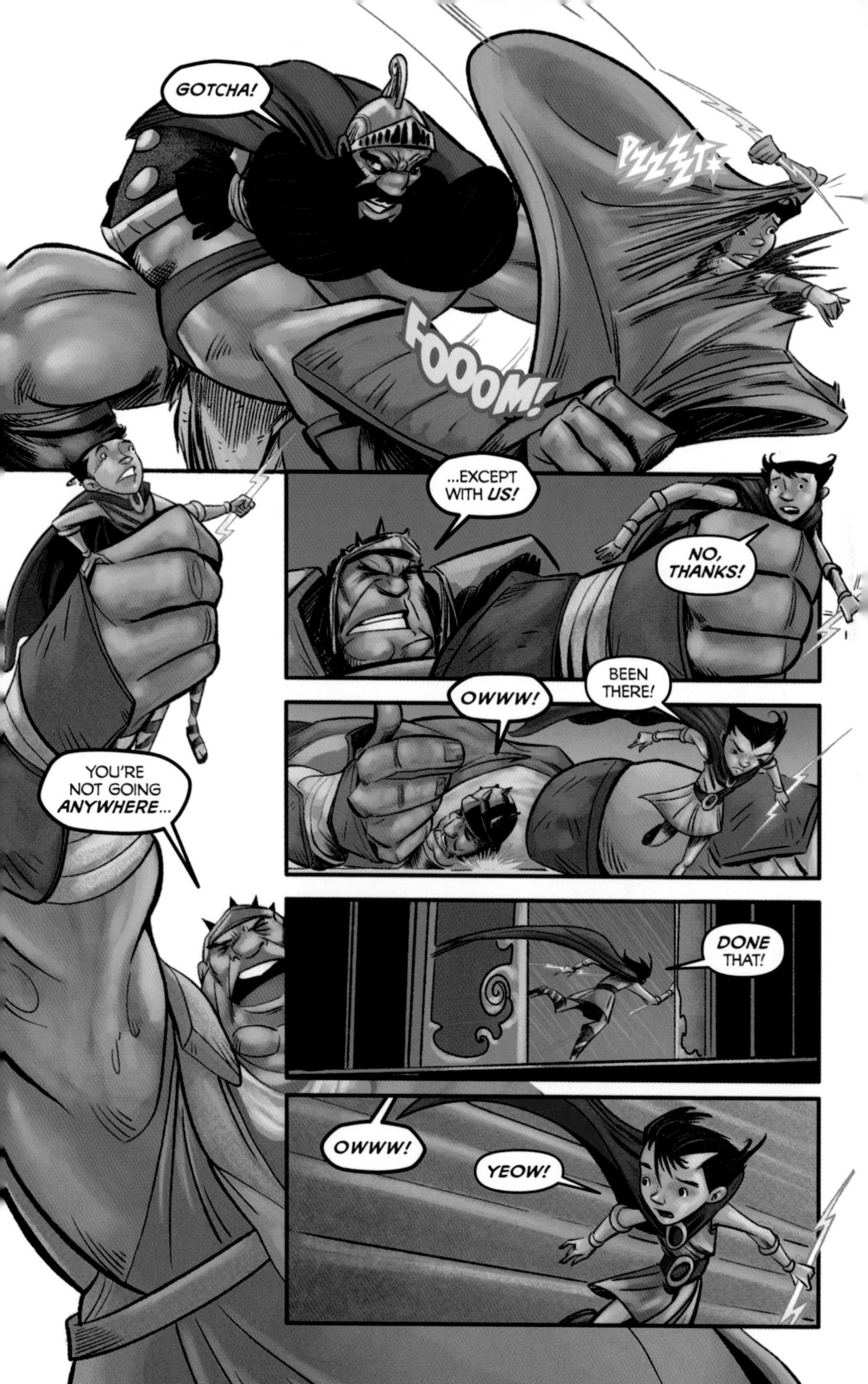

GOTCHA!
PZZZZT
FOOOM!
...EXCEPT WITH US!
NO, THANKS!
YOU'RE NOT GOING ANYWHERE...
OWWW!
BEEN THERE!
DONE THAT!
OWWW!
YEOW!

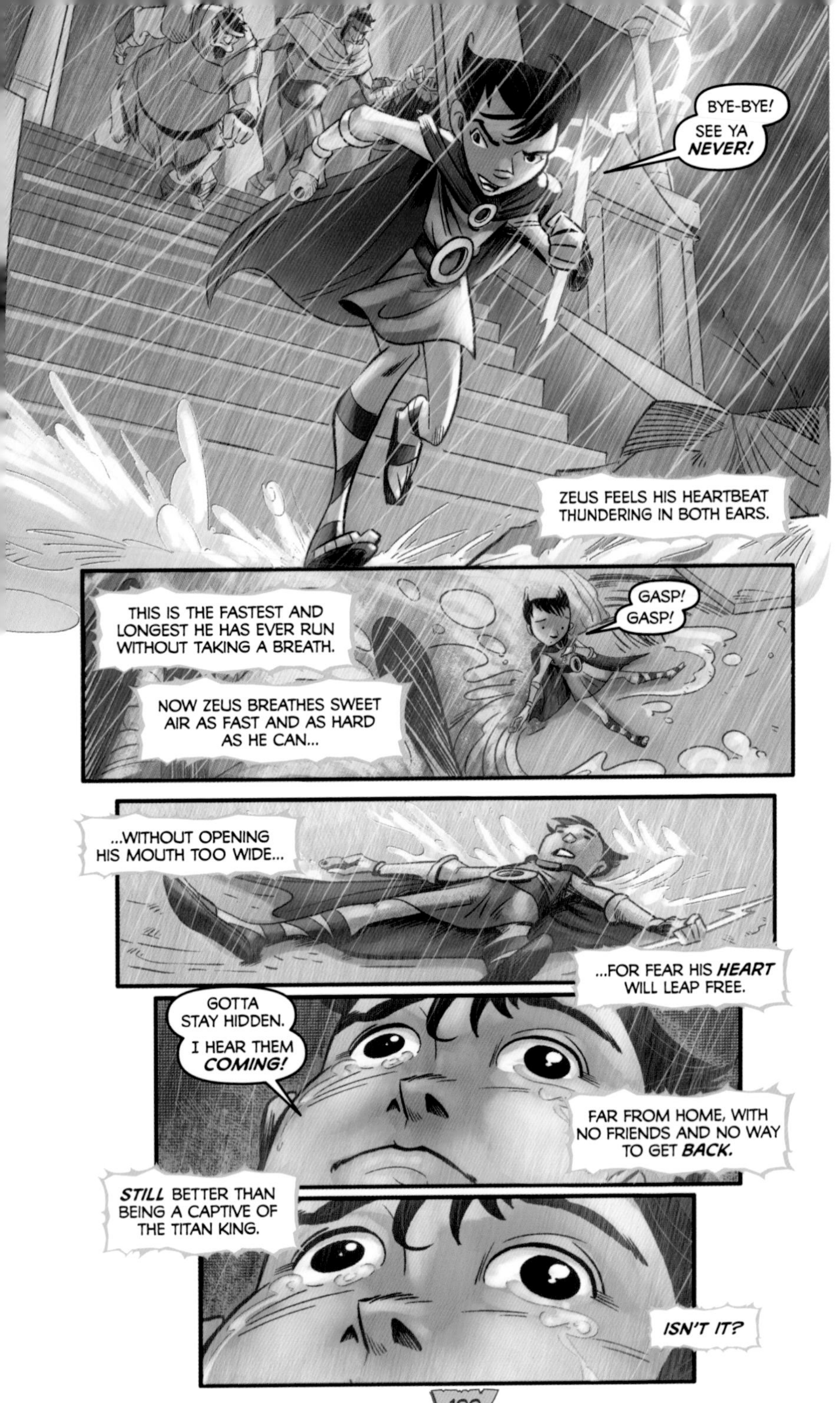
BYE-BYE!
SEE YA NEVER!
ZEUS FEELS HIS HEARTBEAT THUNDERING IN BOTH EARS.
THIS IS THE FASTEST AND LONGEST HE HAS EVER RUN WITHOUT TAKING A BREATH.
GASP! GASP!
NOW ZEUS BREATHES SWEET AIR AS FAST AND AS HARD AS HE CAN...
...WITHOUT OPENING HIS MOUTH TOO WIDE...
...FOR FEAR HIS HEART WILL LEAP FREE.
GOTTA STAY HIDDEN.
I HEAR THEM COMING!
FAR FROM HOME, WITH NO FRIENDS AND NO WAY TO GET BACK.
STILL BETTER THAN BEING A CAPTIVE OF THE TITAN KING.
ISN'T IT?

OWWWW!

IS IT SAFER, *SMARTER*, TO SOMEHOW FIND HIS WAY BACK TO *CRETE*...

ORACLE *PYTHIA* TOLD ME TO GO WHERE THE STONE *LED*.

STOP *GANGING UP* ON ME! I'M TRYING TO FIGURE IT OUT!

AND *YOU*, CHIP, TOLD ME TO "FIND *POSEIDON*."

FOR ALL I KNOW, "POSEIDON" COULD BE THE NAME OF ANOTHER *THUNDERBOLT*!

BRSHH

FRUMMP

OKAY, *FINE*...

...SO THAT HE CAN BE SAFE AND COZY IN HIS *CAVE*?

HOW WOULD HE *GET* HOME? AND IS THAT WHAT HE REALLY *WANTS*?

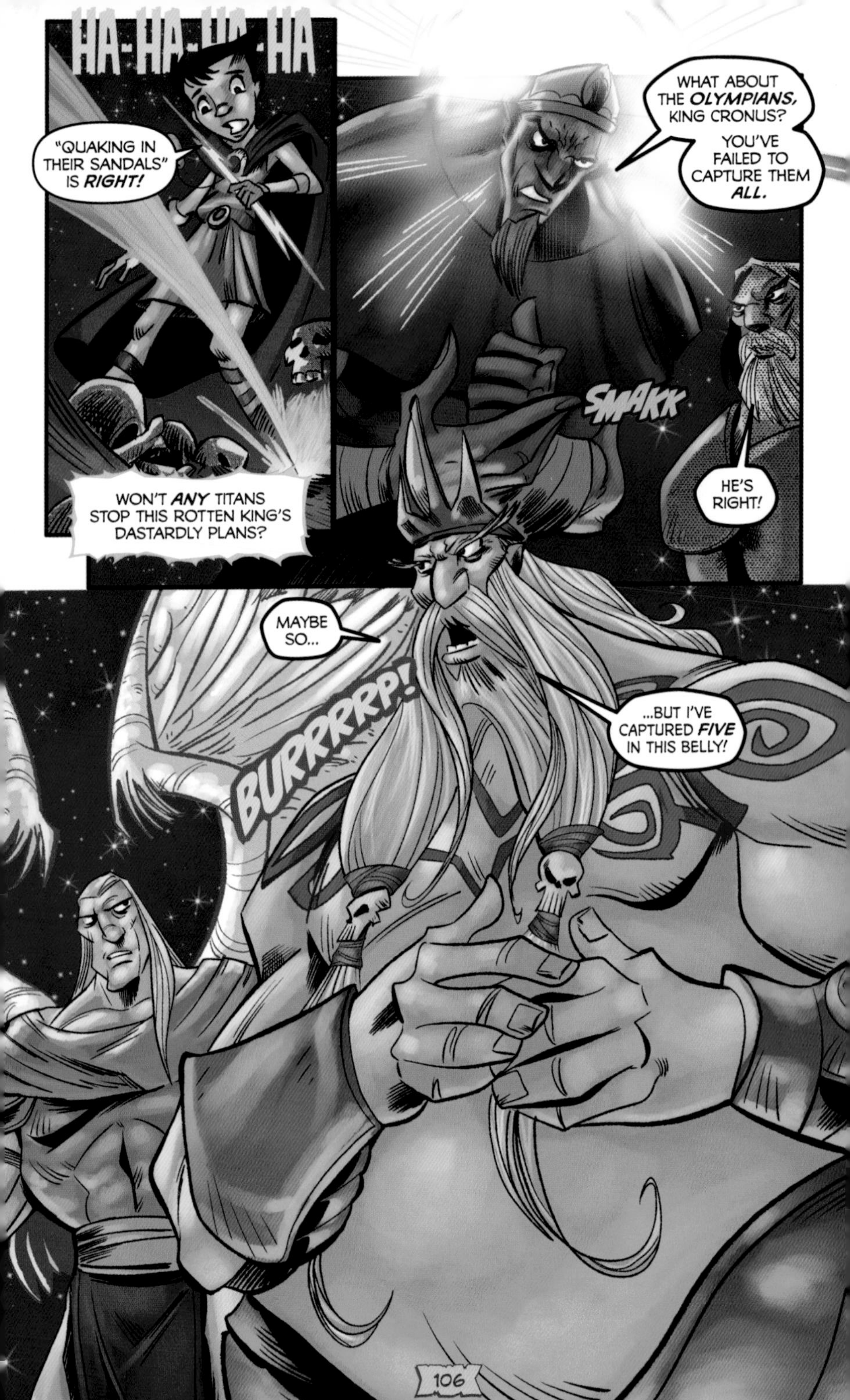
HA-HA-HA-HA
"QUAKING IN THEIR SANDALS" IS RIGHT!
WHAT ABOUT THE OLYMPIANS, KING CRONUS?
YOU'VE FAILED TO CAPTURE THEM ALL.
SMAKK
HE'S RIGHT!
WON'T ANY TITANS STOP THIS ROTTEN KING'S DASTARDLY PLANS?
MAYBE SO...
BURRRRP!
...BUT I'VE CAPTURED FIVE IN THIS BELLY!

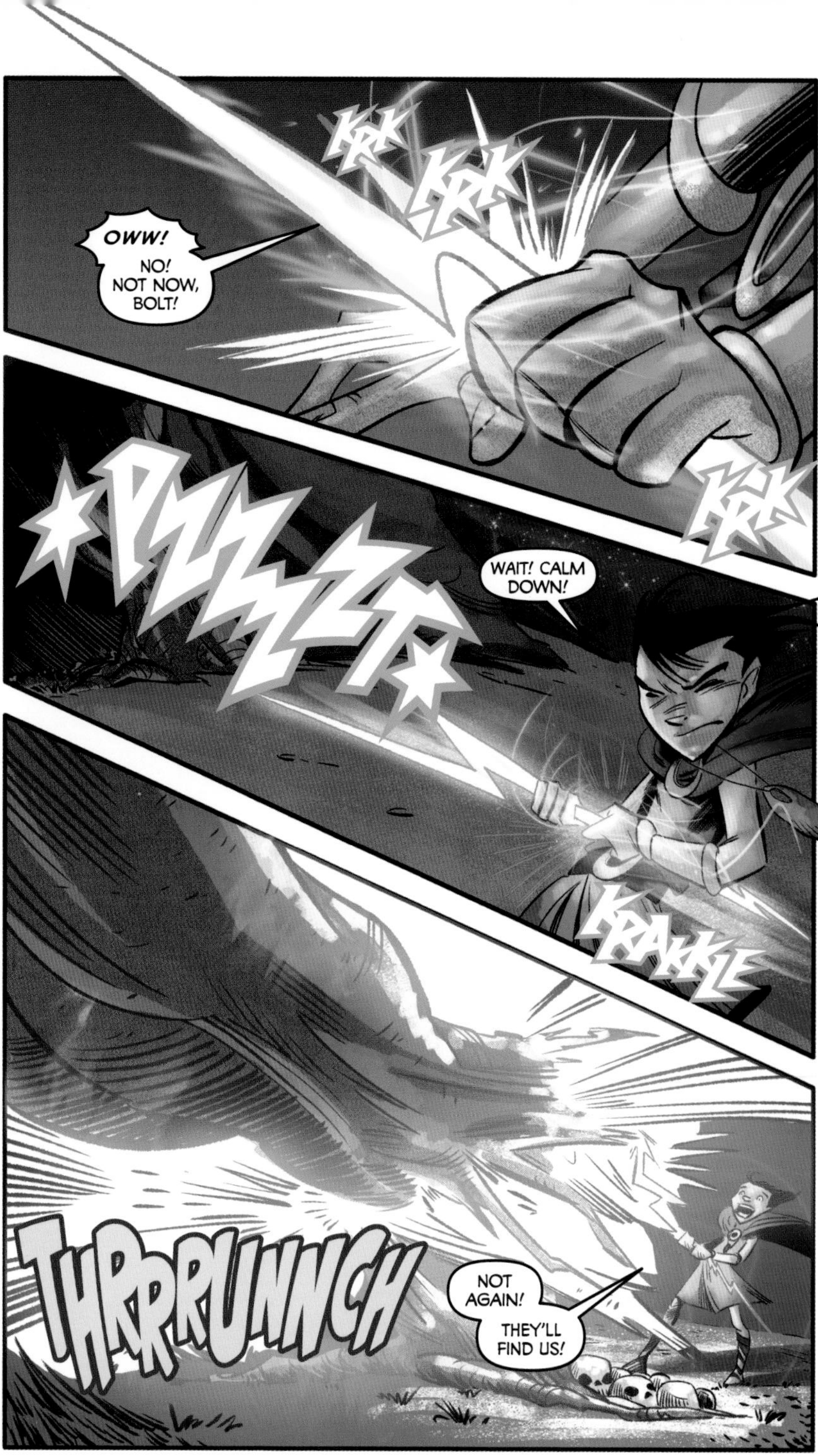
KRK
KRK
OWW!
NO! NOT NOW, BOLT!
KRK
PZZZZT
WAIT! CALM DOWN!
KRAKKLE
THRRRUNNCH
NOT AGAIN!
THEY'LL FIND US!

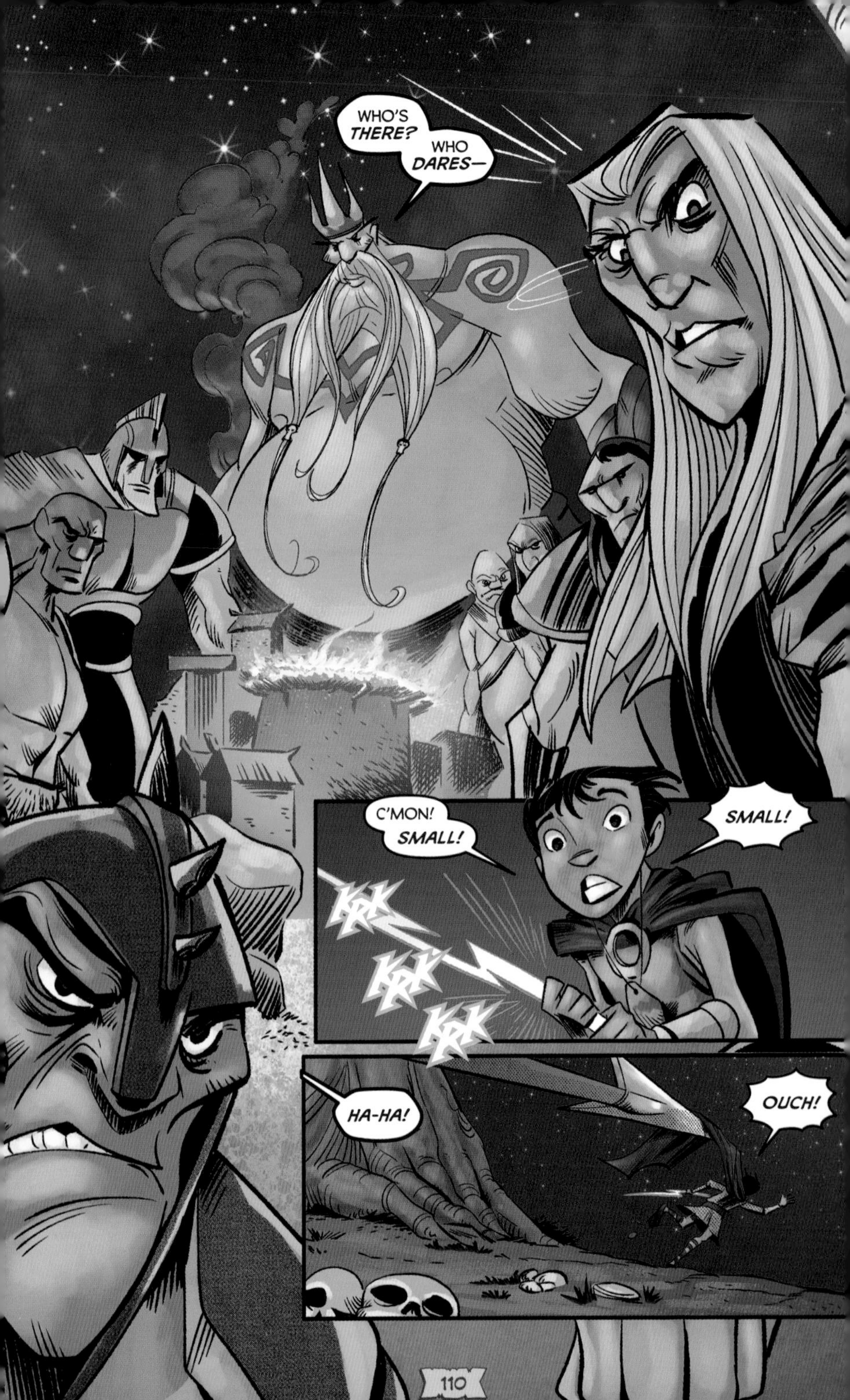

WHO'S THERE? WHO DARES—
C'MON! SMALL!
SMALL!
KRK
KRK
KRK
HA-HA!
OUCH!

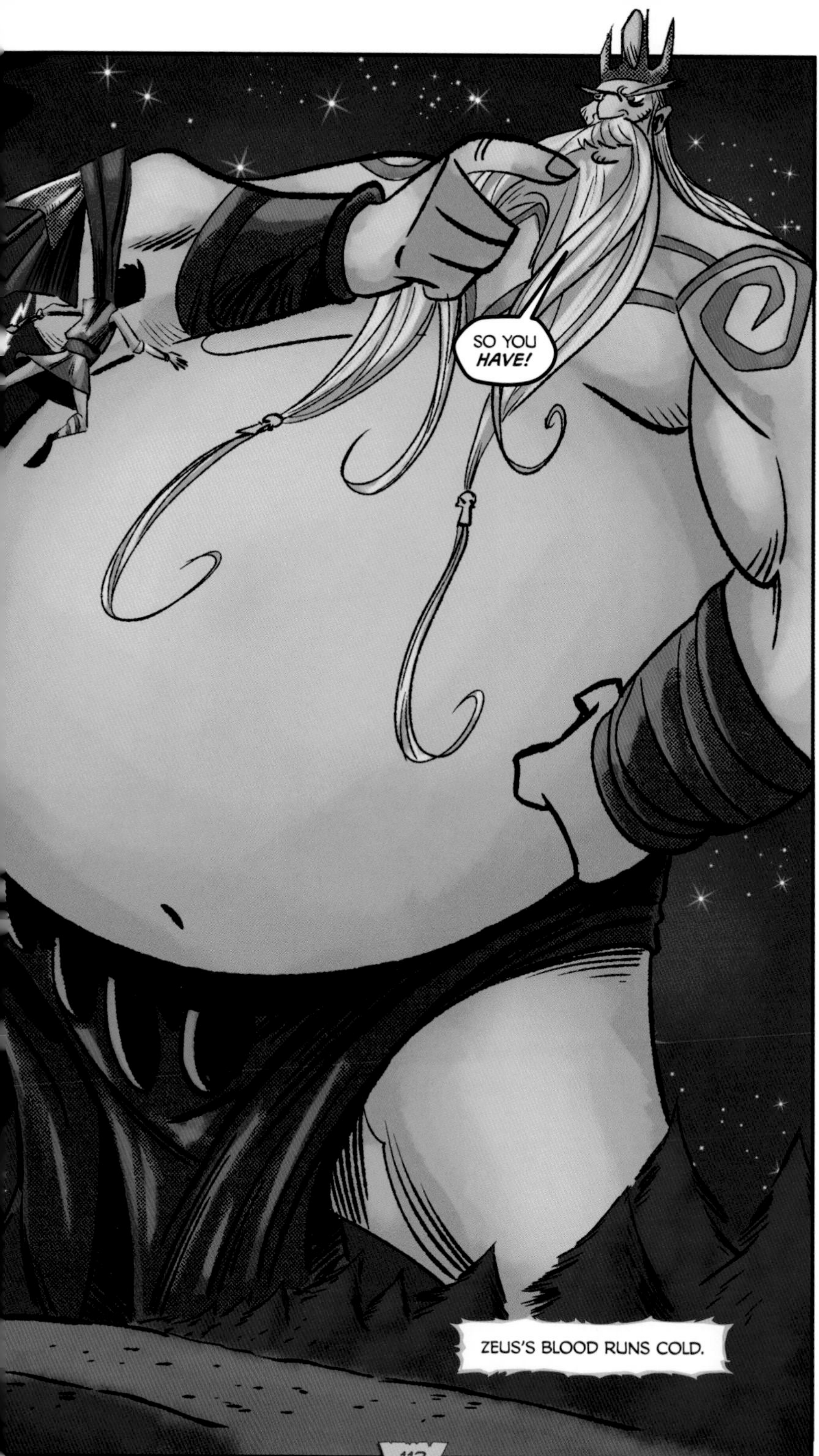
SO YOU *HAVE!*
ZEUS'S BLOOD RUNS COLD.

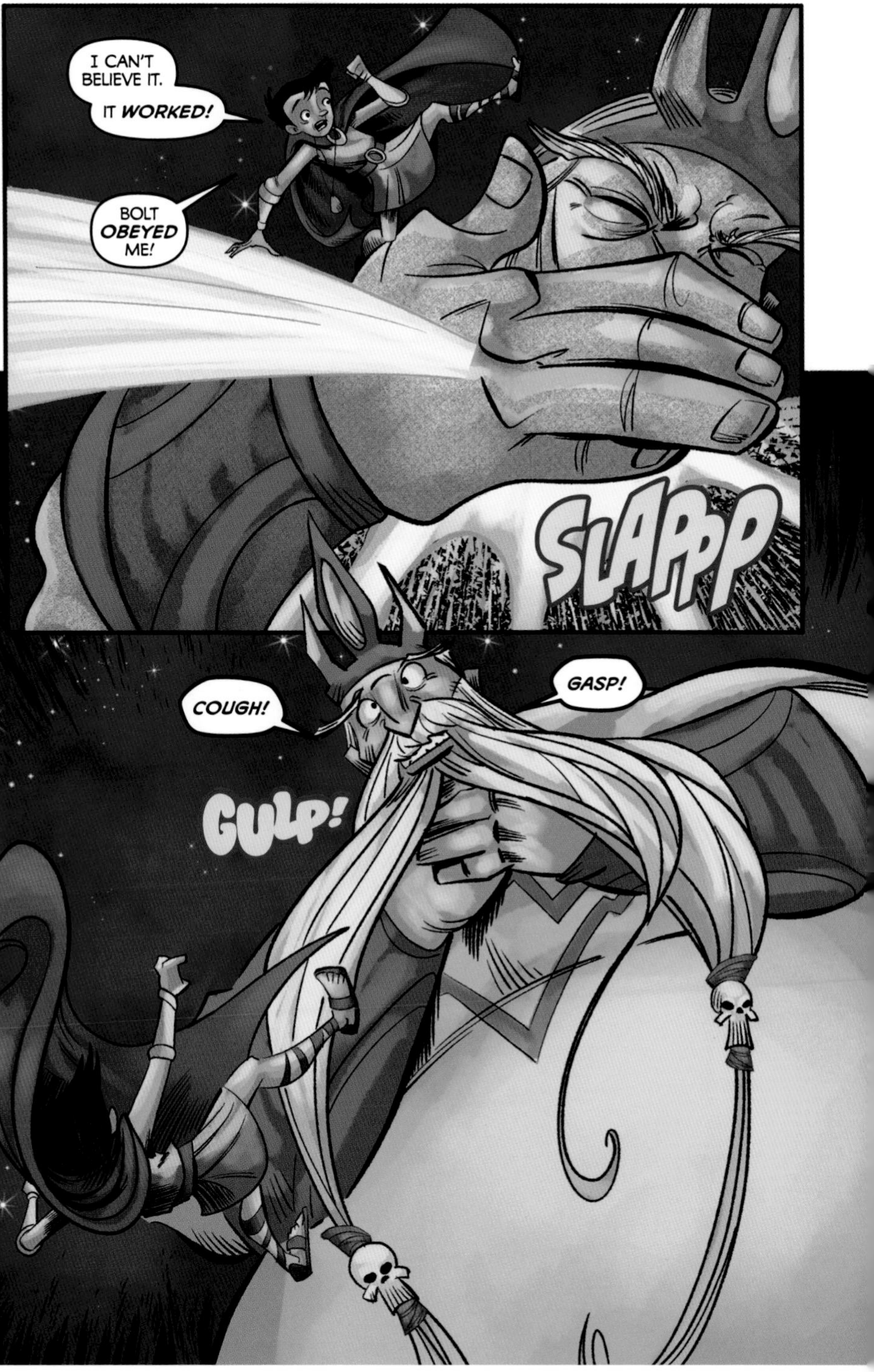
I CAN'T BELIEVE IT.
IT WORKED!
BOLT OBEYED ME!
SLAPP
COUGH!
GASP!
GULP!

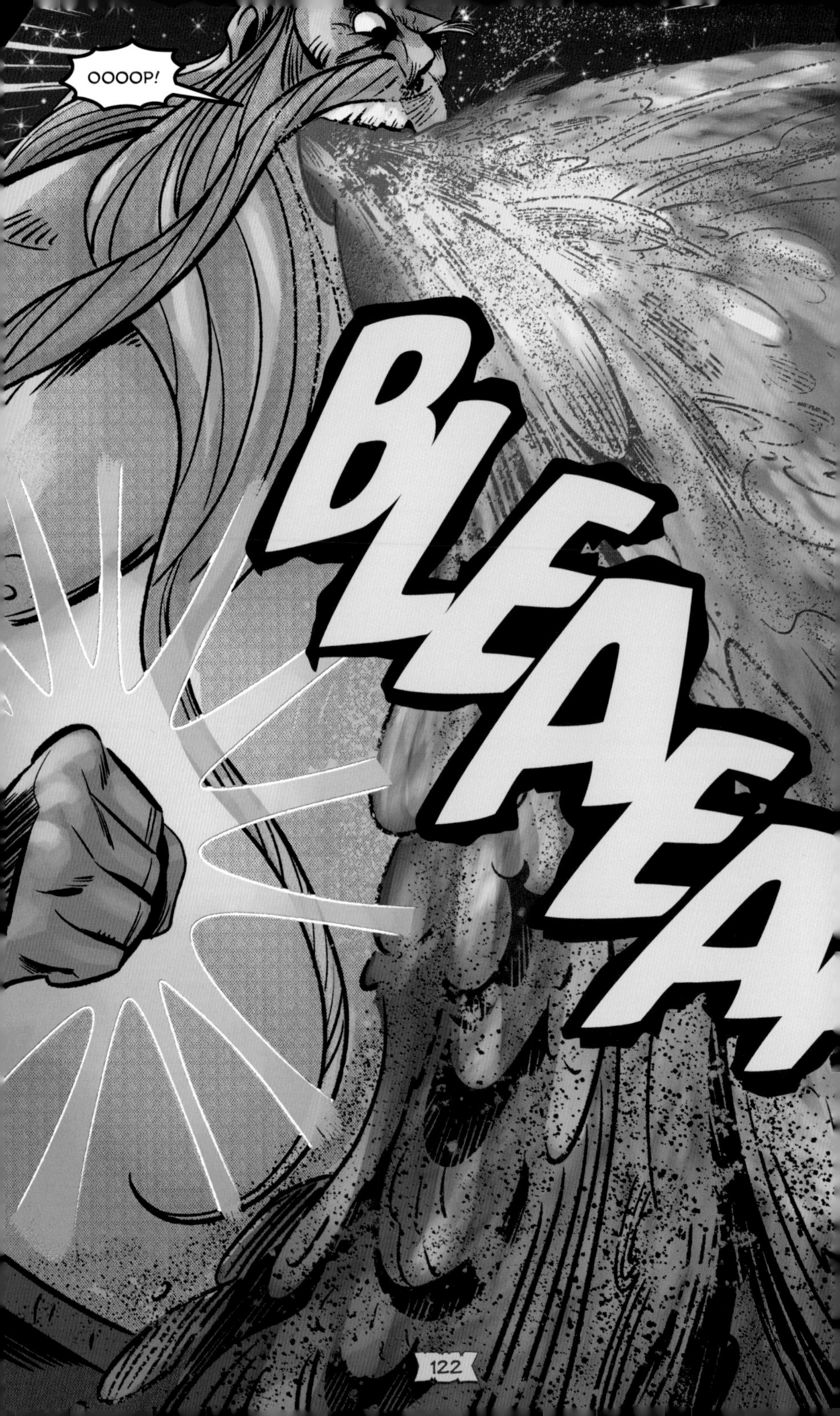
OOOOP!
BLEAAA

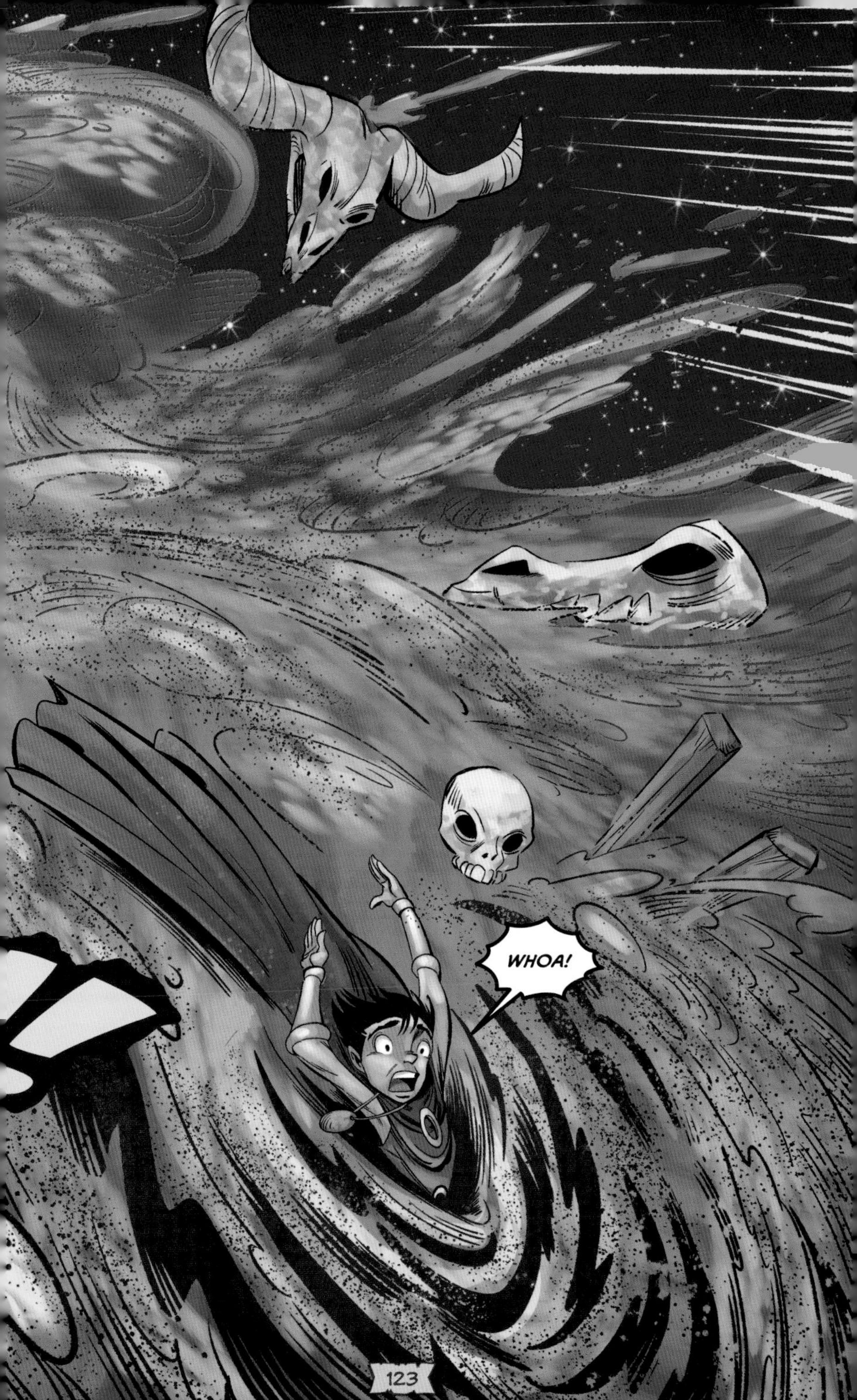
WHOA!

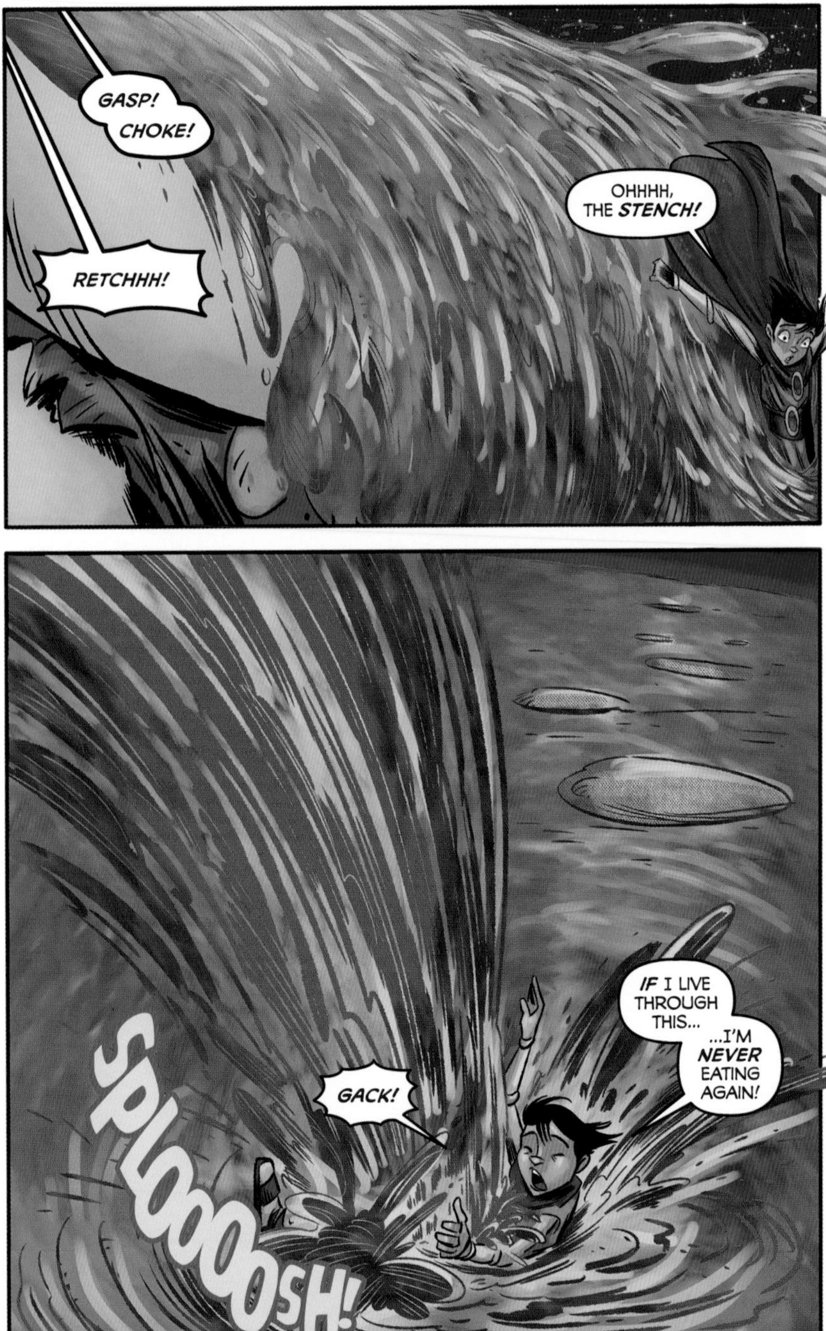
GASP!
CHOKE!
RETCHHH!
OHHHH, THE STENCH!
SPLOOOOOSH!
GACK!
IF I LIVE THROUGH THIS...
...I'M NEVER EATING AGAIN!

CHAPTER TEN:
OLYMPIANS

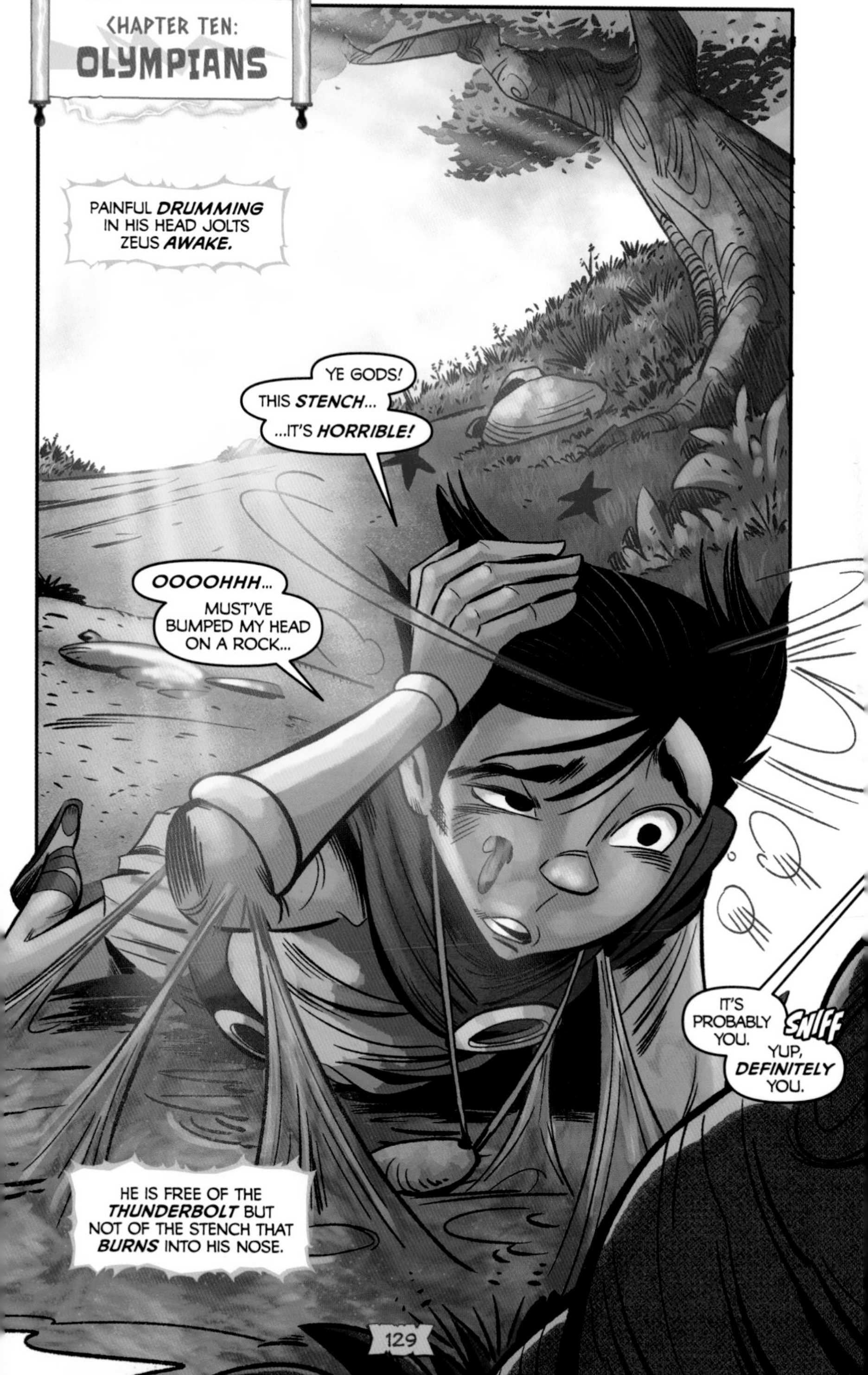

PAINFUL *DRUMMING* IN HIS HEAD JOLTS ZEUS *AWAKE.*
YE GODS! THIS *STENCH*... ...IT'S *HORRIBLE!*
OOOOHHH... MUST'VE BUMPED MY HEAD ON A ROCK...
IT'S PROBABLY YOU.
SNIFF
YUP, *DEFINITELY* YOU.
HE IS FREE OF THE *THUNDERBOLT* BUT NOT OF THE STENCH THAT *BURNS* INTO HIS NOSE.

CHIP HERE POPPED OFF A CONE-SHAPED STONE IN A *TEMPLE.*

HE *TALKS* TO ME WHEN HE WANTS TO.

HE EVEN SPELLS OUT *MESSAGES* WHEN HE FEELS LIKE IT.

SOMETHING ABOUT THIS SEEMS FAMILIAR.

I'VE GOT TO SAY...

...THAT ALL OF THIS SOUNDS PRETTY *PREPOSTEROUS* TO ME.

YEAH.

AND HAVEN'T YOU BEEN LIVING INSIDE THE BELLY OF A *GIANT* YOUR WHOLE LIFE?

YOU HAVE A POINT.

AS ZEUS TELLS THEM HIS STORY, HE FINDS HIMSELF WARMING TO HERA AND POSEIDON...

THE HALF-GIANTS WEREN'T REALLY SCARIER THAN GETTING HIT BY LIGHTNING *EVERY DAY!*

I HAVE *NO IDEA* WHAT HAPPENED TO *BOLT* AFTER I THREW IT DOWN INTO CRONUS'S *MOUTH!*

...FEELING AS THOUGH HE *BELONGS* WITH THEM.

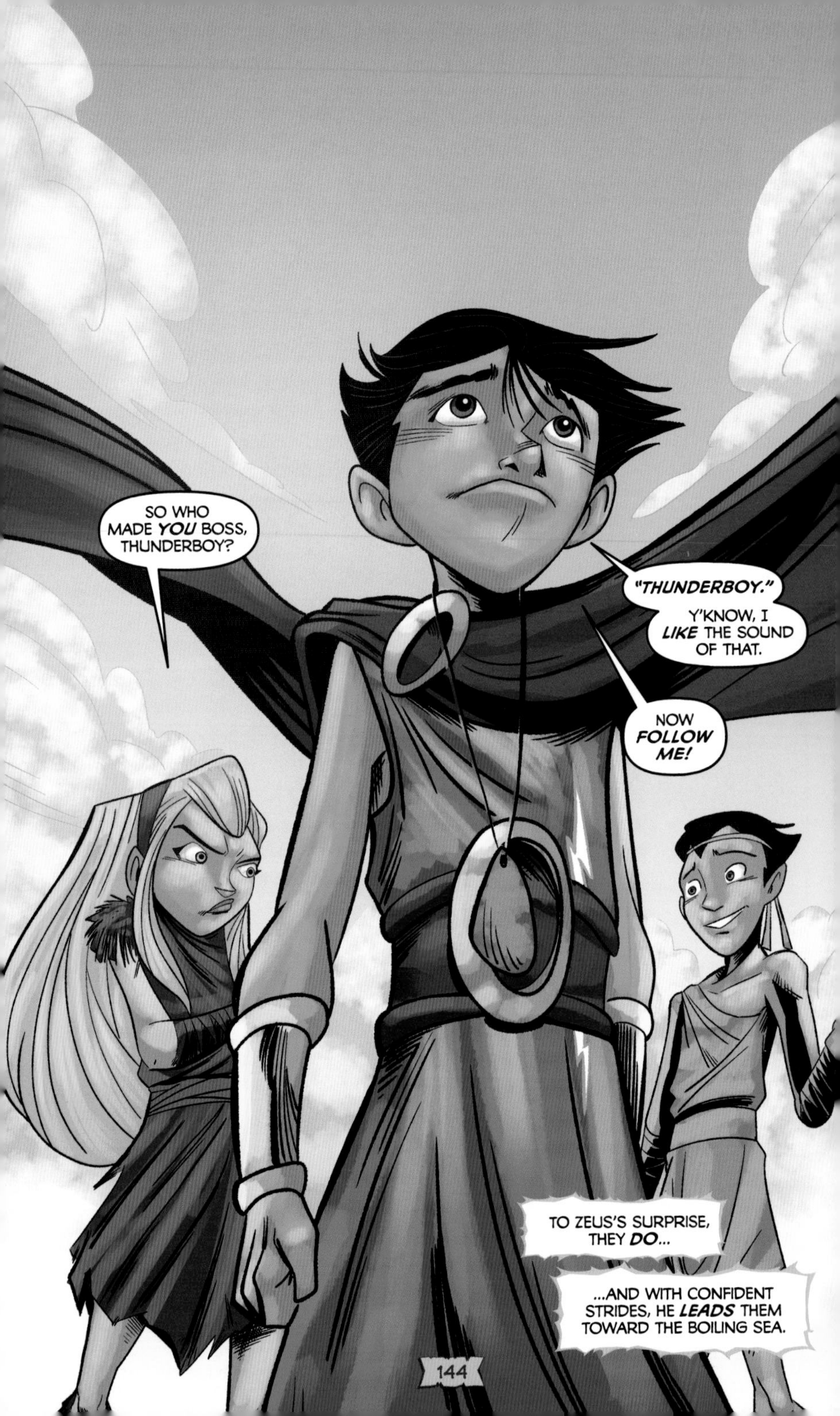
SO WHO MADE *YOU* BOSS, THUNDERBOY?
"THUNDERBOY."
Y'KNOW, I *LIKE* THE SOUND OF THAT.
NOW *FOLLOW ME!*
TO ZEUS'S SURPRISE, THEY *DO*...
...AND WITH CONFIDENT STRIDES, HE *LEADS* THEM TOWARD THE BOILING SEA.